She'd been attacked b
trust them, so why di

"I can smell the leopard in you, Angel," he whispered in my ear, the scars across my chest throbbing in response. My heart raced against my ribs, fear mingling with desire in a way that made me pull my body from his. "Come back to me tonight. Meet me here after your appointment."

"No," I said, opening the door. I couldn't. I wouldn't. "No," I said again, softly, shaking my head. I wasn't going to get involved with the Leopard King. Not in this lifetime. Not ever. "No."

For my husband,
who listened and listened and always believed,
and without whom, this novel simply wouldn't be.

ACKNOWLEDGMENTS

With thanks to my friends and families,
especially my mom, for all of their support and
encouragement, offered freely and forever, long
before they knew for certain.

And also with thanks to the wonderful writers at the OWW,
for giving their time in such abundance,
and for holding my hand without ever holding back,
I'm grateful beyond words.

Forever Crossed

***

A. Leigh Jones

Forever Crossed
Published by ImaJinn Books, a division of ImaJinn

ISBN: 1-893896-24-2

10 9 8 7 6 5 4 3 2 1

PUBLISHER'S NOTE:
This book is a work of fiction. Names, characters, places and incidents are products of the author's imagination or are used fictitiously. Any resemblance to actual events or locales or persons, living or dead, is entirely coincidental.

Books are available at quantity discounts when used to promote products or services. For information please write to: Marketing Division, ImaJinn Books, P.O. Box 545, Canon City, CO 81215-0545, or call toll free 1-877-625-3592.

Cover design by Patricia Lazarus

ImaJinn Books, a division of ImaJinn
P.O. Box 545, Canon City, CO 81215-0545
Toll Free: 1-877-625-3592
http://www.imajinnbooks.com

Prologue

In the dream I am seven.

It's early, and I'm riding my bike through dappled shade. There's a bend in the road, a bloody stain, and right here, this exact place, this is where the images linger, hazy at first, swirling all around me.

I blink, and there's a deer, fear-stiffened, like linens left overnight on the line. He's frozen there, unable to move.

Blinding lights, closer and closer, and then there's only searing white. For a moment there's nothing but that empty light, and then exhaust mixes with pain, and even filtered through scratchy red, it's too much for me.

I know what death is, and I stop my bike just for a minute. The cross around my neck feels cool in my fingers, the sun's light warm on my face. I say a prayer for the deer, but the images keep coming.

A pair of denim-covered legs, the sound of heavy footsteps. The rush of air moving toward the gasping deer before the boot comes down on its middle. A long black gun rises, the oily scent of hot metal, a cloud of linseed and sulfur as the bullet bites through the deer's brain.

Endless dizzy blackness, and then the deer's spirit soars away from the pain.

The man drags his empty prize across the pavement, lifts it into the back of his truck. He whistles, curses with the effort.

I pedal my bike faster now, tears streaming, until I reach my Nana's arms. *Why did the man hurt the deer on purpose?* I sob. *Why are there bad men?*

Nana rocks me to and fro, her red beads swaying between our bodies. She murmurs soft words about gypsies and pretty girls and flowers. She smooths my hair, kissing the tears away from my face.

Nana's voice is as sweet as ever and her hands are warm in my hair, but I don't want the dream to go on. I know what scene is next, and I don't want to go there. Not really, not today.

From a distance I hear the phone ringing, pulling me through time, through the dreamworld, back to where I'm supposed to be, the exact moment, exactly now.

One

10:06 AM. I grabbed the phone, not sure I wanted to know who could possibly be calling this early.

"Olivia Peters," I said, my mouth moving around the words as automatically as most people say *Hello.*

"Liv, sorry to wake you." It was Lincoln Anderson, my boss, and the owner of the Forever Crossed funeral home. Like hell he was sorry.

"I need you to be sharp this morning, Olivia," he said. "Detective Rutledge has a crime scene that needs your attention."

Crime scenes aren't my specialty, people are, but I didn't want to go down that road this morning.

"What's so special about this one that you're dragging me out of bed to take it, Linc?"

"Hey, you're young, Olivia, you'll recover." Sometimes Linc's voice took on a sweet paternal tone when he spoke to me. This was not one of those times. "It's a cop case. It doesn't need to be special. And it's a homicide."

Well, that explained it. I'd go in as a Bereavement Specialist, offer what comfort I could to the remaining loved ones, and poke around the crime scene to see what I could see.

"Another homicide? Does the victim have family at the scene?"

"Like I said, Liv, I don't have the details. Detective Rutledge called, I answered, and you're on the job."

I reached for the aspirin bottle on my nightstand. The medicine wouldn't help. My body would metabolize the painkillers before they had half a chance to work, but the tinkling of the little round pills as they spilled into my hand always made me feel better.

"Damn it, Linc. I haven't slept, and I have a headache. Can't Danny take this one?"

Linc answered me with silence, a sure sign my co-worker, Daniel Sundeen, could've handled the case, but Linc was giving it to me regardless. Well, whatever his reasons for adding to my workload, he certainly wasn't sharing.

I took the address of the crime scene and swallowed

an extra aspirin for good measure. What else could I do?

After I hung up, I cursed myself for not pulling a few more details out of Linc. Never one for telephone chitchat, Linc had said less than usual this morning. An uneasy feeling pulled at my belly, a wisp of a nudge, more of an irritant than a warning.

Linc's family had owned Forever Crossed for three generations, but by the time Linc took over, the business had started to go bad. That'll happen when families pay good money to bury a loved one, only to find Grandpa back in his old chair a few weeks later, rotting zombie-brains from the inside out—or worse yet, roaming the old neighborhood in the darkest hours, Undead and aching for an easy meal.

So Linc did the only thing he could do to save his family's business. He brought in some new blood, namely me and Danny, and these days, Forever Crossed is the hottest funeral home in the Triangle. We haven't had a body rise in the three years I've been here, and we haven't had a single case of unrequested vampirism, either.

I don't stake the dead, Linc and Danny do that. And I'm not a necromancer, although Linc is thinking of bringing one onto the staff. What I do is different.

I speak with crossing souls. Or more accurately, they speak with me.

When I'm in the presence of souls in transition, I catch glimpses of their final reality, reliving in pictures the last few moments before their bodies die. The images linger until the soul leaves this plane of existence—usually about seventy-two hours, just long enough for me to see how they crossed over and whether or not they intended to come back.

I'm also a survivor, not that there's a twelve-step group for people like me, I'm not that kind of survivor. I was attacked by a wereleopard when I was a teenager. He died. I didn't. End of story.

Of course, the attack was big news at the time, a media feeding frenzy, not that the reporters cared about my survival. They wanted a hot story. The problem was, turning sweet little me into a cold-blooded killer wasn't exactly firing up the ratings. So they jumped on the conservative bandwagon and called in their medical correspondents, all of them demanding an explanation for my DNA.

I hated what they were doing, the way they were making me into a victim all over again, but I wanted an explanation, too. Because despite the attack, despite everything I'd ever heard about shapeshifters, I hadn't changed. I was human right down to the last twist of my double helix, and none of the experts could explain why.

I do have some interesting side-effects, more like the shapeshifter's version of consolation prizes than anything else. But, like my mother says, it isn't something we talk about in mixed company. I'm pretty sure Linc knew all the sordid details when he recruited me, though.

Of course he did. He wouldn't have hired me otherwise, and it really didn't bear thinking about any further. Still, as I stumbled toward my bathroom, I wondered if I could make it as a freelancer in this city. There might be enough work for me here, customizing burial rituals and weaving graveside protections. Might be, I thought, but in the mirror, my reflection's hazel eyes looked doubtful.

The last three weeks had brought a rash of vampire murders to the Triangle. Two humans had been murdered, drained completely and unnecessarily of all blood, their bodies displayed in public places for all the world to see. On top of that, three of the local Undead had been destroyed, corpses abandoned to the night, or to the sun, whichever happened to find them first.

Forever Crossed had been called in when the second body was found. I hadn't liked it then, and I didn't like it now, either.

Since I spend more than my share of time around all sorts of corpses, I tend not to socialize with vampires in my off hours. Besides, my ability to communicate with the dead makes dealing with these particular folks creepy on all kinds of new levels, so I keep my distance when I can.

I checked the clock. Time never seemed to be on my side. Nevertheless, I would make it to the crime scene in thirty minutes, as promised.

I'd showered before I fell into bed just a few hours ago, though I hadn't bothered to blow dry my hair. I pulled my fingers through the still-damp tangles, twisting the long strands into a sleek knot at the back of my neck.

It was dark in my bedroom despite the hour, night blinds drawn tight against the morning, but I didn't bother flipping on a light before I peered into the closet. No need. Prepping the dry-cleaning before putting it away was my mother's habit. It was also the only way I could keep the kind of crazy hours my work with Forever Crossed demanded and still feel like a human being when I walked out the front door. Each hanger held a solid color sheath, a matching jacket, and a rope of beads or a pretty scarf around the neck. They were all perfect, and all more or less the same. Some of the jackets even had coordinated earrings in the pockets. I grabbed the nearest one and got dressed.

The only part of my wardrobe not on the hanger was my weapon. Before I got involved in this business, it never even occurred to me that a grief counselor might need a gun. But from my very first day with Forever Crossed, I'd carried Linc's weapon of choice—a 9mm Sig Sauer—in a right draw shoulder holster. Concealed-carry is one of the benefits of being a citizen in the South, and every once in a while the funeral home business truly does get a little hairy. That's why at Forever Crossed, all of our bullets are hydroshock silvers. Between the silver itself and the massive exit wound of this particular bullet, odds are good it'll damage just about everything that goes bump in the night.

I shook my wrist a little as I smoothed my hair, listening to the jingle of the charms on my bracelet. It sounded like peace to me, just a few seconds of floating calm whenever I needed it. Slipping into low-heeled pumps, I grabbed my handbag and headed out. No breakfast, as usual, and I'd have to put my lipstick on in the car.

Plus, I needed to make a quick stop at the office on the way, since I'd left my briefcase there the night before. I hadn't needed it then, and I wasn't thinking too clearly when I left. I'd spent the wee hours at the hospital with a client, doing the type of work that keeps me busy when I'm not helping the city's finest solve crimes.

Last night I'd comforted a widow-in-waiting, describing the images swirling through my mind as her husband crossed over in his sleep. His heart was full of her, his memories of their life together vivid in my mind, and I knew that they would meet again soon. Tears streamed from her eyes, but she didn't try to keep him with her.

Hey, I'm a professional. I see death for a living, have seen it all my life whether I looked for it or not, and mostly, the job doesn't move me. This session did. The short drive back to the office wasn't long enough to clear my head, and my eyes had welled with unshed tears. More emotional overflow than anything else, but they were salty just the same.

Even this morning, in the brilliance of a new spring day, my throat constricted a little just thinking about it. I swallowed hard, wondering if I could blame my reaction on a freak surge of hormones. I tried to pinpoint exactly when I'd last had a period . . . It had been cold then, and dreary. Six months ago? Seven, maybe? Not a new record for me, but getting close. *Well woo-freakin'-hoo,* I thought, making the sharp turn into the parking lane reserved for Forever Crossed staff.

I hurried up the back stairs of the revitalized Victorian and into the business offices of Forever Crossed, a prayer to Desmas, the Patron Saint of funeral homes, already crossing my lips. Late morning light glinted off the windows, and I could feel my professional persona wrapping itself around me with every step. I smiled at our receptionist, Ellen, as I walked in, but her sparkly aura dimmed slightly as I approached. *Damn.* I must have looked worse than I thought.

I detoured into the cubbyhole we all pretend is my private office and grabbed the black leather case I'd come for. File folders, ink pens, and legal pads filled the flip-up section, while a starchy white lab coat, a box of latex gloves, a sturdy plastic toolkit, and extra ammo clips were tucked into the wider bottom. A couple of liters of bottled water, a roll of breath mints, and an emergency makeup case rounded out the sides. Just the basics.

As I came back through the reception area, Ellen handed me a cup of coffee in a tall travel mug.

"Bless you, Ellen," I said, taking that first sip. Strong, but light and sweet, too. Perfect.

So, yes, welcome to my world. Sleep is optional and the dead talk back, but coffee is one of the four food groups, and you gotta love that!

Two

Skinny pines crowded close to the houses as I approached the crime scene. Flowering cherry trees blossomed along the walkways, and Crepe Myrtles stood stark, waiting for their blooms to spring to life. I loved these older neighborhoods. They were warm and solid, with playgrounds up the street and a swim club around the corner. Nothing bad was ever supposed to happen here.

I parked my red convertible on the street, slipping it behind a pickup truck that could've swallowed my little car in a single gulp. As I unfolded myself from behind the wheel, I spotted my special liaison officer, Detective Michael Rutledge. He was standing at the bottom of the driveway beside a younger man, an officer whose name I couldn't recall. They were like time-warped mirrors of each other, one of them in uniform and the other in a suit, separated by the violence and drudgery of about seven years on the force and not much else. Even their auras had the same ragged edges this morning.

I wasn't one of them, but at least my clothes were the right shade of navy blue. Still, at an even six feet, and that's without shoes, I tend not to blend well in a crowd. Not that I'm complaining. Hey, it's a man's world, and with as much leg as my hemlines tend to show, if most men mistake me for eye candy until they get to know me, well, really, that works for me just fine.

These two men should have known better, but it didn't stop their auras from perking up a little as I approached. I took the compliment, smiling a silent thank-you to the gods of small wonders.

"Olivia, glad you could make it," Detective Rutledge said, mixing a wicked grin with his faint Southern drawl in a way that made me flash him a smile of my own. Detective Rutledge was true-blue, practically born blue, if I understood his family line correctly.

"Good to see you, too, Mike. What can I do for you this morning?"

"Have you met Officer Bradley yet?" Mike asked, a smooth reintroduction for both of us.

I smiled again, said we'd worked together a while back. For a few minutes we stood there making small talk, pretending we just happened to bump into each other, feeling each other out, easing into the crime scene.

"So, shall I speak with the family?" I asked.

"No family here," Mike said. "Not much of anything, if you want the truth."

"Meaning what, Detective?" I asked.

"Meaning you're going to have to tell me," Mike replied. "The neighbors called 911 when they smelled smoke. Other than that, I want to hear what you've got to say."

We left the younger officer by the road and walked toward the house. People clustered in small groups, staring silently and shaking their heads. Every once in a while someone spoke softly, a hand stretched out, palm up. They were ordinary neighbors, ready to carry over a covered dish or plate of cookies. Civilians, unprepared for the tragedy before them.

I looked away, and as Mike steered me around the back of the house, I slipped into one of the lab coats I always bring to homicides. Two steps later, the smell of the crime scene crashed over me. Burned flesh, melted fabrics, and something else I couldn't yet identify mingled together, became the familiar scent of wrongful death. Mike hung back a little, letting me feel my way through, and without thinking, my hand reached for something solid, the warm feel of the doorframe just enough to ground me again.

Fresh crime scenes are tricky. Images layered upon each other until I can't tell what I'm seeing in real time and what I'm seeing in my mind's eye. This scene was worse than most. Even after a careful survey, the only thing I knew for certain was that two people had been assaulted here. And only one of them made it out alive.

The pictures in my mind were sepia-toned and bloody, but as I looked closely, there wasn't much blood to be found. There also wasn't much of anything that resembled a body, though Forever Crossed would still hold a service and protect whatever remains the Coroner released, if the family so desired. If there was any family.

I shook my head a little, trying to focus on the surface of the scene. From the looks of it, this room had once been an old-fashioned sleeping porch. I peered through beveled glass doors into the bedroom proper—a woman's room, warm and gingery. A worn quilt draped over a wooden bed, photos and trinkets undisturbed on her dresser. Interesting.

I slipped my hands into cool latex gloves, soft powder slick on my skin. "Has the scene been documented, photographed, all that?"

"The Coroner's waiting on you before he takes the remains." Mike's voice was edgy. "You wouldn't be here if we weren't ready for you, Peters."

"Hey, I had to ask."

Which was true, I did. If I didn't touch the debris, didn't get up close and personal, I might not be able to find the memories locked inside. And since that's what I was here for, I took a cautious step into the edge of the ash, closed my eyes, and waited.

This had been a peaceful place, a sanctuary of sorts. But a well-controlled fire had burned here, charring the furnishings and leaving only ash and twisted metal in its wake. Still, I could see the images before the fire. The victim, an older woman, was running. Panic, sharp and heavy, crashed over her. She burst from the woods behind the house, the predawn light eerie and still. She knew these woods well, knew the presence that didn't belong here was closing ground fast. She sprinted the last few yards, but it was upon her as she lurched across the threshold, calling out to the goddess Cardea as the porch screen tore around her.

She began to chant, and her words for protection echoed in my mind. As I focused on her voice, the lingering buzz of her power slid across my skin. She felt like my grandmother, and I knew she was a witch, too, or something very similar. I also knew that in the moments before she died, she had sent her power outwards, warning another to stay away.

Who was it? I wondered. And why hadn't they listened? Slowly, I reached out to her power with my own. The flood of images raining over me nearly knocked me over, but I couldn't pull myself away. My hand shot out, looking for something to ground me once again. Not the doorframe this time, but the solid arm of Detective Michael Rutledge.

Dizzy and nauseous, I pulled my power back.

"You all right?" Mike gripped my arm, steering me around the back of the house and away from the scene.

"I'm fine," I lied. "Just need some air." Mike couldn't have known what I would see when I stepped into the fray, but he could have warned me anyway. At Forever Crossed, cremated remains are sealed into warded vessels, so it's not like I sift through human ashes everyday.

"Uhm, Mike? You mind telling me what you've got so far? I'm not quite myself yet." I fanned my face with one hand, cold sweat beading above my lip. I was buying time, sorting through the pictures and trying to put them together in a way that made sense.

Damsel in distress? I thought, shaking my head at my own reaction. I was exaggerating for Mike's benefit, but not much. My fingers were like icicles, damp in the late morning heat, and I buried them beneath my crossed arms. All this time, and still, I wasn't immune to the aftereffects of murder. It was part of the job, though, and I swallowed hard, determined.

Mike nodded once, and started on the scene. He told me they suspected the burned remains on the porch belonged to the homeowner, Anya Sorensen. There were no signs of forced entry, no sign at all that the perpetrator went inside the main part of the house. The blood in the surrounding area and tracking away from the scene into the woods was assumed to be the perpetrator's, since it couldn't very well be the victim's. They'd called the bloodhounds down from Greensboro as soon as they found the tracks, thinking that the perpetrator had killed the victim, burned the remains, and then disappeared before the neighbors noticed anything was wrong.

Now Mike Rutledge was a smart cop. I knew he was, but just at this moment I wondered how his first impressions could be so wrong.

I tried to break it to him gently.

"There was a second victim, Mike. That's who the tracks belong to, and I don't think you'll find him with the hounds." Mike raised an eyebrow at that, but he let me keep talking. "If I'm right, they'll lose his scent up a tree not too far from here."

I tried to reconstruct the images in my head, but they

didn't quite make sense to me yet. Again, I saw two deaths, but I was sure only one of them had happened this morning.

I needed to go back in.

We walked through the house this time, winding through the interior rooms until we reached the porch. I opened myself to the images but didn't try to connect with the woman's spirit. I wasn't ready to feel the full force of her power again, not yet, anyway. Using Mike's nearness as a ground, I kept the intensity of her energy at bay, allowing just enough for the images to come through.

Now, when I saw her attacker, I saw his death, too. And that could only mean one thing. The attacker was a vampire.

In a way, that made piecing the events together easier, because although I was seeing the attacker through the eyes of the deceased, it felt as if I were seeing him in real time. It also explained why I was seeing two deaths, when there was only one deceased at the scene.

Vampires are the only people I can read who are still alive, and the experience always freaks me out. The images I get from vamps are pretty much the same as I get from any of the recently deceased, except vampire images shift perspective all the time, because the events are still pieces of their living memory. Sometimes I'll even see death lingering around them, their victims timeless and unknown to me, shadows of who they once were. Those are the Undead who truly spooked me—the ones carrying their ghosts through the decades without ever seeming to notice.

The good news for me is vampires rarely kill humans these days, present circumstances notwithstanding. Even before they'd mainstreamed, the Undead had already become celebrities, the media clamoring for interviews, humans circling in droves for the privilege of warming them after dawn. Januarius Blood Bars popped up all around the country, humans and vamps flocking to the franchise's counters, doing their parts for supply and demand.

I didn't get the attraction, personally, but to each her own. Either way, I already knew this was bad, and I was pretty sure it was going to get worse before it got better.

The vampire who committed this murder was old, and powerful, and if I was sensing him correctly, out of control. Not a good sign, not a good sign at all.

"A few of the pieces still don't quite fit," I said out loud, my eyes flitting to the digital recorder in Officer Bradley's hand. The green indicator light was glowing, and it reminded me of some kind of an armored beetle, black and ugly. Had he been recording the whole time? I hadn't noticed. I hadn't even noticed he was there.

I took a deep breath and exhaled slowly. I figured I might as well start at the beginning. "The remains belong to an older woman, a grandmotherly type." Officer Bradley confirmed that fit the description of Anya Sorensen he'd gotten from the neighbors. I clenched my jaw, trying to ignore him. "She was out for a walk. Maybe she had trouble sleeping? I don't know. But her attacker tracked her through the wooded area behind the house, chased her back here."

The feel of the woman's power echoed in my mind. "I think she may have been a witch. And I think she caused the fire to free herself from the attacker." I rushed on before their objections interrupted my train of thought. "Her attacker was a vampire—an old and extremely powerful vampire. He's not a local, and he doesn't play by the rules." I shuddered, seeing her again, hearing the echo of her chant. "She was terrified of him."

Mike's hand started towards my arm but dropped before making contact. I smiled a little, tried to let him know I was okay.

"When she knew she couldn't escape, she conjured the fire. I think she was trying to kill him, or maybe just scare him away . . . But once she knew she wasn't going to survive, she made sure she wouldn't be returning."

Both of the cops were staring at me now, shaking their heads. They didn't believe me. Hell, I wish I didn't believe me either.

"No one would torch themselves on purpose," Officer Bradley said. "That's insane. There's another explanation . . . You forgot about the blood, Ms. Peters. The blood belongs to the perp, just like we said. When we find him, we'll get the real scenario."

"The blood belongs to a second victim," I repeated

calmly, sure of myself now.

Mike cleared his throat, his eyes piercing the younger man with a silent warning. "What else?" he asked, his chin jutting toward me, advising me to continue.

"Whoever the second victim is, he's a shapeshifter. Probably a wereleopard, but I'm not positive about that. Could be some other sort of shifting feline, a cougar, maybe? Whichever, he tried to save her and took a nasty beating from the vamp for his trouble."

"If there was a shapeshifter involved," Officer Bradley said, a nasty twist playing with his mouth, "I'm sure it'll live. Bastards are damn near impossible to kill."

"Are we through here?" I asked Mike, unable to keep the tension from my voice. "I'd like to get going."

Mike's instincts were sharp enough to know I wasn't telling him everything, but he knew me well enough to know that I'd given him what I could.

"If you need to come back, Olivia, you call me first, hear?" Mike's voice was steady, stretching toward me in an easy Southern arc. "I'll make the arrangements; bring you over myself if I can."

I nodded, smiling despite myself.

We walked back toward my car, planning our follow-up schedule. I was already worried about protection for this victim's remains. Her magic was strong enough even now to draw unwanted attention to itself. Since Linc would need to make arrangements with the Coroner's office right away, Mike put a call in to the medical examiner, arranging access for Forever Crossed staff.

Triangle P.D. would use the hounds to follow the trail through the woods, despite what I'd told them. I didn't argue—they'd only prove me right. Mike and I would meet tomorrow at my office and go through the evidence with fresh eyes.

The delay gave me time to switch gears from Bereavement Specialist to P.I., since it looked like that's the hat I'd be wearing for this one. It would also give Mike time to gather the case files on the other vampire murders in the city.

Determination set Mike's eyes in stone, but I could read the urgency underneath plain enough. We had to be quick, because if we weren't, there would be another crime scene and another body, another media crew camped out in front of the station, ready to pounce. He knew beyond the shadow of a doubt that this vampire would kill again.

We both did.

Three

I drove away from the crime scene, winding out the low gears until I merged onto the belt line. I was anxious to be headed home, desperate to put some distance between myself and the images of Anya Sorensen's death. It was two o'clock, time for the Lady Blues Review, so at least I had that going for me. There are six or seven colleges in the Triangle, and all of them have radio broadcasts, but this was one of my favorites. Bessie Smith's raspy voice poured through the speakers, the pops and fizzles of the old recording like her own special magic.

Traffic on the inner loop was light for a change, and the blues carried me back to the historic district in record time. My apartment sits on the upper story of one of the old brick buildings that line this end of Glenwood Avenue, above the fashionable shops and pricey restaurants where the pretty people like to play. There's parking in the back for employees and residents, and a tiny garden plot where we grow plenty of weeds, herbs, and at least a few tomatoes in the summer.

It was a beautiful afternoon, white clouds high in the blue Carolina sky and the sun just the right shade of warm in my hair. I lingered in the new spring growth for a moment, and the fresh scent of crushed mint clung to my shoes as I made my way up the old wrought iron fire escape.

The two apartments in the front of the building overlook the street, and both were occupied by artsy sorts who could barely keep track of their own comings and goings, never mind pay attention to mine. My apartment is nestled along the back of the building. It doesn't have the people-watching views that the front rooms have, but the floor-to-ceiling windows fill with late afternoon light, and I get to use the fire escape as a patio when the landlord isn't around.

My answering machine blinked its furious red light at me, drawing my eye as soon as I walked through the door. *Please not my mother*, I implored the gods. *Please. Not today.*

I held my breath and pressed play.

"Liv, it's Karen." Her consonants were too quick, her Southern drawl clipped with concern. "Call me back. Okay?"

I exhaled slowly. Karen was attending a conference for female firefighters in Atlanta this week, something she'd been looking forward to for months. Her voice should have bubbled out of the machine, filled with news and friends and fun. Instead it fell flat.

While the front desk rang her hotel room, I tried to work out what had gone wrong. Something with the conference or something personal? I had to find out.

Karen wasn't picking up, the desk clerk advised me, but would I like to leave a private message on her voice mail? Damn straight I would.

Irritation edged its way toward worry. I kicked my shoes off behind the door, careful to cross them left over right. How could she leave a message that virtually shouted, *Help me!*, and then have the nerve to go out? I paced, the wood floors cool under my feet, plucking off my work clothes as I went.

Too impatient to prep my suit for another wear, I dropped it into the stiff white laundry bag on the frame behind the door. Spray-on fabric freshener was a great thing, but it wouldn't be enough to clear away the memory of Anya Sorensen's death.

I promised myself I'd take the lot of it down to Lares Laundries soon and concentrated on convincing myself that Karen was fine, that she was a big girl and could take care of herself. These things were true. Karen lifted weights like it was a part-time job, and we both took boxing lessons two days a week, sparred more often than that. I knew she could handle almost any situation that came her way.

So what would upset her enough to leave me that message? I continued my pacing, bottled water in one hand, the phone in the other. Could it be a problem within her coven? Something that had come up since she'd left for Atlanta?

Her coven meant everything to her. More, even, than her job, and I knew how important being a firefighter was to her. The first time Karen saw a real fire, a fire raging out of control, she was ten years old. She told me she felt a circle of protection spring to life around her as she watched that old warehouse burn to the ground, sparks popping into the night and thick smoke billowing closer. She knew right then that she would be a firefighter. From the beginning, she understood the flames, what they wanted, where they would flare next. There was nothing else she ever dreamed of doing.

I'd dreamed of being a ballet dancer when I was a little girl, and now most nights I dance with the dead. Well, sort of, anyway.

I cleared the clutter from my coffee table, sorted out the magazines I might still read and tossed the others in the recycling bin. The air around me sparked with impatience. I opened a window, the old casings groaning their protest. Then I opened another one. And a third, until the crisp breeze whisked it all away.

Goose bumps prickled my arms. I shivered, but left the windows up.

The last time I was this tense was when Karen had confronted me about my magic. I'd had to confess what I really was, not that I completely understood it all myself, or risk losing her as a friend.

I remember shivering then, too. It was cold and gray, a Wednesday, and a steady drizzle had been falling all week. Collars up and hands stuffed into coat pockets, the chill held conversation at bay. Karen slowed her pace and then stopped walking altogether, her energy a tentative tug against my own. I turned to face her, cold rain pooling around our feet. I could see my breath in the air, like steam rising from my body after a long workout. I shivered anyway. I knew what was coming.

"Olivia. This is ridiculous. When are you going to tell me what you are?"

Fear fell over me, and I was soaked through in an instant.

"I don't mean to be rude, but you know I can feel that you're . . . different. You're more than a witch. More than even a powerful witch. I know you don't call yourself that, don't practice in a coven like I do. But there's something boiling under the surface, and I'm worried for you."

Concern etched her face, throwing me off guard. I had expected the question, but not the kindness behind it.

Maybe that's why I told her. I couldn't think of how to explain it all, so I just told her what happened, and hoped it would be enough.

The summer before I left for college my life was full of ballet skirts and happily-ever-afters. Memories of my Nana's magic were tucked away at the far end of my closet, with the sweaters I never wore and the nightmares I didn't talk about. It was the beginning of August when all of that changed. My girlfriends and I decided to take a trip to see the New York City Ballet one last time before we all went our separate ways. We were out late, later than we should have been. But we were lost in the night, in our innocence, pirouetting through our hotel's back gardens.

Laughter hung in the air, landscape lights flickering around us, but in the sudden stillness, the click of my shoes on the stone walkway was too loud. Tree limbs crashed, snapping into the darkness. Screams surrounded me, spun me around. Something leapt out of the night, knocking me to the ground. Hot claws locked around my ankles, sank into my skin. Cold granite scraped across my cheek, shredded my palms. I reached for something to hold on to, anything. I found the skinny trunk of a white birch, wrapped my arms around it and held on.

My ankle twisted, pain singing over fear until my hip popped, the empty boom echoing over them both. The beast stopped pulling at me and I buried my face in the cool mulch around the tree. Stiff fur brushed my shoulder, the low sound in its throat feral and deadly. Claws like razors slashed through my flesh, ripping across my arm, baring my chest.

My hands gripped the earth beneath me, my blood pouring into the rich dirt of the garden. I opened my mouth to scream again, the tastes of white birch bark and blood filling my mouth, turning the terror into prayer.

In that moment, magic surged like a storm in my belly, and my attacker was thrown fifteen feet, catapulted headfirst into a stone wall.

How? Don't ask me. The only thing I can figure is the combination of prayer, blood, and fear caused some kind of supernatural flare. All I know is it was purely spontaneous. I've never been able to duplicate the effect.

When I came to in a hospital, there were restraints

locking me in place and sedatives keeping me groggy until the full moon passed. That's how I learned the attacker had been a wereleopard. When the full moon came and went and I didn't change, the police interrogated me. For days.

My girlfriends hadn't been harmed—seriously freaked out and recovering at home, though not harmed. They'd run for help when it happened, but by the time the hotel security guards arrived I was a bloody mess and the wereleopard was dead. The police found the circumstances highly suspicious, but I didn't have any answers for them. I didn't understand it, either.

I did know that I was healing faster than I should have been. Plenty of doctors were coming around to poke at me, recorders in hand to document all of the gory details. And the nurses took vial after vial of blood, too, but all the testing was pointless—there wasn't anything unusual about my chemical makeup. Really.

Plastic surgeons spoke to my parents about new and expensive procedures to minimize the scarring, but I didn't see the point. With or without the scars, I would never forget, and I would never be the same. The hospital counselor recommended continued therapy sessions and promised my dad I was well enough to start college as planned, so long as I followed up with the counselor on campus. She also suggested I enroll in a self-defense class.

I thought it was maybe a little late for that, but I enrolled in boxing instead of ballet, which was as far as I was willing to go at the time. My sophomore year came and went before my World Religions class introduced me to Tai Chi, and I got involved with the martial arts. I doubt it's a self-defense combination the hospital counselor had in mind, but so far it's worked out pretty well for me.

Anyway, it turned out I'd come away from the shapeshifter attack still human, but only just, and still a teenager to boot. Damned if I didn't wear those blazing new scars like the badge they were, and proudly, too. For both protection and shock value, sure, but also to prove a point—to myself and to anyone else who cared to gawk in my direction. *I am human. Hear me roar.*

So that was that. I'd told Karen the truth about why I felt different to her, why her senses stood up and took notice when I walked into the room. She knew as much as I did about what lurked beneath my skin, and we'd been best friends ever since.

I set the phone down, finally, worn out with waiting and tired of the memories, and just let the images from this morning's crime scene filter in.

Anya was running. Branches blurred by, scratching her arms. Her back porch came into view. The screen ripped. She was too late. The rogue vampire stretched his hands toward her, and the distance between them vanished. She was lost in his eyes, swirling blue pools in an alabaster face. He smiled, his face contorted by breaching fangs, and Anya tensed, tore herself away.

The spell broken, she conjured the fire. The rogue blinked away, and for a moment she didn't know where he'd gone. When his fangs sank into her neck, she used the searing pain to loose the flames. He howled, and the sound tore through her bones, black rage so thick I couldn't see my way through.

Gulping the sharp clean air streaming in through my window, I jumped when the phone rang, cracking my knee on the coffee table in my hurry to reach it.

"Olivia Peters," I answered.

"Liv, I have a favor to ask you." Karen sounded breathless, like she'd run up the hotel's stairs instead of waiting for the elevator. She probably had. "Davis called me early this morning. Antonio Vesci wants to see you tonight. It's business."

So, the Undead Ruler of the Carolinas had issued a summons for me. Huh. It wasn't the sort of appointment I could refuse, not really, but I didn't have to make it easy, either.

"What kind of business?"

"What kind do you think?"

"I don't know. That's why I asked. And why are *you* calling me about it? Doesn't he have minions for this sort of thing?" I asked, rubbing my knee and knowing full well why she was calling.

Karen's latest lover, Davis, was one of the local vampires, which meant he was linked to Antonio. Personally, Davis made me uncomfortable. He was kind of creepy in the usual Undead way, but I figured he'd been a creep when he was alive, too. He just had that kind of look.

Plus, the whole vampire dating a firefighter thing seemed like overkill to me, but who was I to judge? My own dance card wasn't exactly full these days, not by a long shot. And not just because my creep-detector was set on stun, either.

I sighed. "First, tell me what you know. I'll make a decision about working for Antonio when I have all the facts."

"Okay, but it's complicated." Dread filled the space between her words. "I'm not sure I can explain."

"Try."

"You've heard me talk about Luka Niere, one of the owners at that bar we go to sometimes? Feeling Blue? The one with the bands?"

"Yeah," I said, nodding impatiently. "What about him?"

"Well, he's a wereleopard."

Oh, really? I thought.

"Actually, he is the local clan's Ra'Jahn."

Say again?

"Sort of, the uhm, Leopard King."

Naturally.

My mind whirred and clunked, but couldn't seem to connect all the dots.

"Early this morning, their Shaman, Anya, was murdered. And one of the wereleopards was attacked." The edge in her voice was all but gone, and in its place was a sad shaky sound I liked even less.

"I know. And I'm sorry. I didn't realize you knew her." But I should have. I knew Karen's coven had ties to the wereleopards' Shaman. I should have put two and two together.

"Thank you." She sniffled, and then it hit her. "Wait a minute. How do you know about this already?"

"Well, I didn't know anything about the wereleopard clan, but I saw Anya Sorensen this morning. I'm working the case with the police."

"You saw her? Was it bad?"

I couldn't bring myself to answer her, not directly, not even as a grief counselor. "There's a rogue vampire involved. She tried to take him out, but she didn't get him."

Karen's breath caught in her throat, the details in mine. I couldn't tell her the rest of what I knew. Instead, I turned the tables. "I get the feeling there's something else you want to tell me?"

"You won't like it," she warned.

"That's okay." It wasn't, really, but I couldn't think of anything better to say. "Just say it quick. Get it over with."

"Working with Antonio will put you in close contact with Luka Niere. They're business partners, and, uhm, they're close." She hesitated. "I guess there's a blood link of sorts? Antonio has some type of bond with Luka, and maybe the rest of the clan, too. I'm a little hazy on the details."

She paused, and I bit down hard on my lip. It was a sore point between us, and I didn't really want to acknowledge it. Not now. Karen had always thought it would be good for me to make nice with the wereleopards. She was sure I had unresolved issues about the attack. I didn't, and I wasn't in denial, but there was no convincing her otherwise once she'd declared it true. Either way, this wasn't the time.

"The blood link, it's, like, an ancient connection," she went on, her voice rushing in to fill the silence. "I think it's supposed to be passed from Ruler to Ruler, or something. Like I said, I'm not real clear on the details."

Again, she paused. Again, I said nothing.

"Davis says it's nothing like in the movies."

I took a deep breath, and then another one. "Thanks for clearing that up, Karen." Well, I had to say something, didn't I?

"You're missing the point. The local wereleopard clan is part of Antonio's power base. So this rogue vampire attacked Anya to get to Antonio."

"I didn't miss that one, actually. I just don't see what it has to do with me."

"The rogue has got to be stopped, Olivia, and Antonio believes you're the only person who can do it."

Truthfully, I didn't see how, but I was leaning towards taking the meeting. I figured whatever I could learn from Antonio tonight would only bring me closer to where I needed to be anyway.

"You've got what it takes, Olivia, I know you do. You just have to let it out. Trust me. This is something you have to do. Not for Antonio, but for yourself."

At least seven witty replies came to mind in the thirty seconds of silence that followed, but I swallowed them all. Rogue vampires and wereleopards and burning Shaman vied for position with the images from my dreams, and just now none of it seemed real.

"I'll meet with Antonio," I finally agreed. "I suppose he's already decided when and where?"

***

I didn't like meeting at Feeling Blue, but I didn't have a better idea. I really didn't want to bring Antonio into my office at Forever Crossed, because truly, vampires and funeral homes are not my favorite mix. I did need some control, though, so I insisted on meeting at seven instead of ten. Go me.

Still, I figured the bar would be less crowded, and after, well, I might be able to salvage the rest of the night. With a little luck, I could turn the investigations part of this case over to Mike Rutledge tomorrow and focus my energies on Anya Sorensen's final services. Unfortunately, I wasn't usually that lucky.

The seven o'clock meeting left me with some time on my hands. Not enough for a sparring match at The Ring, so I settled for a quick run. I pound the pavement for the endurance training, of course, to push myself farther and faster than I did the last time, but also for the sheer joy of my body in motion, the blur of speed remaking the world in watercolor. Beautiful, sure, but I can wax poetic about just about anything. It's a natural side effect of being in the funeral home business.

After a quick shower, I spent a long time blow-drying my hair, delaying the inevitable. The wood-handled hairbrush felt warm in my hand, smooth, like a wooden tool ought to feel. When I was young, my Nana and I would sit together in the evenings, and she would brush my hair forever, telling tales and laughing. I remembered her hair, steely gray and long, and how she would let me braid it with flowers after she had done mine the same way.

Finally, I got dressed. There was really nothing to think about. Broken-in Calvin's and a crisp white tee always look good, and I wasn't going to Feeling Blue tonight to make an impression, anyway. A loose sport coat that belonged to an old boyfriend covered the Sig. It held an extra clip in the inside pocket, and it was a staple this time of year, when the air-conditioning made inside temperatures unpredictable.

I took a last look in the mirror, my fingers floating over the charms decorating my bracelet, nervous, and a little eager, too. I'm a practicing Faithologist, which means I Believe in all the gods, but the truth is, everyone has favorites. Personally, I'm partial to the gods of small things, but this bracelet was an old one, and mostly the major gods were represented. Like the deities, each charm had its own energy, like a steady pulse, giving me the focus I knew I would need to face Antonio tonight.

Four

Feeling Blue wasn't a landmark nightspot, but it was getting there. Already it was one of the best places in the Triangle for watching live bands and hot firefighters, which meant I'd been here more than once. On those nights I'd been comfortable, hanging out with Karen and having a good time. Tonight I was here on business, and that was an entirely different story.

I scanned the length of the room, peering into the corners just to be sure, but if Antonio was here, he wasn't in plain sight. My jaw clenched, the tiny popping sound echoing in my ears as I worked hard to pry my teeth apart. The plaintive note in Karen's voice echoed in my mind, helping me fight the urge to spin away from the door and hightail it out of there.

At this hour, the house lights were up and the battered stage was swallowed by the shadows in the far corner. Later in the evening I knew the stage would flare to life, dancers closing the space between the tables and bathing the room in a warm glow. I'd never been here this early, and for a moment, I wished I'd left Antonio's time-frame alone. I missed the band in the background, the feel of a space filled with rhythm and soft light.

Still, the bar itself was the same. Rich mahogany polished to a warm sheen, it stretched across the length of Feeling Blue and separated the live music crowd on the left from the quieter companion tables on the right. Hand carved details proved its age, and tall stools called out to all who entered.

I sat towards the end of the bar, closest to where the band would set up, and when the bartender slid over, I ordered without a second thought. I didn't have to worry about the alcohol affecting my judgment. Like swallowing aspirin when I had a headache, it was more or less window dressing. Cool side effect, huh? It didn't matter how much I drank or what proof the alcohol, I wouldn't get drunk. Not that I hadn't tried.

An abandoned newspaper rested on the bar a few seats from mine. I flipped through it, automatically looking for the Sports section. *They ought to call it the Basketball section,* I thought, scanning the March Madness reports. As usual, the Triangle was well represented at the Dance. The Duke Blue Devils were the title favorites this year, but the Demon Deacons had done well for themselves and Wolf Pack fans had nothing to be ashamed about, either. I found the hockey scores eventually, buried three pages in. It didn't look as good for the Hurricanes, our NHL franchise. They still needed three late season points to edge into the playoffs, but they'd taken a 2-1 loss to Washington the night before. I shook my head, disgusted, and tossed the paper aside.

"On the house," the bartender said, setting the glass down in front of me.

He nodded toward the far side of the room. The man's back was toward me, but I could see the delicate green aura outlining his form. His power stretched toward me, like a cool breeze on a late summer night, and I knew this was Luka Niere. The wereleopard Ra'Jahn.

He turned, displacing the air around him in a shiny rush I shouldn't have been able to see. He was tall, lean and long like a swimmer, with broad shoulders and narrow hips. Karen had warned me about the Leopard King, but it was clear now that she'd left out all the really important details.

The black suede of his coat whispered as he approached, and the cuffs of a linen shirt showed at his wrists. Honeyed hair slicked away from his face in loose whorls, finger-raked perfect, like he woke up looking this good.

I caught his eyes, pine green in the off-light of the bar, and watched his aura shift darker. His power rolled over me, smooth and tingly.

Already I was starting to revise my opinion of wereleopards.

"Manhattan sour?" he asked, casually stretching a few fingers toward my drink. "It's a little old for you, Angel, but I love its scent."

I wondered if he could smell it from across the room, and if so, what other scents hovered in the air around me.

"Come to my table while we wait for Antonio." He took my drink from the bar and started to walk away.

I followed. What choice did I have? But I left cash on

the bar to make a point. I pay for my own drinks.

Silence stretched between us, thickening as we sized each other up. I sipped my drink, swirling the ice cubes and listening to them clink against the glass. I pretended to be comfortable, hoping the truth didn't show.

"So," he said finally. "You're the witch."

"I'm not a witch," I said. "I'm just a friend of Karen's."

His expression didn't change, but the light in his eyes danced, made it clear he didn't agree. He was too smug, this Leopard King, and I countered with a question of my own. "Why are you here, waiting with me?"

"I'm here because Antonio asked me to be here." His aura clouded over. Then he raised an eyebrow, and just like that, the tension fell away. "But, really," he said, white teeth flashing in a full smile. "If you aren't a witch, what are you?"

I didn't like this game. I had power, that much I knew, but it wasn't associated with an avatar or catch phrase or even a religion. And I didn't like the casual inquiry, either, like a challenge, like he'd rummage through my history if he felt like it, with or without an invitation.

"My driver's license says I'm human," I replied, trying not to sound as edgy as I felt. "What's yours say?"

"The same of course." He laughed, a rich warm sound that made the hair on the back of my neck stand up. "If you can pass for human, Angel, I can, too."

Luka stood, nodded toward the bartender and a moment later the houselights dimmed. Candles flickered to life on the tables, making the bar feel cozy and familiar. He shrugged out of his coat, black suede draping from his fingers like an old flannel robe. He raised that eyebrow again, his arm outstretched, waiting for my coat as well. *Why not?* I thought.

My chair scraped against the wood floor, covering the whoosh of my jacket falling from my shoulders to my wrists. I'd exposed not only my gun, but the raised scars that tore across my shoulder and disappeared under the scooped neckline of my shirt. In the bar's dim light they seemed stark, a shiny white I wasn't expecting.

Suddenly shy, my eyes darted away from Luka's. A moment later, Antonio Vesci stood between us, smiling as if he hadn't appeared from thin air.

Goose bumps flowered over my skin, and my arms crossed in front of me as if by rote, my thumb and first two fingers flicking beneath my collarbone. Antonio's hand rested lightly on Luka's shoulder, their bodies close. He turned his face toward me, and I blushed, embarrassed, although I wasn't sure why.

"Ms. Peters, I presume?" The Undead Ruler walked behind my chair and held it out for me. "I see you've met Luka. I trust your wait hasn't been too unpleasant?"

I wanted to ask for my coat back. I wanted to leave and forget about this whole business. In my mind I wove a spell for clarity, sent it swirling through my thoughts. Lowering myself back into that chair was easier than I expected, making me wish I'd fought myself a little harder.

"I don't appreciate the way you set this up, Mr. Vesci." This time, I did fight, fought hard even, making myself meet his eyes.

"Whatever do you mean?" Antonio smiled graciously, as if I were a small child or an amusing companion—attractive, but not too bright.

He held one of my business cards in his unwavering fingers, the clean black print facing out so my own name stared back at me, *Olivia Peters, Bereavement Specialist.* The flashy Forever Crossed logo and the funeral home's contact information were embossed over a hologram on the other side, as garish as my side was plain. *Good gods,* I thought. I hated those cards.

"Your services are for hire, Ms. Peters. And that is what I intend to do. I'm hiring you to track down a predator and bring him to justice."

I didn't like the way he sat cross-legged and motionless, looking at me through eyes so brown they were almost black, trying to appeal to my sense of duty. I didn't like him trying to appeal to me, period. Yeah, he might look perfect, but that's how it is with the Undead. Looks could be deceiving, and in my business, that was never a plus.

"I'm a Bereavement Specialist. That means I'm more like a grief counselor than a hired gun."

"You're also a private investigator, are you not?"

"Well," I began, choosing my words carefully. Truth be told, I am a P.I., but that isn't supposed to be public knowledge. "My services are for the survivors, Mr. Vesci.

Occasionally my work leads in an investigative direction, but that's not really my forte."

"Please," he said, his smile erasing my denial. "Please. Call me Antonio. Vesci is a legality, nothing more."

"Fine. Antonio." I struggled to keep my voice level and sure. I could feel his eyes pulling on mine, like a dare I was afraid to take. "I'm sorry, but I can't help you."

"I think you can, and I'll pay you handsomely for your efforts."

He held my gaze, and despite my agitation, my eyes softened. I remembered this feeling. It was how Anya Sorensen felt looking into the rogue's swirling blues. Except now, with Antonio, magic didn't mingle with terror. A calmness that wasn't my own settled over me, a smooth relaxing energy, like snow flurries on a sunny afternoon.

For the most part, an average vampire's tricks don't impress me much, but average wasn't the sort of word I'd use to describe Antonio. Power rolled off him like foam-tipped waves, and just being in the same room with him made my skin crawl and my own power flare to life around me. He was the Undead Ruler of the Triangle, this was his territory, and he was offering to pay me well for a job I was almost certainly going to do anyway.

Still, I didn't like it. And I didn't like him, either.

My fingers whispered against the condensation on my glass in steady flicks. *Away, away, away.* It was a small protection, a childhood reflex, and it had absolutely no effect on Antonio.

"I'd be happy to recommend a professional you can trust," I said, trying on the sort of smile I usually reserve for the perfume girls at Nieman's. "In my line of work, I've encountered one or two."

"Can you recommend another with your talents, Olivia?"

He spoke with a slight accent, rubbed round and smooth, brought to the surface by the sound of my name. I let his question hang between us, unanswered, a spark of brightening stillness. Neither one of us spoke. The background sounds of the bar hummed into our silence, and his power seemed to pick up that steady thrum.

Suddenly, the candle on our table sputtered in its wax, and in my mind's eye, I watched Antonio die. The images in my vision were broken, frustration seeping around jagged edges, frayed with his effort to keep them hidden.

He was so young, a boy really, and innocent of the ways of the world. His eyes followed a slim woman sauntering across the street. She was dressed in costume, sparkles and feathers, a wand-held mask. The air was thick with torchlight and music as the shadowed man approached him, pressed warm coins into his palm. Antonio smiled, motioned the man toward the canal, where the gondola waited. Antonio turned his head back toward the woman for just a moment, and behind him terror descended. I could feel his shock, the searing pain of fangs sunk deep into his neck, the swirling pleasure of vampire magic as the life force drained from his body.

The vision blurred, and I pulled away.

It was hard to reconcile the naïve boy in my mind's eye with the smooth vampire sitting across from me now, but they were in fact one and the same. Antonio had aged well over the centuries, and to the casual eye, he appeared to be an affluent businessman, a thriving model of twenty-something success.

He smiled at me now, his features sharpened by what he had become, unmasked power veiling the fangs I didn't want to see.

Sweat sprang to life at the base of my neck, slick strands of hair clinging in the damp heat. Blinking hard to clear the remnants of his magic from my mind, I focused on his expression. A puzzle played with the corners of his eyes. He was surprised, maybe even concerned. I'd be worried, too, if I were him. His power was infinitely stronger than mine, but with a single shudder I'd cleared his magic from my eyes.

I took a deep breath, gathered my own power close before I shifted my gaze back to his. Antonio's eyes were like melted chocolate, tempting, but bittersweet when my magic touched them. Replaying the scene in my mind, I pressed the images toward him over and over, until Antonio's hand blurred across the table, and I jerked away from the movement, breaking the link.

"This is a not a game you can win, Olivia." He smiled when he spoke, but it was not a pleasant smile. "I must advise you to stay out of mind. I don't think you'll like what you see."

Antonio's voice radiated authority, but he pulled his power inwards, creating the illusion of distance between us. He stretched his arm casually along the top of Luka's chair. Luka leaned back, like he was settling in for a good movie or a long flight. I inched my chair further from the table.

"I wish I could stay out of your mind," I said. "But you're the one who's broadcasting here. I can only block out so much."

"Fascinating." Antonio ignored my slight. "I underestimated your talents, Olivia. I'll work harder to control my thoughts in your presence."

Luka's mouth twitched at the corners, his power dancing toward me, sending a warm shiver along my spine.

"Most of the time, I only see flashes of a vampire's human death," I told Antonio, my stomach churning with nervous energy. "My visions of the Undead aren't usually so . . . *Complete.*" I stumbled a little there, but I didn't know how else to describe it.

"Extraordinary." Antonio seemed pleased with himself, pleased with me, too, and I regretted the disclosure immediately. "Shall we get down to business, then? I've already worked out the details of our arrangement with the owner of Forever Crossed. Mr. Anderson, is it?"

Was I the only one who doubted I'd agree to this? Probably, but Linc still should have discussed it with me first. I shook my head, making a mental note to talk terms with Linc later.

"Exactly what is it you think I can do for you, Antonio?"

"There is a rogue vampire in this city, Olivia. He uses the name of Feine. Perhaps you have heard of him?" I shook my head. "No? Well, you will, I'm sorry to say. He wants the Triangle for his own, and he'll do anything to get it. Many people, mine and yours, will be hurt in the process."

He had a point. I didn't like it, but I knew he was right. At Forever Crossed we guaranteed the dearly departed we buried would stay both buried *and* departed, so if anything unusual is suspected in a death, the Triangle Police Department often call us in for consultation. We'd had two such calls in the last three weeks, both of them vampire attacks, and there could very well be others that hadn't hit our radar yet.

"The rogue will do substantial damage to me, Olivia, but not only to me. Many innocents will be killed. Don't let your fear of what you do not understand prevent you from doing what you know is right."

I blinked, the motion of my eyelids lousy cover for the truth in his words. Suddenly Antonio was leaning close to me, his breath cool in my hair.

Who said I didn't understand what I was afraid of?

"You are well connected to the city's law enforcement, Olivia," Antonio said. "I believe you will catch my enemy and see he gets the punishment he deserves. I want him executed."

I sipped my drink, wishing I could still hear the ice cubes clink against the glass, wishing I was anywhere but here.

"I could kill him myself," Antonio continued, "but I want this handled legally. Feine's misdeeds have had the effect he desired. The public is beginning to lose confidence. They doubt my ability to rule a peaceful vampire population."

He paused, reining in the power that swirled around him. "I won't tolerate that, and I won't have the Council interfering, either. No, Feine must be legally executed under the watchful eye of the media. You are in the media spotlight, my dear. You are perfect."

Forever Crossed gets it share of local press, but I wasn't exactly a media darling. At best, I gave a reluctant interview, and I'd been told by a few reporters that it was lucky I was photogenic. In my case, at least, a picture was more than worth a thousand words.

"Media relations aside," I said. "The truth is, I'm not much of a private investigator, and I'm certainly not an L.V.T." Nor did I have any plans on becoming a Licensed Vampire Terminator, and if Antonio, or Linc for that matter, thought otherwise, they had better think again.

"I wouldn't ask such a thing of you, Olivia. Please." Antonio's eyes crinkled and his power pressed outward again, like a cocoon around our table. "What I'm asking you to do is help the police catch a rogue vampire. Which you would do regardless, I might add. The rest will take care of itself."

Antonio seemed too confident. It irked me. If there was nothing to it, why the big push to put me on the payroll? He already knew I was involved through the police.

"If your Council wants this resolved, why not let them handle Feine?" I countered.

"No."

Antonio volunteered nothing else, and the silence hung between us. Luka's expression was hidden behind his glass.

"What aren't you telling me?" I demanded.

"Humans." Antonio spoke the word like a sigh, sending fresh shivers up my spine.

Luka grinned, tilting his head just slightly, like a question he shouldn't have to ask.

"I will not invite the Council to solve my problems," Antonio said. "They would destroy what I've worked for here, install another in my territory and send me to who knows where to start again."

I didn't know much about vampire politics, but I didn't like the sound of that. Antonio was popular in the Carolinas. He was outgoing, with an interest in furthering vampire-human relations. And he was good for the economy. Business travelers were starting to bring their families with them now, and tourists stopped in the Triangle on their journeys between the coastline and the mountains, thrilled for a glimpse of the city where vampires roamed free in the night.

Not all areas of the country were so lucky, and I knew that, too. Still, I had some questions of my own.

"May I ask why Feine thinks he'll succeed? Is the Triangle simply positioned for takeover, or is it a personal thing?"

Antonio sighed. "I wish I had a simple answer for you, Olivia. Suffice to say there are many who would like to see me fail. Feine has simply found a way to do it." He paused. *For effect?* I wondered. "The Council will be advised when this threat has been expunged. Not before."

My pager blared to life, the sound jolting from my pocket, startling me. I busied myself checking the display screen, hoping they hadn't seen me flinch. Linc's message indicated that he'd scheduled a last minute appointment for me. *Damn it!* The last thing I needed tonight was another client.

I couldn't put the appointment off, as much as I'd have liked to. The Undead notwithstanding, there's a brief window of opportunity to see whatever a soul has to show me, and this particular death had occurred yesterday. Tomorrow was inconvenient for the client. So it would have to be tonight.

"Is there a phone I could use?" I wanted to let Linc know I would be there within the hour. He could pass it on to the client himself. "It seems I left mine in the car."

"You can use my office," Luka answered. It was subtle, but I saw Antonio give a slight nod before Luka rose. "I'll show you the way."

Luka steered me through the tangle of bodies in the bar, steady pressure on my arm guiding me toward the back stairs. My skin burned beneath his hand, and I both wanted and didn't want to pull away. It had been a long time since a man's touch had made my skin react. Too long, really.

Yeah, I admit it. So what?

I date now and again—a firefighter I met through Karen, the bass player of a jazz band that comes through the Triangle every so often. Nothing like my college days, where lanky athletes and moody artists moved in and out of my life at regular intervals. *Ah, the good old days . . .*

"So, how'd you do it, Angel?" Luka's voice was soft, hushed in the sudden quiet above the bar. He stepped in front of me and opened the office door.

"Hmmmm?"

"He had you in his eyes, just like any other human. I saw it in your face. He had you. Next thing I knew, you had him."

"I really don't know."

He closed the door behind us, the click of the latch like a punctuation mark I couldn't decipher. I picked up the phone without waiting to be invited and sat down behind the desk. His office was organized, used, but not messy, and I frowned into the phone. Even with the desk between us, I could feel the cool heat of him. I wasn't the least bit happy about my physical reaction to Luka Niere, but there was no denying it.

Of course, Linc wasn't available to take my call, which was probably just as well. He knew I'd be furious with him for making arrangements with Antonio behind my back. Not to mention scheduling this client tonight. I left a message with the night receptionist and set the phone back in its cradle.

Across from me, Luka seemed at home in the dark leather side chair, like he spent more time there than behind the desk. Maybe he did. He didn't seem like the desk-jockey sort.

"All set?" Luka lifted his body from the chair and stepped toward the door in a single fluid movement. He had the smooth speed all shapeshifters do, not blinding like the Undead, but graceful and boneless, like water on a winding path.

I swallowed hard and followed him.

***

Downstairs at Feeling Blue, the house band was setting up. On the other side of the bar, two petite blondes, both human, were clinging to Antonio. The majority of the crowd was human, but there were a few shapeshifters in the mix as well. So far, Antonio was the only vampire I could see. I watched his smile broaden as we approached, watched the slow reach of his arm send his admirers back toward the press of bodies by the band.

"You didn't have to dismiss your evening sweets, Antonio." As usual, my nervousness took refuge in sarcasm, but when I looked again, I knew it was true.

Behind my eyes, I watched Antonio awaken this evening, young blondes curled on either side of him, warm and tingly. He fed leisurely, their bodies wrapped lightly around his own. Antonio turned his head, reached absently to rub his hands over living flesh, sift his fingers through the pale hair spilling across his pillows. I shook my head, made an effort to clear away the image.

I started over, hoping something slightly more professional would come out of my mouth this time. "I've got business elsewhere, so we'll have to continue this another time."

I reached for my coat on the hook where Luka had hung it earlier, but Antonio was already holding it out for me. I considered snatching it out of his hands, but figured that would only make me look ridiculous. Instead, I let him help me into it.

"It occurs to me," I said, "that Feine probably isn't working alone." Antonio's face was a stony mask. I pressed on, "He was alone when he attacked Anya Sorensen, but as injured as he was, there must have been another with him to wound the wereleopard."

For the first time, it also occurred to me that Luka might be here for reasons of his own, that maybe he wasn't simply Antonio's beck and call boy. The deceased was his Shaman, and though I didn't know exactly what that meant, I assumed they'd been close.

"I am sorry for your loss," I said to Luka, becoming the Bereavement Specialist once again. "And I hope your associate is healing well. If there's anything I can do, please let me know."

Luka nodded at me, his green eyes cloudy for a moment. "Thank you."

Wasn't I doing enough, already? I wondered, giving my head a mental slap. But my manners, and my training, had taken over. My mother would be proud.

"You are right, of course, Olivia." Antonio's voice brought me back into the moment. "Feine would not have entered my territory alone. He's likely to have half a dozen of his own people with him." His power bristled. "They are all here without invitation."

I knew that should mean something to me, but it didn't, and I was pressed for time.

"Tell me what else you have determined about my adversary, Olivia."

The command in his voice was unmistakable, but I didn't have time to argue. I decided to cut to the chase.

"He's old," I said. "Older than you, but not as powerful." I paused a moment while Antonio soaked up the compliment, giving me time to switch gears. "That tells me just one thing, Antonio. If he believes he can defeat you, he not only brought help with him, he already has help here. One of your people has turned on you, maybe more."

"Yes." In Antonio's mouth the single syllable sounded sharper than it was. Power stormed around him, explosive.

I backed away. "I will find the one who has betrayed me. There are fates worse than death for a vampire, Olivia, of that you can be sure."

White hot pain flashed through my mind, and with it, dark gray fear. Terror gripped my insides. A cool sweat raced over my skin. I'd never experienced anything like this before, and I was quite sure I never wanted to again. But there were fates worse than death for all of us, and I was pretty sure of that, too.

Luka laid his hand on Antonio's shoulder, and his power wrapped around Antonio in a cool blue-green sheet. He spoke quietly, his words moving like sand in an hourglass, though I couldn't quite hear what he said.

Antonio pulled his power back within himself, shook his head and smiled. He was all confidence again, making an effort to meet my eyes.

I don't know why, but I allowed it. My right hand strayed to the Sig at my side, but his eyes were just eyes now, large and lovely dark brown eyes. Understanding washed over me. If we were careful, Antonio and I could find a balance.

"Please allow Luka to see you to your car. I know you have another engagement this evening." Antonio was careful to keep his power away from mine as he sent tendrils toward the bar, lightly touching the patrons with a happy vibe, making sure no one was disturbed by our encounter.

Luka was a half step behind me as we walked toward the door. Again he had his hand on my arm, steering me through the crowd. And again, even through my jacket, I could feel the heat of his hand. Even after we'd left the bar, Luka didn't speak, didn't break the buzzing quiet of the city at night. His arm rested against the small of my back, his fingers dancing a delicate pattern at my waist. I was lost in the moment, mesmerized by his easy manner, the graceful way he moved, and the cool touch of his power along my skin. Even if I could have found my voice, I don't think I would have used it.

I stopped at my car, not stepping away from him until I had to unlock the door. He moved quickly, wrapping his arms around me from behind, holding my body against his. The lean muscles of his chest and stomach pressed into my back, his thighs solid against mine. His fingers brushed the swell of my breast, hot through the soft cotton of my shirt, electric. My nipples stiffened in response, my body sure of itself, sure of him.

Luka nuzzled his face behind my ear, inhaling. In the span of his breath, I knew I could drown in that moment, our bodies pressed together, veiled by the shifting city night, and never notice I'd forgotten to come up for air.

"I can smell the leopard in you, Angel," he whispered in my ear, the scars across my chest throbbing in response. My heart raced against my ribs, fear mingling with desire in a way that made me pull my body from his. "Come back to me tonight. Meet me here after your appointment."

"No," I said, opening the door. I couldn't. I wouldn't. "No," I said again, softly, shaking my head. I wasn't going to get involved with the Leopard King. Not in this lifetime. Not ever. "No."

Luka stood on the sidewalk, one hand in his pocket, a lopsided smile showing the soft curve of his mouth.

I cursed a blue streak under my breath until he disappeared in my rearview mirror, and then I opened the convertible to the cool spring air, letting my frustration out into the night. When my pulse finally slowed to something like a normal rhythm, I punched the client's address into my GPS and let out a long breath. I'd gone at least five miles out of my way, and the loop was inexplicably backed up in the direction I should have been heading, and of course, there wasn't a viable alternate route.

Of all the damn luck, I thought, knowing it probably wasn't going to get any better. Not for me, anyway. Not tonight.

Five

Linc's last minute client hadn't dragged me away from Feeling Blue for nothing, although she hadn't been completely right about her stepfather, either. Like many of the people who call Forever Crossed for a Bereavement Specialist, she hadn't really wanted my services as a counselor. She wanted validation.

Determining right from wrong was never as easy as it seemed, even with an inside track like mine. However, this client was convinced that her stepfather had murdered her mother, and she insisted on contacting the police. I saw nothing from the deceased that suggested she'd been tricked into an overdose, but neither was there evidence that she had intended to die. So when the officers arrived at the scene, I reconnected with the transitioning soul, allowing their digital recorders to document my findings.

Again I saw the deceased sitting up in her bed, dressed in a pretty pink nightgown, a white duvet over her legs. She stretched her hand out to her husband. He emptied several pills into it, then handed her a tall glass of milk. She swallowed the pills, returned the glass, and held his hand as she settled back on the pillows. She heard him read to her from a book of poems, the pages worn and yellowed with age. And then she slept. She felt no malice, and she died without pain. I thought she probably went knowingly, but it wasn't my call.

The police ordered an autopsy and waited for the stepfather to return from the mortuary. I verified that this was the man I saw providing the pills to the deceased, and he was taken into custody. I squeezed my client's hand, trying to impart as much comfort as she would allow. Her mother's body would be delivered to Forever Crossed from the Coroner's office, and Linc would be in touch with her about further arrangements. I invited her to contact me directly if she needed additional documentation, since we'd have to try to connect before tomorrow evening, and I left as soon as I could.

I hoped she didn't want anything else from me, since I thought pursuing charges against her stepfather was a mistake. But she was paying for my vision, not my opinion, and I wasn't exactly the moral authority around here.

That's what I was thinking about, standing on the fire escape and unlocking my kitchen door at two in the morning. Again. And then a hollow whir spun in my ears, heat prickling a warning along my spine.

Too late, and a silent blast smashed my body into the door. Slick pain seared through my left leg. I crouched lower, twisting to get my back against the solid door.

Shot? Shot! Gods be damned, I've been shot!

The thoughts raced through my mind so quickly I wasn't sure which one came first. My hand roamed over my leg, assessing the damage. Shrapnel shredded denim; hot blood streaking through gaping flesh. Sweat rolled off my face, icy trails burning down my back.

Adrenaline pushed the pain to the background and forced me into action.

My fingers were cold and sticky, but the Sig was steady in my grip. I peered through the darkness, scanning the lot for my shooter. A lone figure ducked behind the recycling bin, stock still and solid. I took a deep breath, willing him into motion.

I had no problem shooting back. I just wanted to see the gun in his hand first, wanted to be sure I hit the right target.

C'mon, you coward, I taunted, my mind racing a mile a minute. *Move!*

In the blink of an eye his body slammed into the fire escape. Startled, my hands flew back to cover my mouth, the weight of the Sig splitting my lip. His feet pounded the stairs, shaking the rusted metal against the quiet of the night. The air around me was charged, scented hot with blood and gunfire.

He turned the bend in the stairs and paused, directly below me. The shiny silver of his gun flashed against the black backdrop of his body. I heard my own breathing, quick and jagged, and his, unnaturally slow, a steady counterpoint. I clenched my jaw, waiting until his foot hit the next step.

My leg ached, the pulse of blood slowing to a heavy beat against my temples. Sore from holding the Sig steady, my arms began to tremble. My muscles screamed, tense from waiting.

He lunged toward me. Instinct took over, and I fired. My brain lurched, unable to catch up.

Time slowed as I watched my bullets find their mark. Flesh gaped stark white, then filled with blood. Bright red against the black knit of his clothing.

He sagged against the rail. Time rushed forward, tumbling him over the stairs. Peering through the metal grating, I saw him fall, heard his body hit the pavement with a solid thud.

I was still staring down into the night when his body twitched twice and rolled over. I blinked hard, scrubbed grimy hands over my face as he picked himself up and disappeared around the corner.

Cool air burned my lungs as I hauled myself upright. My leg roared in protest, my body slouched against the door. Sheer will forced my fingers to turn the key. Finally, I limped into my kitchen. Raising a shaky finger to the door, I traced a circled pentagram with my own blood, words of protection spilling from my mouth.

I didn't want to see my leg in the bright light of the kitchen. I didn't really want to see it at all. I stripped off my Calvin's in the dark, the denim clinging wetly to my throbbing leg. I left them in a heap on the floor, a bloody mound covering my shoes. Ruined.

In my peripheral vision the blinking light of my message machine called to me. Habit took over, compelled me forward. From a distance, I watched my own index finger pressing play.

Karen. My mother. BellSouth customer service. I half listened to the messages, leaning against the wall, until Mike Rutledge's cop voice demanded my attention. He'd faxed the relevant case files to my office and would meet me there at ten in the morning. He said I should call him first thing if the timing wasn't convenient.

It wasn't, but it would be less convenient to get up early just to reschedule. I couldn't decide if I should report the shooting now or just tell Mike about it in the morning. And then the phone rang, derailing my train of thought.

I grabbed the handset and dragged myself into the master bath, bracing myself for the flood of light as I flicked the switches for both the overhead fixture as well as the bulbs surrounding the mirror. Too bright, way too bright, but I really needed to get this wound cleaned up. It wasn't bleeding much anymore, but it wasn't looking so good, either. I was drifting, and my teeth hurt, and the ring of the phone vibrated through my fingers.

"Olivia Peters."

"Did I wake you, Angel?" Luka's voice breathed into my ear. Tears sprang to my eyes.

"I've just come in." My voice was calm, steady, as I shook three aspirin tablets into my palm. I slipped off my jacket and tossed it into the dry cleaning bag.

It suddenly struck me funny that I was on the phone with the local Ra'Jahn, wearing not much more than my undies and a 9mm, and trying to figure out how to keep my gun handy but still get in the shower.

"Hey, Luka?" I knew I was interrupting, but I had no idea what he was saying. "Could you come over?" Now I had no idea what I was saying. "Some guy shot me on my way in, and I need to get cleaned up, but I kinda don't want to put my gun down to do it." The words were just slipping out now, I couldn't stop them, "It's not bad, just a flesh wound." And why was I still talking? Gods, why was I telling him this, telling him anything? I had better be in some kind of shock, because that was the only excuse for this kind of babbling.

I wanted to hang up while Luka swore under his breath, then spoke quickly to someone away from the receiver. "One of the Ja'Nan will be there in ten minutes," he said, clearly speaking to me again, and I knew I'd missed my chance. "I'm sorry I can't come myself, but I'm sending Cole. You can trust him, Angel. He'll look out for you."

"No," I said, sorry that I'd told him. "Don't send anyone. I'll be fine. I'm barely bleeding now." I meant it, too. I didn't want this from him. I tried to tell myself I didn't want anything from him.

"Too late, Angel. Just stay on the line with me until Cole gets there, okay?" I didn't say anything. "Don't be mad," he soothed. "Let me do this."

I didn't usually inspire this kind of protective instinct in men. Then again, I didn't usually ask to be protected.

I listened to him talk, about nothing mostly, just words, just his rich voice pouring into my ear. I hobbled to the bathroom, set my gun by the sink. Shrugging out of the holster, I pulled off the not-so-white shirt I'd worried over this afternoon. With the Sig tucked into the right-hand pocket of my robe, I leaned back against the counter, exhausted.

My fingers itched at the gash on my thigh, and it was all I could do to focus on Luka's voice. I rubbed at the drying blood, lost in the thick brittleness of it. When I noticed the rusty flakes on the floor I forced myself to stop. It would only make more of a mess when I stepped out of the shower.

An eternity passed before I put together a coherent thought, another before I voiced it. "Luka?" I asked. "What makes you think I'll feel any better taking a shower with a wereleopard watching over me?"

"You probably won't," he admitted, "but I'll know you're safe."

The knock on my front door had to be Cole. Through the peephole, he looked to be about my age. Tanned warm and golden, streaky hair falling over one eye, he seemed more like a stranded surfer than anything else. I opened the door and waved him in.

"Hey," he said. "That Luka?" When I nodded, he nodded back, locking the door behind us. That earned him a couple of points in my book. Details matter. I handed him the phone.

While he spoke to Luka in low tones, I limped to the kitchen and put the kettle on to boil, careful to avoid the bloody jeans by the door. Bunched muscles throbbed with a fierceness I could barely stand, drawing my attention away from crushing the herbs I knew would help.

Gripping the counter, I watched my knuckles poke at my skin. My breath was ragged. My heartbeat marked time in pale, uneven beats. I searched for a focus, desperate not to faint. The whisper of the kettle was soft, a steam-filled secret, lulling my racing pulse back to a steady throb.

I poured the hot water into a bowl, tied the herbs in a muslin square and dropped them in to steep. The water swirled, ribbons of color blurring my vision until I closed my eyes against them, the warm vapors filling my mind.

I didn't look up until I felt Cole in the room. He lounged in the doorway, curious blue eyes following my every move.

"It's for healing," I said. He nodded again. "Would you

carry it for me? There are hot pads in the drawer by the stove." He moved, and the doorway seemed bigger than it was, empty. I hobbled past him, keeping my right hand on the gun in my pocket.

He followed behind me, carrying the steaming bowl easily. He didn't bother with the hot pads. "You can set that down," I told him when we reached the bathroom. "I'd like some privacy. Do you mind waiting out there?"

I wasn't really asking.

For the first time he looked uncomfortable. "I can't," he said. "Luka told me to stay with you."

"I don't think he meant we should shower together." This was exasperating. I didn't even want him here.

"You could fall, hurt yourself . . . Luka would blame me." He jammed his hands into his pockets. "You've been shot."

"If I fell you would hear me," I countered. "Besides, the bullet barely grazed me. See?" I pulled the robe away from my leg. My thigh was swollen, angry red, a horrible gash splitting lean muscle in an ugly line. It was rough, but the bleeding had stopped and the wound wasn't gaping anymore. It could have been a lot worse. Even so, bits of denim and shrapnel and other debris would be knit right into the fabric of my skin if I didn't get it cleaned up in a hurry.

I looked up from my leg, surprised to see the color rushing into Cole's cheeks.

"It's true?" He swallowed hard, his voice close to a whisper.

"You think I'd fake taking a bullet?"

"No! Of course not . . . That's not what I meant."

"I don't have time for this. Get out so I can get cleaned up." He didn't budge. "Please?" I added, an afterthought.

He just stood there, eyes wide, staring at me. I leaned past him and opened the linen closet.

"If you're not going to leave then you're going to help," I told him. "Grab a few towels and a wash cloth."

He did as I asked, setting a neat stack of towels on the vanity. "I'll go," he said. "But I'm waiting right outside the door. If I hear anything, I'm coming in."

I shook my head. I didn't want him lurking around my bedroom. "Would you mind going back out and making sure everything is locked up?" I turned my back to him and started the shower. By the time I turned around again, he was gone.

I waited for the steam to drift up toward the ceiling before I inched on the cold tap and stepped under the streaming water. I didn't bother taking my hair down from its twist. I was in no shape to wash it now and the thought of drying it made my head hurt.

Hot water beat over my skin, the needling pressure soothing my aches away. When the water swirling around my feet turned from red to pink, and then finally clear, I nudged the showerhead to a fine spray and angled it carefully into the gash across my thigh. The whole area was raised and dark, but the swelling had gone down some. The good news was my body wouldn't have to fight off an infection on top of healing the wound. The bad news was I would have another nasty scar. Guess I'd either have to get comfortable with that quick or buy some longer skirts.

Like I had time to shop.

Finally, I turned off the water and wrapped myself in a thick cotton towel. Good linens were one of my first post-college indulgences, and back then, I'd actually bought white. Hey, live and learn, right?

Now my towels were black and I didn't worry about stains, I just dropped one of them in the herbal soak I'd prepared, gave it a quick swirl and then eased it over my thigh. I lowered my self to the edge of the tub, leaning against the tiled wall for support, and stretched my injured leg across the ledge. Between the hot towel and the herbs, I figured I'd be walking around by morning.

I closed my eyes, wondering for the first time since it happened, who the hell had shot me and why. In theory, any number of people in this city could have it in for me.

More than a few folks in these parts had religious objections to the work we did at Forever Crossed, claiming our actions to keep the dead in their graves gave credence to other risings, and therefore devalued The One Truly Risen. Or something. Since the logic of the Righteous always confuses me, I wouldn't put hiring a hit man past them, but the idea just didn't feel right this time.

The only active cases I had were the two I picked up tonight, and I doubted that my client's stepfather had hired someone to take me out. He didn't seem the type, which meant this had something to do with Antonio. Or more precisely, with Feine.

Just at this moment, though, I needed sleep more than I needed answers. Despite the sharp soreness in my leg, I edged upright and shuffled to my bedroom. Wrapped into a soft quilt, the Sig tucked under my pillow and cool air playing over my leg, I was almost asleep when I remembered the leopard in my living room.

"Hey!" I called out. Cole appeared faster than I could sit up. "You really don't have to hang around. I don't think that guy is coming back."

"I'll stay anyway." He shrugged, jammed his hands in his pockets. "Luka," he said, as if that explained everything. I guess it did.

I couldn't decide if it would be easier to send him back out to the living room and try to pretend he'd left like I'd asked him to, or if I might actually sleep better knowing he was here. I went with the latter.

"How is it?" he asked, moving closer to get a better look at my leg. "Does it hurt?"

"Yeah," I admitted. "It hurts. But it'll be better in the morning." I reached out and set the alarm clock for nine. If I was quick, I could get ready in an hour and still have time for coffee. Cole was still standing over me, by the foot of the bed. He was starting to freak me out.

"You're afraid of me." He grinned and shook his head, surprised. I looked in his eyes, saw them slide yellow, shiny and iridescent. Then he blinked, and his gaze washed over me again, soft and sweet blue. "Why are you scared?" he asked. "I'm here to keep you safe."

I didn't want to explain, so I put the fear out of my mind. I told myself I was safe, letting the words repeat over and over in my mind. Still, I couldn't stop my hand from straying under the pillows, my fingers flicking against the sheets.

"Forget it," I said. "Tell me about the Ja'Nan."

I tried to get comfortable again. The words of a childhood rhyme filled my head, something my Nana taught me years ago that used to keep the bad dreams away.

Cole crossed the room, switched off the overhead lamp.

The only light spilled in from the bathroom, enough to watch him look around the room, searching out all the corners. I closed my eyes. When I opened them again he'd pulled a chair beside my bed and curled into it, his feet tucked beneath him. Just then he reminded me of a dancer, graceful and limber, comfortable with himself.

He took a deep breath, let it out slowly. "We are the Kaluu Ja'Naa," he began. "We are the Noble People. We were here in the beginning, and we will be here in the end." His voice took on the musical quality of an often-told story. In my head I heard the now familiar cadence of Anya's chant, and I knew this was a shaman's story. "We are free on the land, the waters. We are the people of the trees. Protected and protecting, always."

Cole's hand reached across my pillow, quick, and shapeshifter smooth. His voice didn't waiver as he removed the wooden sticks still holding my hair twist in place. He set them on the dresser, light fingers pulling my hair across the pillows. He settled back into the chair, still lulling me with his story, whisper-rounded words finally carrying me into sleep.

Six

I sauntered through Forever Crossed dressed in my workday usual, bare legs daring my coworkers to mention the shiny red ridge blazing across my thigh. It was still sore, and touching it was not a good idea, but my body had accomplished overnight what it would take the average person weeks to do.

Ellen looked concerned, taking a bit of the wind out of my sails, but she didn't say a word. I draped a cloak of confidence over my shoulders, and meandered over to the fax machine.

Danny whistled from the doorway, low but rising, like a liquid smile.

"Nice going." He took a closer look at my leg, nodded his approval. "Wanna talk about it?"

"Not so much," I replied, smiling. "I think it speaks for itself."

I gathered the files Mike had faxed last night and took them into my office. A quick glance through the paperwork told me the two victims who preceded Anya Sorensen were female, too, though a closer look revealed that's where their similarities to the Shaman ended. Still, I couldn't shake the feeling that they were all connected.

The coroner had measured bite spans and compared imprints and whatever else coroners do, all of which determined conclusively that the same vamp killed the first two. By the size of the bites, I was guessing the perpetrator was likely female, or a young male turned vampire before he'd hit puberty. That thought alone made me shudder.

Of course, it was impossible to say for sure, but from what I'd seen through Anya's eyes, I'd say Feine's jaw was too large to have made those marks. Which meant I'd been right after all. Feine did have accomplices in his quest for the Triangle, and at least one of them was willing to kill for him.

So far, the police hadn't found a single witness to the vampire's crimes, nor did they have any leads on who the murdering vampira might be. Naturally.

On the plus side of the case files, the coroner had

collected quite a bit of forensic evidence. Both victims had multiple secondary bites, and on the second victim, Jaclyn Dupree, some of the bites dated back a number of years. Interesting. The old bites were healed over, but a viable DNA sample from the newest wounds wasn't impossible. The proliferation of fang scars was a good sign that both victims were Undead groupies, so unless they were unusually discreet, it wouldn't be too tough to find out which vampires they'd been hanging with lately.

The first victim, Sabrina Ross, also had ligature marks at her wrists and ankles. The coroner speculated sexual bondage. It wasn't pretty.

As for the vampire remains that had been found, the police hadn't expended much manpower on looking for the perpetrator. The files contained photos, though. All three corpses had been brutally dismembered and the examiner on-scene had photographed the bodies in various stages of rot.

Despite popular belief, vamps didn't burst into a cloud of dust and blow away the moment they died. Instead, they began to decompose. The longer they'd been Undead, the faster the rot took them. It could be anywhere from several hours to a week for a vampire's corpse to reach that cinematic ashy stage. An instantaneous dusting meant the body had been thousands of years old, ancient even by vampire standards. These three weren't that lucky.

I'd have to find out who these vampires were, of course, and maybe talk with the individuals who'd found the bodies. It was possible their souls were still hanging around, though I doubted it. I noted the names on all the files, from the victims to the callers to the cops who'd been assigned the cases, but none of them matched up.

Damn.

I'd have to run them by Antonio and see if he had any insight. I'd put money down that the folks who found the dead vamps couldn't be interviewed until sundown, and if that was the case, I definitely needed more caffeine.

While I was stirring sugar into my already lightened coffee, Mike's heavy black shoes on the back steps announced his arrival.

He nodded at me and said hello to Ellen.

"You take it black, right?" I asked, holding out a fresh

mug, a good excuse to keep him at arm's length.

Mike smiled, and I knew I was in trouble.

"You got something you want to tell me about, Peters?" he asked, not a minute after I'd closed the door to my office. "I can't help noticing you didn't have that scar yesterday."

He settled into the chair opposite my desk, careful to keep his expression neutral. The rapid healing was hard to swallow, and Mike wouldn't be the first person to walk away from it thinking that maybe I wasn't quite human after all.

"A stray bullet may have found its way through my leg last night. It's not a big deal."

I tried to laugh it off, but Mike was a cop's cop. He couldn't stop himself from bristling about my failure to report the shooting. Even so, I knew better than to let him talk me into it. I didn't have a shred of evidence on my side, not even a bullet wound, not anymore. There wasn't a whole lot of incident left to report, nowhere near enough to make an official explanation worth my while.

To take Mike's mind off the shooting, I shared a few details from my conversation with Antonio last night. I didn't like concealing his contract with Forever Crossed, since I was already walking a fine line here, but I couldn't risk it. The Undead Ruler was essentially using us as pawns in his plot to rid himself of Feine, something a guy like Mike wasn't about to take lightly. Come to think of it, I didn't much care for the sound of it myself.

According to the reports Mike brought with him, the coroner had nothing to add to my findings regarding Anya's death. Not a surprise, since there wasn't a body, and all of the evidence was burned black and ashen. The police had no leads on who the blood at the scene belonged to, either. No identifiable prints in the house, and the dogs hadn't been able to track him through the trees.

A cocky grin seemed in order, but then I remembered I could have verified my theory about the wereleopard last night, and I didn't feel like such a hot shot anymore. I'd been distracted by the Ra'Jahn, damn it, and then afterwards I'd forgotten all about it. Hey, taking a bullet will do that, but I had no excuse for my lapse at Feeling Blue.

I cleared my throat, tried to focus on the next step. "Maybe we should concentrate on the first two victims? The coroner thinks our killer is a female vamp, so that narrows the field by half." Less than half, actually. The Undead population was disproportionately male. "The bodies were left in public places, so she wanted us to find them . . ."

"High drama factor," Mike agreed. "She's in it for the attention."

"Power hungry, too. If Feine succeeds, she'll be right by his side."

"She won't be hard to track down, Peters. Not with a crackerjack *Bereavement Specialist* like you on the case, eh?"

Mike wasn't a big fan of my position at Forever Crossed, but he never treated me like some sort of funeral home freak. He'd always given me the same crappy treatment he'd give any P.I. horning in on one of his cases, and I liked him a little more for the extra effort. I tossed the folder at him, laughing, but I hoped he was right about tracking the vampira.

Now that the police were looking at all the cases on the same timeline, it was obvious that the space between attacks had narrowed to just a few days. Mike suspected there'd be another victim within forty eight hours.

I suspected he was right.

"So," Mike started. "I'm thinking your shooter isn't attached to this thing. It's a break in the pattern, and it doesn't make sense. Whoever heard of a vampire hiring a hit man?"

"First time for everything?" I said, and then it dawned on me. The shooter wasn't a hired gun.

I bounced the idea off of Mike. First, the guy was a lousy shot and carried a flashy gun. Second, I shot the guy twice at a fairly close range, and he'd walked away, even after a nasty fall from my fire escape. Third, he left the job unfinished—lucky for me, but not very professional.

"Let me get this straight. You're saying that the shooter is a vampire? Well, that's just not natural, Peters." He laughed at his own joke. "Get it? Not natural?" He cleared his throat and tried to suppress the grin. "Cop humor. Sorry."

"Cop humor," I agreed, smiling more at him than at the joke.

Law enforcement was never easy, but for a guy like Mike the challenge was greater than usual. Working the Triangle's supernatural cases separated him from the other cops in the city, forced him to the edge of that circle. Besides, I knew how important it was to keep finding the laughter. When you couldn't joke about the job, it was time to get out. That Mike considered me joke-worthy was actually quite a compliment. Like using my last name, the jokes were his way of making me one of the boys. It was kinda nice, really. Mike was kinda nice.

And if he decided to pursue the vampire angle, this case could be headed into interesting territory. It would bring the question of jurisdiction into play, and until now that question hadn't really been answered. In the eyes of the law, vampires weren't any different from other citizens. Not technically, but the reality was local cops didn't get involved in vampire grievances. The vampire population had its own laws, and the Ruling Undead acted as judge and jury for his territory. Executioner, too, if he chose to be.

But now we had two dead groupies downtown and Anya Sorensen's burned remains way out in the burbs. Things were about to change in the Triangle, and Antonio was smack in the middle of it.

Vampire crimes were on the rise in big cities around the U.S., and so far the Courts had shown little tolerance for the Undead in these matters. Crime, like everything that the vampires did these days, was big news, and in nearly every case that splashed across the wire a Termination Warrant had been issued. The controversy raged, breathing new life into the death penalty debates and making my blood boil.

I understand better than most exactly what kind of animals stalk our city's streets, but I wasn't about to start advocating for court-ordered killings. Not with my family tree. Still, the Criminal Justice System hadn't found any other way to deal with the Undead, and as it happens, they'd sort of changed the way the rest of us thought about cruel and unusual punishment.

Antonio had thought all of this through already, I

mused, only half hearing what Mike was saying. That's why he'd hired me. He wanted a public execution, and he knew the media's insatiable appetite for sensationalism would give it to him. Meanwhile, he would take care of the betrayers in his midst, punish them for whatever rules, written or unwritten, that they'd bent or broken.

"Peters?" Mike's voice cut through my haze. I got the feeling it wasn't his first try, either. "Hey, you with me or what?"

"I'm with you, Mike," I lied, trying to cover it quickly with the truth. "Just thinking about jurisdiction."

"Yeah, okay. Jurisdiction." He stood, the contact list I'd made earlier still in his hand. "So. You want to see if any of these folks can be reached during the day?"

"It's a long shot," I answered, standing up to walk him to the door. My leg was stiff, sure, but I was up for a little recon. You bet I was.

"True. But we might get lucky."

"What's this *we* crap?" The office seemed smaller than it was, the two of us towering over the furniture and my energy bouncing off the walls. "If you think one little bullet scratch has me out of commission, you're dead wrong!"

"Ease down, Peters." A grin toyed with the left corner of his mouth. "Try thinking of this as a joint investigation. Don't get your panties in a bunch."

Which is exactly why I'm strictly a thong or nothing kind of gal. And Mike calls himself a detective. Hah!

***

I spotted the unmarked cop car in the parking lot, a shiny white Ford, and headed for it without a word. I didn't like not taking my own car, but my display of ego in the office made this an easy concession. Besides, I was grateful to be a passenger for a change, and it felt damn good to stretch my leg out.

Mike was an aggressive driver—go figure—but he knew his way around the city. Even though I'd been living in the Triangle for a few years now, I still needed directions wherever I went. Maybe it's me, or maybe it's a chick thing, but I figured I'd keep on paying for the GPS subscription that linked my car to the best mapping technology the world had to offer. Because, yeah, I'm directionally challenged. So what?

Both of the human victims lived in a rundown section on the city's east side. Sabrina Ross, victim number one, had resided in a converted motel that now offered weekly and monthly rentals. A few beat-up cars littered the parking lot, and when Mike cut the Ford's engine, strains of a rhythmic bass beat pulsed toward us. The Triangle might be populated by the Undead, but it was certainly alive with music. Especially now, in the early days of spring, when windows were flung wide to the flower-scented wind, everything around us rustling with restless energy.

Despite the rhythm, and the sweet blossoms blooming on the stoops even in this beat-up section of the city, Mike was all business. His eyes were cold, and his mouth was set in a firm but pleasant half-smile. It was his cop face, honed to perfection and radiating authority. I did my best to match his expression and knocked on the door.

It opened in, a swell of sound pushing forward to fill the void, revealing a woman about my age with a baby on her hip and a toddler's chubby arms wrapped around her leg. She was beautiful, in an exhausted sort of way, and the thrum of music bouncing around her made her skin seem shiny and bright. She bent, whispering something in the toddler's ear, and he disappeared behind her. The three of us looked at each other for a few seconds, waiting, assessing.

Mike flashed his badge, and I watched her good mood evaporate. He introduced us as the music edged lower, faded into the background, and the little boy returned with a remote control wobbling in one hand, his arms snaking back around his mother's thigh.

"Are you Bandie Cede, ma'am?" Mike asked, glancing quickly at the notebook in his hand. I was impressed.

Bandie only nodded, meeting Mike's eyes, then mine. I smiled. She didn't.

"We'd like to talk to you about one of your neighbors," Mike said. He paused, both of us watching her face. "Sabrina Ross."

Her eyes softened, and she moved the baby to her other hip.

She spoke after a moment, and her voice was sweet and gravelly, the rounded words flowing from her mouth. "I tol' that girl, keep cleara the blood suckers, but she have her own min'. Most ones around here poisonin' they lives with drugs, but not Bri. She like to bleed. Girl was crazy." The patois was a local mix, an island dialect stirred into decades of Southern culture.

"You ever party with her?" Mike asked.

I doubted it, but I knew it was a standard question. This woman was too earthy, too connected to herself, for the blood thrills Sabrina Ross sought.

"Once. And once enough for me. Not my thing, nah mean?" She played absently with the beads in her baby's hair. "I got a full life. I tol' her I don't go for that mess, tol' her she ought leave it alone. But Bri wasn't mucha listener."

"You know of anyone who might be able to tell us more?"

"She have friends, I s'pose, but none who came around this way. Sometimes she'da come here, listen to music, talk about men, love . . ." Her voice trailed off and she looked at me. "Girl stuff, nah mean?"

I nodded. My thoughts strayed to Karen for a moment, and I reeled them back in, quick.

Her hips swayed slightly with the music, keeping the baby drowsing as she spoke. "She workin' cocktail downtown, some nasty place, fulla vampires. The Double Down? She have friends there." Her face clouded over, and in response the baby on her hip started to whimper. "Bri have problems, sure, but she don't deserve it like this."

"Was Sabrina seeing anybody in particular? Any special friends?"

"Nah. She close wi' the bartender, Jackie. Maybe she tells you more?"

"Thanks for your time," I said, handing her my card. "If you want to go to the cemetery together, give me a call, okay?"

"Y'all would do that for Bri?" she asked.

"Sure would," I said, and I meant it. I'd go visit the gravesite by myself, if I had to. She'd made some lousy decisions along the way, but Sabrina Ross had opened her heart in this world, and a body's final resting place needed to declare the soul's truth. Maybe she'd been a

Believer, maybe not, but I'd weave my own protections for her either way. It was the least I could do.

***

The air conditioning in Mike's car hummed quietly, an easy silence I almost didn't want to break. I did it anyway, because really, open windows would have been fine by me. "Jackie, huh?"

Mike grinned. "Who knew?"

Jaclyn Dupree was the second victim—had to be Jackie the bartender. Both bodies were found within a mile of each other and, according to Mike, within a mile of the Double Down.

This was almost too easy.

"We're on a roll with this one," Mike said, easing the car back onto the belt line. "Let's get some lunch, then go talk to whatever staff is working at this hour at the Double Down. The way this is going, we could have the name of our perpetrator today, maybe even find her tonight."

We grabbed sandwiches at a corner shop that catered to cops and served dark-roasted coffee all day long. Pictures of the boys-in-blue, wearing softball uniforms and holding bowling trophies, decorated the walls. Music played softly from a jukebox in the back, mostly older stuff. Mellow, not much bass, not too risqué. Cop tunes.

***

Mike was right. We did get a name from the day boss at the Double Down. Between accepting deliveries off the loading platform in the back, Ron White told us that Sabrina Ross and Jackie Dupree had been hanging around an Undead dominatrix who called herself Adrienne.

"What do you know about her?" I asked.

"She's been in the city for a few years. Don't know where she came from, but she's pretty old. Doesn't seem all that powerful, but she's a looker, you know?"

He waited for us to agree, so I nodded my assent. Besides, I did know—vampire magic covered flaws and accentuated the positives. Even a Plain Jane could become eternally attractive as a vampire.

"Adrienne's got a pull on certain folks," he continued. "I've never seen anything like it. They take one look at her, and she owns them."

"That's unusual for this scene?" Mike asked. "I thought

Blood Bars like this one were all about submission."

He seemed to know what he was talking about, which made me give him a second look. Maybe there was more to Mike than I'd thought.

He caught me looking. "When I first made Detective, I worked Vice," he explained.

"Sure you did." I nodded, trying to look sincere. Ron White grinned. Mike frowned.

"So what's special about this Adrienne?" Mike prompted, getting us back on track.

"I can't explain it any better. I just run the place. I'm not into this mess myself. It's like her magic is all about her looks. When she's prowling, it's like she glows. Come back tonight and maybe y'all can see her for yourselves."

"You think she could be responsible for what happened to Sabrina and Jackie?" I asked.

"Maybe." He seemed to be thinking it over. "But those two were into the danger. It was bound to catch up with them sooner or later."

He was probably right.

"So where can we find Adrienne now?"

"Lady, you think I know where they sleep during the day? You have any idea what a human has to do to get that kind of information?"

Antonio's breakfast of blonde flashed through my mind, just as disturbing now as it had been the first time. I shrugged away from the images, hoping it looked like nonchalance.

"You want to come to the club tonight and see if Adrienne's here, I'll put your name on the list at the door. I've told you what I know. You want more than that, you'll have to question Antonio." He looked smug, like questioning Antonio was something we probably wouldn't do.

Which was good news for me. It meant word wasn't on the street that I was on the Undead Ruler's payroll.

"We'll do that," Mike said. Then as an afterthought, he asked, "Any chance Antonio will be here tonight?"

"Nah." The manager laughed. "Not his kind of place. He'd close it down, but that would just open the market to a chain like Januarius."

"So?" I asked.

"Antonio doesn't want a franchise like that in the Triangle. Don't you read the papers?" He led us back through the front of the bar. "He was quoted the other day, said those places make it tough on the locals who own bars and other businesses down here."

"Interesting."

"More than interesting," he said. "Januarius brings in the big bucks, no doubt about it, but there's problems come with all that money. Especially for little guys, like us. Antonio won a lot of support voicing that opinion."

Very interesting.

Ron White reminded me I'd be on the guest list, then locked the Double Down's front door behind us.

It was about five hours until the sun set, when the Undead rose and the Double Down opened its doors to the public. Five hours on top of that before the place would really get hopping.

I could hardly wait.

Seven

"Not without police backup, Peters." Mike's deep voice was clear in the fading light. The thunk of his car door closing lent his words an authority that made me bristle.

"Fine by me." A cool breeze blew across the funeral home's lot. "Send all the backup you can spare, Mike. But send 'em tonight." My jaw ached, sweetness pouring through a smile that wasn't meant to win him over. "I'm going to the Double Down."

"I'm suggestin' that you wait." The edge in his voice crept into his eyes, turning them to steel as I watched. He wasn't making a suggestion at all.

"Can't," I said, shaking my head as I stepped away from the white sedan. "Ron White put me on the guest list for tonight, remember?"

I felt Mike's stare drilling into my back as I walked toward the building. He wasn't happy with me, but he wasn't mad enough to turn away before I was safely inside Forever Crossed, either.

Linc was out of the office, but Ellen penciled me in for half an hour between tonight's viewings, which was fine by me. I was looking forward to an afternoon at home anyway, and thirty minutes with Linc was more than enough. I only needed time to chew him out for taking on Antonio's case without consulting me, with a little left over to butter him back up. I had a favor to ask, after all.

Linc had taken me shopping for the 9mm when I first got my P.I. license, and now I needed help finding a second weapon. Fast.

***

I parked my convertible on the street instead of in the resident's lot, even though the closest spot I could find was a block and a half from my building. On an ordinary day, I'd have enjoyed the walk—pink cherry blossoms swirling to the sidewalk, and the late afternoon sun warm in my hair. But my leg was sore, the shops were busy, and the horrified looks my spankin' new bullet wound attracted lit my face beet red with something close to shame. Even so, the sound of the wind whistling through my fire escape wasn't something I was in a rush to hear again. Not today. And maybe not tomorrow, either.

The dull ache in my thigh was screaming revenge before I was halfway up the wide front-entry stairs. Classical music wafted from beneath my neighbor Max's door. As I edged through the hallway, I wished I felt up to an afternoon of people-watching through his kitchen windows.

Instead, I limped into my apartment, ignoring the crumple of stained denim in the kitchen and the scent of dried blood lingering by the door. My lungs burned, and I let out a breath I hadn't realized I'd been holding. I glanced down the hall, thankful the message light on my machine was silent this afternoon, and programmed the coffee maker to start brewing in two hours.

Getting comfortable on the sofa was easy, since I'd actually found a piece of furniture long enough for me to stretch out on. I would have purchased it for that reason alone, had I not fallen in love with the covering first. Soft, and so dark it was almost black, but with the afternoon light streaming through the windows the rich velvet radiated deep purple hues.

For unknown reasons, my mother despised this sofa. She'd never seen it, but I'd heard her wince over the phone the day I described it to her. Within a week of the purchase, glossy magazines had flooded my mailbox, cluttering my coffee table with pictures of beautiful houses where nobody lived.

My mother and I have since had a shocking number of conversations about the merits of a neutral palette in the home versus the extravagance of abundant color, none of which particularly interested me, and all of which ended with a reference to 'that hideous beast in your living room.'

If she only knew. I rolled to my side, smiling to myself, the soft whoosh of skin on velvet—smooth, like a sleepy whisper.

But velvet could be discussed, a hope for redemption held out like a candle on a dark night, and my other oddities weren't quite so simple. After I'd come home from the hospital way back when, the unpleasantness of my attack was swept promptly under our handwoven rugs and never spoken of again. Ever. Denial kept my mother's world turning, and the rest of the family played along. We had to.

Lucky for me, my older sister was the daughter of their dreams. Rose was six years my senior, married to a lawyer and raising two little boys in the same town where we'd grown up. Naturally, my mother had assumed that after I finished college, I would marry a nice boy, too, and settle down just like Rose.

If moving almost a thousand miles from home didn't burst my parent's dream-bubble, I think my job description finally did. They were face to face with the fact that I favored my paternal grandmother in more than just looks, and it wasn't sitting well. This had long been a source of discontent to both of them, but particularly to my mother, and I didn't exactly know why. I sighed, wishing I could change for her, and knowing I wouldn't anyway, not even if I could.

My fingers curled beside my cheek, still, finally, the warmth of the sun on my face sliding me into sleep.

***

There's really nothing like a nap when you're exhausted, and mine had worked wonders. My leg felt fantastic. I raced down the front stairs and into the night, and the brisk swirls of spring air didn't scare my muscles a bit. My new scar glared raw and awful, but it would fade soon enough, and I could live with that.

It was only six-thirty when I pulled into the lot behind Forever Crossed. I was hoping against hope that Linc would be early, but I didn't see his truck. Ellen's parking space was empty, too.

I could kill half an hour gossiping with Ellen and not even realize I'd blinked, but I didn't know the night receptionist nearly so well. She was new, and young, and I didn't like the way she juggled my schedule. To make matters worse, I could never remember her name.

She was on the phone when I walked through the door, and I smiled at my luck as I slipped by the front desk with a quick nod in her direction.

She tapped her fingers on the desk and bobbed her head, exaggerating impatience for my benefit. "She's just become available, sir. Would you care to hold a moment? I'll transfer you now."

She mashed a sequence of buttons, wide eyes smiling at me. "You can get that call in your office, Ms. Peters."

"Uh, thanks?" She might be efficient, but this one had a lot to learn about the fine art of Reception. Ellen would never have put a client through to my office without asking me if I wanted to speak with the caller first. "Could you tell me which client is on the line, please?"

"Oh! I forgot to ask! I'm really sorry . . ."

Her voice trailed behind me as I turned into my office. Good thing for her I had bigger fish to fry with Linc tonight, and I didn't want to waste a second talking to him about additional training for the new receptionist.

I grabbed the phone and pulled open a filing cabinet. I figured I'd clean the older cases from my desk while I spoke with whoever was on the line. "Olivia Peters."

"Keeping me waiting already, Angel?"

Luka's voice took my breath away. I didn't know why, couldn't even begin to explain it, but I couldn't deny the effect he had on me, either.

"Not intentionally," I answered. With any luck he couldn't hear my heart pounding through the phone line. "What can I do for you, Luka?"

"Business, Angel? Are you certain?"

I wasn't, but I didn't think phone sex with the Ra'Jahn would do it for me. Besides, I was due in Linc's office in fifteen minutes.

"Antonio needs to see you tonight."

I leaned against my desk, relieved to talk shop. "Sorry, but tonight won't work for me. How about tomorrow?"

"Eight o'clock. Tonight. I just confirmed the appointment with your receptionist."

Damn! "She's new, and she doesn't know my schedule yet. Could I talk you into tomorrow night?"

"Sure." His voice filled the word with suggestion, making me dizzy. My ear pulsed red hot against the receiver. "But Antonio's appointment stands."

I bit my lip, remembering the heat of his hand on the small of my back, the rush of his breath behind my ear. "Fine." I squeezed my eyes closed. "Antonio, eight o'clock."

My mind was reeling with wereleopard, unable to adjust to him as easily as my body had.

"Come back to me, Angel. I want to see you tonight."

"I'm working tonight." It was a lame excuse, but it also happened to be true.

"Which kind of work?"

"I'm going to the Double Down." A low thrum buzzed in my ear, static, like a silent roar. I swallowed hard. "We have a lead on a vamp who might be involved. Adrienne? I need to check her out."

"No."

Just one word, and spoken softly, too. But the race of his power echoed through it, changing everything.

Who asked you? I demanded silently, shaking my fist into the empty office. *No one, that's who!*

"The Double Down is a nasty place, Angel, and Adrienne is a nasty vampire. Let Antonio handle it."

I made an attempt at counting to ten, but even a quick count was too slow. I made it to six, which wasn't bad under the circumstances.

"This is my job," I said evenly. "It's why Antonio hired me."

"No," he growled. "Antonio hired you to find Feine. Adrienne is another matter."

Tension racked my muscles. I was sore, achy all over, and the silence stretching between us was killing me. "I'm not asking for your permission, Luka. I'm going."

I tossed the phone into my chair and stormed into the reception area. It was five to seven, and I was determined to get better acquainted with the night receptionist.

***

"What would you have me do, Olivia?" Linc asked, "Turn perfectly good clients away simply because they're Undead?" His tone was light now, trying to diffuse my temper. Truth be told, I wasn't angry with Linc for taking Antonio's case anymore. It was the principle of the thing I was after.

"First, you should have asked me. And second, now the cops and the vamps are paying us for the same case. It's not right, Linc." I hoped I sounded more indignant than I felt. "That said, and since the case has taken a personal turn," I gestured to my leg, "I need suggestions for a backup weapon. What do you think?"

"If you like the Sig, we'll get you another one," Linc offered. "Use a waistband holster, left draw. It's a solid piece."

"I'm thinking something smaller, strictly backup." But I filed the waistband suggestion for future use. A second 9mm wasn't a bad idea.

"You could go for a .38 ultralight. Taurus makes one that'll fit in your jacket pocket, or you could try an ankle holster." It sounded promising. An ankle holster meant pants, so that was out for tonight, but it was something I'd like to try. "It has a two inch barrel, weighs about a pound. If you've got limited conceal options it's a good choice, although I know you can handle a bigger gun."

I smiled. "You say the sweetest things, Linc."

He made a phone call to the gun shop where he'd taken me to buy the Sig. The owner of the shop, Johnson Ryals, had been an old man when he sold Linc his first gun way back when, and he was positively ancient now. I suspected he and Linc had a crisscrossed network of clientele, but that was their business, not mine.

Mr. Ryals would be expecting me at ten o'clock tonight, and he'd reserved an hour on the shooting range so I could get used to my new gun. At Linc's suggestion, I'd take the Sig as well. A little practice with both weapons wouldn't hurt.

"That should put you at the Double Down around midnight," Linc said. "You sure you don't want company? It so happens that I'm free tonight, and I've been wanting to check that place out. Professional curiosity, of course."

"Oh, really? In what way?"

"Seriously, Liv. Don't go alone."

"I won't be alone, I'll be in a crowded bar. I just want to get close enough to read Adrienne, see if she's the killer."

Linc raised an eyebrow at that. A week ago I would have done everything I could to avoid getting close enough to a vampire to see its past.

Things had changed.

"If she's the one, I'll follow her to Feine. After that, I'll turn her over to the authorities."

I didn't say which authorities, human or vampire, but then again, it wasn't a distinction that mattered a whole lot to Linc. Forever Crossed is in the business of the dead, and it certainly didn't hurt to have contacts on both sides of the line.

***

I poured myself another coffee and settled in to wait for Antonio. I focused on my breathing, hoping for a flash of inspiration. None came. Restless, I stood and stretched my arms wide, fingers open to the air. Magic pooled in my belly, rose like a cool mist through my chest. It pulsed through my blood, steady and a little more frightening than I was used to.

Moments like these, I was desperate for more time with my Nana, but she'd died long before I was old enough to understand most of her teachings. It wasn't just that she knew more about spells and herbs and how to use her gifts than I did. Those things were true, but she also knew exactly who she was, and she'd embraced it.

I didn't. Not fully, not yet. But I was working on it.

The buzz of Antonio's power announced his presence, drew me out of my reverie. Twirling quickly, my fingers drew a circle of energy through my office. I opened the door as he entered our waiting area, waved him over.

Even with his long hair and delicate complexion, he exuded masculinity. Maybe it was the way he wore the night like a second skin, or maybe it was those dark chocolate eyes. Or maybe it was simple vampire magic and a few hundred years of practice, I reminded myself, shaking my head.

Maybe that was also why it took me an extra moment to realize he wasn't alone. Worse, the man by his side wasn't Luka. Not even close.

"It's lovely to see you again, Olivia." Antonio breezed into my office. His Undead companion followed.

"Thank you." I closed the door, trying not to panic. After all, closing the door was my choice, not theirs.

Antonio smiled, the white of his teeth distracting me. "Olivia, have you met my associate? This is Michael."

I turned away from Antonio and looked Michael dead in the eye.

He appeared to be in his late twenties, though I'd put his true age closer to seventy-something, if I had to guess. He was heavily muscled, darker skinned than most of the vamps around here. Alongside Antonio's alabaster, this one's ivory looked positively swarthy. His power washed over me, the warm feel of it so much like Antonio's that I knew if he played his cards right, he would rule a territory of his own someday.

I eased my mind open and watched him die. Rich olive skin, hair clipped short enough to prickle, long limbs straining against a scratchy white uniform. A sailor maybe, on leave for a night or two. He struggled against the vampira who made him, cursing her until he was too weak to move.

She smoothed his hair long after his body went limp, her fingers tracing the outline of his face. She cared for him, that much was clear, although she hadn't used her power to ease the pain her bite inflicted. Her features softened as she wiped his blood from her mouth, and I realized she was extraordinarily pretty, almost fragile, like spun ice or a sugared web.

I kept the images to myself.

"Pleased to meet you, Michael," I said, resisting the urge to address him as Mate. His Naval career, if that's what it had been, was so far behind him it probably wasn't worth it. I didn't extend my hand, though. I didn't want to touch him.

I glanced at Antonio. Our eyes locked for a moment before we looked away, both of us constructing hasty mental barriers.

"What can I do for you tonight?" Irritation rubbed my voice. This meeting was a bad idea, but at least it wasn't one of mine.

"I'd like to know what you saw when you looked at Michael. Show us both. Now."

My heart froze for a moment, skipped a beat in its natural rhythm. Whether I could project the images to both of them at the same time was beside the point. Antonio's voice carried a command, and I'd already had enough of being told what to do for one day. Besides, what I'd seen was private, too personal to broadcast. It was bad enough that the images came to me, sharing them should have been out of the question.

Still, Antonio was a client. "I didn't see much. Nothing you wouldn't already know. Nothing useful."

Antonio smiled, the expression lilting into his voice. "Then would you be so kind as to look again, Olivia?"

I looked at Michael, trying to gauge his reaction. He

looked mildly uncomfortable, but whether that was leftover from my initial stare or from Antonio's request, I couldn't tell.

"Do you mind?" I asked Michael.

He shrugged, and the word insolent popped into my mind. "I have no idea what you're talking about."

So. Antonio hadn't taken the time to explain my powers to him. Interesting.

I met his eyes a second time, easing my mind open to the images. Again, the delicate beauty of his maker belied the viciousness of her kill, and I found the contrast striking. Without the lull of vampire magic, being bled was sheer brutality. She watched him suffer, her own pleasure burning bright behind her icy eyes.

I tried to keep my opinions to myself as I pushed the images back toward Antonio. The connection was easier this time, and I felt his mind open to accept it. There was more resistance on Michael's end, but I managed.

"What the hell?" he demanded, leaping from his chair. He looked hard at Antonio, his eyes flashing anger in all directions. "You allow this? It's unheard of!" His head tilted toward me, the words slithering from his mouth. "It should be stopped."

I didn't like his implication. I didn't like it at all. Without thinking, I'd drawn my gun. Looking down the lean line of the Sig, I held the weapon in a steady two-handed grip and aimed at Michael's head.

"Call him off, Antonio."

A silver bullet through either the brain or the heart could kill him, and anywhere else might slow him down long enough for another shot to finish the job. The question was, could I fire even once before he flew over the desk? Would he tear me to shreds if I couldn't, or would Antonio stop us before it came to that?

"I won't be threatened in my own office, not by this Ruler wannabe. And not by you, either." My chin jutted toward Antonio, but I kept my eyes on Michael.

Antonio flashed that gracious smile of his, his hand resting on Michael's arm, warm waves of his power circling the room. I took a deep breath and lowered my weapon. Michael sat perfectly still, his head turned away from me, his focus on Antonio.

My leg throbbed, muscles bunching in protest of the sudden strain. I tucked the Sig back into its holster and found my chair.

"So, now what? I have other work to do, if that's all you came for." Trying to sound bored, I took a sip of tepid coffee and leaned back in my chair. Michael's outburst still prickled along my skin.

"You are a jewel, Olivia. How did you manage to escape my attention the last few years?"

I wished I knew. I really did. I'd like to go back to doing everything just the same way and see if I might slip back under his radar.

"Truly, I only wanted to see if it was a fault of mine that allowed you to pass images to me," he continued, "or if it was simply a power of yours. I chose Michael because I knew what you would see, and I wanted you to see it."

Ah.

The fragile twisted blonde was Adrienne. Of course. I should have recognized the mix of pleasure and pain. And now I had a face to go with the name Ron White had supplied this afternoon. "I see," I said. It was the most noncommittal phrase in my repertoire.

"Do you really?" Antonio's hand roamed over the back of Michael's chair, his fingers disappearing in the other man's hair. "Luka advised me of your plans for the evening. He does not approve. He'd like me to prevent you from going to the Double Down tonight, but you already knew that, didn't you?"

He paused, waiting for me to answer.

"I figured as much," I admitted.

"I am the Ruler here, Olivia. Do you know what that means? Each of the vampires who live on my lands have sworn their loyalty to me. In exchange, they have permission to hunt on my grounds, to live as they choose—within the limits of the law, of course. And they have my protection."

He paused again. I raised an eyebrow and tried to keep my fingers from flicking as I sipped my coffee.

"My vampires may not be harmed without the right to my vengeance. Should I find that one of my people has betrayed me, I will turn the full force of my power on them, but not until I'm certain that there has been a betrayal.

"Do you understand this, Olivia? I cannot guarantee your safety at the Double Down tonight. I can offer you a bodyguard, but I cannot take action against my own people without just cause." He paused again. "And neither can you."

"But I do have just cause, Antonio." I smiled sweetly, my voice sticky even to my own ears. When I stood up again, I let my hand brush the angry pink scar across my thigh before I reached for a file in the cabinet behind my desk. "Besides, I'm going to the Double Down as part of a matter I'm working on with the police. I shouldn't have mentioned it to Luka. It's not your concern."

It was only half a bluff, and it wasn't for Michael's benefit alone. I was going tonight with or without Antonio's approval, and if Adrienne or anyone else threatened me, I would do what needed to be done. I may be more of a Bereavement Specialist than a P.I., but I could take care of myself if I had to. Linc made sure of that when he hired me.

The silence built as I stretched my power out toward Michael again, pushing away the reflexive jolt of meeting his eyes. I wanted to see something besides his death, something that would tell me more about his life as a vampire.

He was edgy still, and uncomfortable around me, a little less in control of his power than he'd been earlier. The wisps of magic curling away from him ebbed into my own, and I watched him stalk the dark streets of the Triangle. The images were recent. Last night, maybe? He was agitated then, too, and I realized with a start that he was hunting.

I reached again and found what I was looking for this time. Michael's fangs sank inside his victim's thigh, her back arching against a swirl of his magic. A dull ache pulsed at my temples, and I cut the connection before I saw anything else.

The woman was a willing participant, and I'd seen enough to be reasonably sure Michael was otherwise occupied around the time I'd been shot. The rest of it made me feel queasy, and more than a little like a peeping-Tom.

I recalled Antonio's casual feeding, and couldn't help wondering if the thrill of the hunt wore off in time, or if stalking just wasn't his style. My eyes darted over Antonio, his skin stark white and perfect even in the fluorescent light, and hoped I never found out.

Eight

I parked around the corner from the Double Down and patted the pocket of my black leather jacket, again, just to be sure. The new little bulge surprised me every time. It was the ultralight model Linc had suggested, and I couldn't believe something so tiny was actually a real gun. I'd spent the better part of an hour at the shooting range watching it tear up the life-size targets, but the comforting weight of the Sig still felt good against my side.

I caught a glimpse of my reflection in the glass of a neighboring building, and I had to admit I looked damn good in the clothes I was hardly wearing. My hair fell long and straight to just past my waist, with a few strands twisting away from my face and held in place by a trendy little clip. I wasn't used to seeing myself this way, but between the black leather dress and the spike-heeled shoes, the ridiculously long hair spilling around my body didn't seem out of place at all.

My fingers strayed to my chest, seeking the absence of the cross around my neck. It had been a gift from my father, a link to my childhood that I'd worn for the better part of the last two decades. I left it at home tonight because this was a vampire bar, and I wasn't about to hand it over at the coat-check like some thrill-seeking tourist. I only hoped the bouncers wouldn't pay much attention to my bracelet. I shook my wrist a little, feeling the charms fall securely beneath my sleeve.

The closer I got to the entrance of the Double Down, the edgier I felt. Club-hoppers lined the street in the front of the building, decked out in black leather, bits of color and lace dotting the crowd here and there. I smiled to myself. For once in my life, I'd blend right in with the crowd.

I took a few deep breaths, cloaking myself in confidence. A simple spell of protection swirled easily in my mind, but I was placing myself in a dangerous situation, and the magic I used wasn't enough to save me from my own lousy decisions.

The vamp doorman was an overly muscled type in an open leather vest, no shirt. He was so newly dead he still seemed fleshy to me, and I could see the fangs poking from under his top lip when he spoke. A Goth-looking girl in pasty white makeup and a long black dress leaned against him, smiling sweetly into his eyes. I wasn't impressed. Any vamp could bespell an average human, and one who went looking for it was no challenge at all.

"Hi!" I chimed, walking right up to the doorman, trying to look cute and not too bright. I hardly ever succeeded at cute. It just didn't go with my size. But most men didn't have too a hard time overlooking my brain, especially when I had so many other assets in plain view. "Ron White put me on the list. I'm Olivia Peters."

"Sure thing," he said, gripping the Goth-girl to his chest as he looked into my eyes. "Admission is one kiss for the doorman." He bared his fangs, too new to notice his magic had no effect on me.

I stepped closer to him, playing along, and then slipped sideways through the door. "Nice try," I said. "But I don't think so." I was inside before he realized what happened.

The Double Down had been transformed from its daytime shabbiness to a dark and glistening nightclub. Fast, heavy music assaulted me as I made my way into the bar. Thick smoke and fresh sweat hung in the air like rancid cologne, fresh air from the door chasing it toward the rafters.

The sign over the coat-check stand seemed to flash in neon just for me: *No Weapons or Holy Items Beyond This Point.* I gave my sleeve a tug to make sure my bracelet was hidden and buried my hand in my jacket pocket, neatly covering the new .38.

One of the girls taking coats and passing lockboxes over the counter for other assorted items caught my eye and held my gaze for a few extra seconds. She was cute, a redhead with warm hazel eyes and lean muscles stretched tight across her arms and chest. Stacie, according to her name badge. Wereleopard, according to my instincts.

The surging crowd carried me into the depths of the Double Down, where colored lights swirled through a mass of dancers, moving like pieces of some strange machine. Strobes flashed in rapid fire, an epileptic nightmare I didn't want to share. Many of the necks in my line of sight were bruised and swollen, showing bite marks in various stages of healing, but none of the faces seemed familiar. These gyrating vampire-snacks made my stomach crawl. They were hangers-on, groupies, maybe even addicts. But as long as they weren't unwilling slaves, it wasn't anybody's business but their own.

I leaned into the bar and waited. When the bartender approached, I mentioned I was a friend of Sabrina's and said I wanted to hookup with anyone who knew her. She smiled knowingly and poured me a shot of tequila, lime on the side and seltzer back.

I tossed down the shot and chewed the lime, scanning the crowd and trying to ignore the guy next to me. He had a dog collar around his neck and a vicious plague of acne, and he didn't smell too fresh, either. There were dancers in pretend cages and a few chained to the walls, shiny metal links wrapped around bite-bruised wrists. They twisted and writhed, synchronized to the deafening beat. I made a mental note to talk seriously with Karen about dating the Undead.

Trying not to let the death-flashes from the vamps in the place overwhelm me, I sipped at my seltzer and signaled for more tequila. I had a theory that I'd be able to recognize the feel of the one who'd shot me from whatever images came my way. It was more wishful thinking than any sort of cohesive plan, but it was all I had.

And with the possible exception of the fierce throb at my left temple, that wisp of a theory was still all I had an hour later. The industrial noise that passed for music at the Double Down beat a relentless rhythm. Mind-numbing bass stabbed through my brain in one endless loop after the next, until even my pulse raced within the matrix.

My new friend in the dog collar had decided to match me shot for shot, and no amount of cold-shouldering discouraged him. Could've been worse, though. He could've been drinking the warm AB positive this place kept on tap, and that I wouldn't have been able to stomach. As it was, he drooped over the bar, a lime-wedge hanging from limp fingers and his half-closed eyes unfocused. He was beginning to lose his balance altogether, and then suddenly, he snapped upright. His lopsided smile reanimated as he turned a rapt face toward the crowd.

I followed his gaze across the mass of dancers and

found myself looking at none other than the lovely Adrienne. She wore straps of white leather crisscrossed around her body, covering her privates and not much else. It was hard to tell where the leather began and her skin ended, except that the white straps were dull beside the sheen of her body. Ron hadn't exaggerated this afternoon. Not only did she seem to glow, she had the attention of nearly everyone else in the place.

Her power shimmered around her, intensifying the effect of my perspective. I watched tendrils of her magic creep through the crowd, feeding the desperation of those who most wanted to be claimed by her. I wasn't surprised to see one of those tendrils dancing around the man next to me. He basked in her presence while she drained his essence from across the room. I edged away from him, wondering how consuming a person's submission compared to drinking his blood. Looking at Adrienne, I thought it must be a close second.

She couldn't live without the blood—no vampire could—but I didn't guess she'd like to give this up, either. She needed their desperation all right, needed to be adored and desired and obeyed like I needed air to breathe and coffee to drink. But was she in league with Feine? What could she possibly gain from the alliance?

I had to find out.

The bartender set down another seltzer and lime, poured me another shot of tequila. She seemed unimpressed by Adrienne's presence.

"You still looking for people who knew Bri?" she asked, leaning across the bar a little so I could hear her. I leaned in, too, eager for whatever she had to say.

She directed my gaze behind Adrienne, to a male vamp in a dark red shirt, slick in a field of stark white.

"He's with Queenie up there," the bartender said. "Bri was attached to him for a few weeks." She shook her head once, sharply, then pulled away.

I thanked her and left a generous tip before I started through the crowd. I couldn't filter the images from their minds through the mass of bodies between us. I needed to get closer.

"Hey!" Cole's voice reached me a split second after his hand gripped my left arm, and my right hand was on the

9mm before I realized it was him.

He looked different tonight, dressed in a black silk shirt and skin tight pants, sun-bleached hair slicked away from his face. He seemed almost fierce with the heat radiating off his body, and I didn't move my hand away from my gun.

"Hey yourself," I said carefully. We were pressed together by the throng of bodies around us, my left hand on his shoulder, my head inclined to his ear. This close, he smelled salty and hot, like the beach, and like something else, too, something furry and still unknown to me. "Why are you here?" I spoke into his ear, shouting to be heard even this close. "I thought I was clear with Antonio. I don't need a bodyguard."

"You look fantastic, Olivia! I almost didn't recognize you." His hands slid down my sides, rested against my lower back. I told myself we were just blending in, but I kept my own hands where they were.

He hadn't answered my first question, but I let it go. I'd rather assume he was here watching me than find out the Double Down was one of his usual hangouts. It would bother me to think of him in this place night after night, alone. Or not.

"Do you recognize the vamp in the red shirt, behind Adrienne?"

He turned in a flash, lifting my feet off the floor for a few seconds and setting me down with my back to Adrienne. I was impressed. Not many guys I knew could move me around like that. Then I realized he could probably lift half the bar without too much trouble. Still, it was a good feeling. If I continued to hang around wereleopards and vampires, at least I wouldn't have to worry about my own strength damaging any egos. I smiled, taking a moment to congratulate myself for finding a way to look on the bright side. *Way to go, Livvie!*

"Shit!" he swore, refocusing my attention in an instant. "I know all of the vampires in Antonio's company, and I've never seen that guy before. We should get out of here. Now."

According to Cole, just bringing this uninvited guest into Antonio's territory was enough proof against Adrienne. That the bartender had told me the guy had been around for a few weeks was icing on the cake. But this was my cake, too, and I wanted a bigger piece.

"Listen," I explained. "You can either do this my way, or you can leave without me. I don't care which. But there's no way I'm leaving before I get what I came here for."

I watched conflicting impulses move across Cole's face. He was here to protect me, all right. And I wasn't making it easy. *Too bad.* I leaned against him and relaxed, feeling his grip loosen around my waist. I let out a long breath.

With a quick turn, I spun to my right, out of his embrace. Lucky for me, I caught him by surprise. Otherwise I wouldn't have beaten his reflexes. Still smiling, I eased my way toward Adrienne. I didn't look back, but I was pretty sure Cole was there.

I searched along the edge of crowd until I found a bit of space to lean my shoulder against the wall. I kept my eyes on Adrienne's glowing energy and opened my mind.

Her human death was unspectacular, except for the killer. The same pale eyes, the same harshness of his features as he killed. It was Feine, all right. Ages earlier, but exactly as I'd seen him through Anya's eyes.

There was nothing familiar about the feel of Adrienne's power, though. Either my theory was wrong or she wasn't my shooter. I waited for more, but without meeting her eyes I couldn't see anything else. Her power surged as she siphoned energy directly from the crowd, and I knew I didn't want to see her eyes tonight.

Had I not been terrified, the vampira would have been impressive. Like Antonio, she was a Ruler, but if she was in Antonio's city it meant she didn't have a territory of her own. I scanned her entourage for shapeshifters and came up empty. Maybe not all Ruling vamps were linked to shapeshifters? I didn't know. What I did know was the days of separating myself from the Undead were over, and from now on, the more I knew about them the better off I'd be.

My eyes drifted over the dark red shirt still hovering in Adrienne's shadow. This one was young and not overly powerful, just what I was looking for. I opened my mind to him and felt a familiar buzz. *Yes!* Lifting my eyes to his face, I willed him to turn in my direction. If he would only look at me, I'd know for sure. Instead he turned to

Adrienne.

In that moment, I knew he was absolutely hers. The need to serve her, to please her, went well beyond devotion. He was every bit as submissive as my new drinking buddy back at the bar.

I was still willing him to look at me when Adrienne met his eyes, held him there in the same way she'd hold a human. I felt him sinking, swirling, lost in the pleasure she gave him. I pulled my eyes away from them and shifted my focus, shivering despite the heat.

She was too damn powerful for me, and I knew it. With my head lowered, I focused on breathing, making room for the stillness inside me to grow.

I raised my eyes, hoping to find Cole close by. Instead I fell into a swarm of blood red silk. I guess I'd caught the young vamp's attention after all.

I jammed my hands into my pockets, the .38 secure in my grasp. Since I couldn't back away from him, which is what I really wanted to do, I forced myself to meet his eyes. Unless I was willing to pull the trigger in a crowded club, my only chance was to catch him by surprise. Despite the fact that he wasn't very old for a vampire, he was still Undead and I was still human. Well, mostly human.

His eyes were no danger to me, and as he registered the shock, I edged away from the wall and into the crowd. I'd put a few bodies between us, but there were plenty more between me and the door. Cole was here somewhere, and though I couldn't see him, his energy pressed through the crowd.

I spun around, grabbing the vamp's arm as he reached for me. I threw my body to the side, using his own momentum to knock him off balance. Fangs flashed as he skidded into clinging dancers, knocking several off their feet. I didn't stick around to see more.

I ran, weaving my way to the back exit. Crashing shoulder first through the door, I sucked fresh air into my lungs. The alley was nearly empty. If there was still a crowd waiting to get inside, I couldn't see or hear them from this side of the building.

I raced down the alley at a full run, didn't stop for a second breath until I slammed face-first into a solid wall of Undead red.

He'd moved fast enough to pass me, and I hadn't even noticed. His hands gripped my arms, squeezing muscle against bone. With his foot wrapped around my ankles and the force of his forearms pressing me backwards, my waist wrenched until I thought I'd snap in two.

Gone was the submissiveness Adrienne elicited. Alone in the narrow lane behind the Double Down, he was every bit the vicious fang-faced predator of legend, and I was more scared than I'd been in years.

Nine

"Bitch," red-shirt sneered. "I should have killed you last night."

"Too bad you're a lousy shot," I spat back. My back was bent at an unnatural angle, forcing me to look up at him though my feet were just barely touching ground.

"Too bad you don't scare easy. But you're afraid of me now. You reek of it." He took a deep breath and laughed out loud.

Damn straight, I was afraid. Terrified. Who in the world wouldn't be?

"Adrienne ordered me to leave you alive last night. Tonight, I don't have orders. Tonight, you're mine."

I was trapped on a deserted side street by a sadistic vampire who would most certainly kill me now. He had no reason not to, really. Adrienne had already drained two women and left them for dead on the downtown streets, so why not add another one to the list? Besides, he was in the Triangle without permission. He'd face a death sentence the moment Antonio found out. Or worse. Probably much worse, if Antonio was half the vampire I thought he was.

My power spiraled outward, searching for the familiar feel of Cole. But the energy rolling off the red-shirted vamp clouded my senses. He was amped up and flying, power surging around him like gale force winds on the blackest night.

Sweat poured off my body, soaked in terror and feeding his predatory instincts. I'd seen this guy with Adrienne, and I had a pretty good idea of the kind of games she liked to play. But he ruled this night, and he was going to enjoy being in control for a change.

He gripped my wrists with one hand, his fingers an icy vise behind my back. His other hand reached into my hair and pulled hard, then snaked under my jacket and pulled at the Sig, bending my head back even further. The gun came free of its holster with a pop that echoed in the empty street. I swallowed, made an effort to keep breathing. Without the 9mm my chances of getting out of this alive were less than great.

The good news was he'd probably only handled a gun a couple of times in his entire Undead lifespan, and he didn't seem to know quite where to put it now that he had it. Plus, he wasn't at all intent on shooting me, which left me feeling a little less thankful than it would have under other circumstances.

"Why don't you put that gun down before you hurt yourself with it?" I suggested.

He slammed the barrel across the side of my head.

Sharp flashes faded bright to red. Blood pounded through my temples. Bile burned my throat. My knees buckled, and I pitched forward. Dazed, I moved my head experimentally, the slick feel of his shirt beneath my cheek. Even that slight motion cost me, and I swallowed hard to keep from throwing up.

I felt his fingers in my hair, and his breath cool against my neck. Fangs scraped across my skin like nails on a chalkboard, taunting me. Red-shirt licked the blood as it dripped down my neck. He was pleased with himself, all right.

He'd already fed tonight, that was clear, and truly, I was grateful. If he hadn't, I'd be drained by now, so he was taking his time about it, enjoying the game.

I wiggled my hands in his grip, worming my fingers up the sleeve of my jacket until I touched one of the charms dangling from my left wrist. Red-shirt ignored my struggles, focused as he was on the blood pouring from my head. I yanked at the bracelet until a six-pointed star fell into my palm, weightless and white hot.

Black dots swam through my field of vision. I gasped for air in ragged stretches.

I concentrated on pinching the tiny star until the grooves imprinted in my flesh held it there. And then I pinched it even tighter. I wrenched away from the icy hand that bound my own, the charm flaring to life with a blast of light and heat that jolted us both.

His mouth jerked away from my neck, and I forced the pointy star into the only bit of Undead flesh I could reach. The holy object smoked against his wrist, shadowing the sudden burst of light.

Fire smoldered through his arm, the crackling flames almost enough to drown out his screams.

Between the rotten stench of burning vampire and the pounding in my head, I lost the battle with my stomach. I heaved, a violent rush of tequila and lime pouring over the pavement. Worse, I could hear red-shirt's howls turn to curses. He would kill me now, without preamble, and I grabbed for the .38 in my pocket, the only weapon I had left.

He crashed over me, slammed me backwards into the street. The world turned black and silent, no echoes, no shadows. Only the feel of the gun in my hand, trapped between our bodies, solid and cold. The ground beneath me slipped away, a loose spiral of power pulling me swiftly through its tides.

The .38 shivered under my fingers, and I fired, praying to all the gods the gun was pointed in the right direction.

***

I screamed, as loud and long as I could, but my ears rang with silence and my mouth didn't move at all.

Blurred images floated around me, assaulted by light and sickening waves of motion. I wrenched away from the body restraining my own, struggled until my stomach lurched into my throat, empty but not appeased.

Mercifully, I sank back into the void.

Warm hands brushed the hair from my face and a familiar coolness washed over me. Luka. I closed my eyes, dropped my defenses. Luka was here.

And then nothing.

When I opened my eyes again, Luka's face hovered over mine, his mouth moving. I tried to smile, but my face didn't feel quite right. From what I could see without moving my head, I was still outside the Double Down. Voices edged closer, questions rising and falling, club-hoppers trying to catch a glimpse of the action.

"Can you sit up, Angel?" Luka's voice was far away.

"Yeah," I replied, but didn't move. "What are you doing here?"

"Cole called. He lost track of you in the bar, didn't know what to do."

"Not his fault . . ." I dragged myself to a semi-upright position, the ground spinning faster with every inch.

"Shhhh." Luka caught me before I dropped back down. "Don't think about that now."

With my head resting snugly against his chest, I couldn't think about anything. There was only Luka, his power thrumming through my body like the beating of his heart, a steady whisper, secure.

Then there were sirens tearing through the night, disrupting the balance of sound. Luka tensed, and dark clouds swirled through my eyes. I heard myself moan, a low painful sound that made my teeth hurt.

"Police?" I asked.

"Gun shots," Luka explained. "I'm sorry I couldn't get you out of here before they came." Irritation crowded his voice. He was more worried about the cops than the vampires? Somewhere in the back of my spinning brain, I filed that question away. I'd think about all this later. Much later, if my stomach had anything to say about it.

"You should go," I said. "I can handle the cops. It was a clean shoot."

And it was, but fear burned my lungs, and I gasped for air, unable to get my next words out. "He's dead, right?" I heard the tremble in my voice. I hated it, but there it was. "Tell me he's dead!"

"Dead and rotting just a few feet away. You put a bullet through his spine. A couple of them, actually."

I'd been hoping to hit his heart, but I was glad to add the spine to my short list of lethal locations to bullet the Undead.

Thick-soled black shoes pounded into my field of vision, and I braced myself against Luka's chest, but when the cop bent to my level there wasn't an ounce of accusation in his eyes. I recognized his face, but I couldn't see clearly enough at the moment to read the name on his uniform.

"Ms. Peters? Is it you?" He wiggled a flashlight over my face and Luka's, the movement of the light causing my stomach to clench again. "It's Officer Bradley, from yesterday."

"Stop," I gasped. Luka covered my eyes and held my head very still. The cool rush of his power steadied the air around me, let me breathe through the waves of nausea.

"What the hell?" Officer Bradley demanded. "Did you feel something funny?"

"Bradley," I gasped. "Has Detective Rutledge been

called in yet?"

"Yeah. He's on his way."

"He'll want a full report." I had his attention now. He rubbed his bare arms as if the play of Luka's energy lingered on his skin. "He'll want a full report from both of us," I said again. "I haven't got enough energy to do this twice, so maybe you could check out the other evidence until he gets here." I managed a wave of my hand in the direction of the corpse.

I needed to stroke his ego a little bit, make him forget about Luka's little display.

"You'll find my 9mm on the corpse, but I'd like it back when you're through. Here's the weapon I fired." I let him take the .38 from my hand, watched him drop it into a clear plastic evidence bag. "I want this one back, too. Just bought the damn thing a few hours ago."

Office Bradley grinned. Luka shook his head.

I handed over my jacket, or what was left of it. I hadn't taken the .38 out of the pocket before I fired. Besides, it was covered in vampire blood. Vomit, too, but I tried not to think about that.

"All right, Ms. Peters. The paramedics will be here soon to check you over. We'll talk to Detective Rutledge after they're done with you."

I waited for him to move toward the rotting vamp and out of ear shot. I had to stand up before the paramedics got here. If they found me like this, there would be ER talk for certain. I didn't know what else would happen tonight, but I knew I wasn't going to the hospital, not if I could help it.

I managed to find my feet without losing consciousness, but it wasn't easy. Wrapped in the circle of Luka's arms, with the warmth of his body against mine and his spicy-sweet scent like a cloud around us, the dark fuzz around the edges of my vision faded.

I faced the paramedics without turning my insides out again, even with their sharp little lights flashing in my eyes. Under normal circumstances, I like to think I could have prevented their full body fang-mark and broken-bone examination, since I knew I had neither. But tonight was not normal, and as it was, I couldn't do much more than blush.

What I did have was a concussion, a cracked rib, and a nasty slash over my right ear. The paramedics pronounced me damn lucky and agreed to let me skip the ride to the ER. They addressed their questions to Luka, as if I couldn't be trusted with my own welfare, which didn't seem exactly fair. Could he guarantee I wouldn't spend even a minute alone for the next twenty-four hours? Would he ensure I went straight to the hospital if my symptoms worsened?

Luka promised, sounding solemn and responsible despite the light dancing in his eyes. I nodded my head at nobody in particular, but gently, and just to prove that I could.

I should have saved my energy.

Mike Rutledge was on the scene and mad as hell.

"Damn it, Peters." His eyes flicked over me, made a rapid assessment of my condition. "I ordered you to steer clear of this place. This is a goddamn police investigation, in case you'd forgotten!"

Actually, he'd only suggested I wait for backup before going in, not to mention that I was a civilian and he couldn't really order me around. But I was in no shape to point out either of these inconsistencies. Still, I took a few steps away from Luka. It was hard to play with the big boys if you couldn't stand without help.

"I'm not really hurt, Detective, but thanks for your concern." When all else fails, my trusty friend sarcasm is always around. I wasn't up for much of it, though. "I promised Bradley a statement once you'd arrived on scene. I'm ready when you are."

I glanced at Luka. He glared at Mike, and Mike returned the favor. *Interesting.* Still, I made a quick decision to keep it light.

"Mike, this is my friend, Luka Niere. He brokered a deal with the paramedics to keep me out of the hospital." I turned to Luka and introduced Detective Rutledge as my friend and co-worker. They both seemed to relax a little. I needed this macho posturing like I needed a hole in the head, and since I already had one of those I just wanted to give my statement and go home.

"Let's get your statement, Peters. You sure you don't want to do this at the station house?" I couldn't tell if he was joking. Surely, he was.

He gestured for Bradley with a wave of his hand, and the officer appeared beside him.

I stated my name for the record and the digital recorder validated my voiceprint. Although I wasn't being charged with a crime at this time, I acknowledged that my rights under the New Miranda Act had been explained to me and my understanding of those rights was complete. This was all standard procedure. I'd seen it plenty of times in the last few years, but it sure looked different on this side of the recorder.

I gave a semi-accurate version of what happened, leaving my reasons for being at the Double Down in the first place somewhat vague. I also kept my mouth shut about red-shirt admitting he'd taken a shot at me last night. Revenge complicated everything, and I needed this investigation to be simple.

Finally, though it about killed me twice to do it, I admitted the vamp stripped the gun from my side and beat me to the brink of consciousness with the barrel. It was embarrassing as all hell, but it justified the rest of my actions. I set the scene for the record, careful to keep my voice steady but true. I'd been afraid for my life, gushing blood and at the mercy of a vampire who'd stalked me through the club and attacked me without provocation.

I even let Mike pressure me into describing how I'd managed to put enough distance between myself and the Undead creep to ignite half a limb in holy fire. Besides, I figured the coroner was bound to notice the scorch marks, anyway.

Mike handed the Sig back to me, watched while I tucked it into the holster where it belonged. As expected, my .38 was impounded as evidence. Then Mike switched off the recorder and told me he would check in with me in the morning, which meant he'd want to know everything I'd left out of my official statement. Still, I was grateful for the extra time.

"If I was you, I'd give Linc a call," Mike said, his voice low. "The press are gonna feast tonight, and it doesn't look like you're up to the swarm, Peters. Not even with your friend's help." He smiled, looking a little too pleased with himself for a cop with a rotting corpse on his hands.

Then he shook Luka's hand and stalked off toward the yellow tape.

"Nice work, Ms. Peters," Bradley added. "Not many civilians could have done what you did." *Not too many cops, either,* I thought, but I kept the comment to myself. My bracelet dangled from his fingers, charms flashing quick and light. "This yours?" he asked.

Luka's power seethed beside me, twisted in on itself and pulled away. Silver? *Hot damn.* For a moment I'd actually forgotten he was a shapeshifter.

"Thanks, Officer," I said, the broken bracelet pooling in my palm. I flashed the warmest smile I could manage, "Good night." A quick nod and he turned, embarrassed maybe, and trotted back to where Mike was huddled beside the coroner.

Wrapped in my fist, the silver felt cool and sweet against my skin. A deep breath rattled through my chest, then another. Luka's arm slipped around my waist, his power smoothing itself out and stretching around me once again.

I closed my eyes and tried to remember what it felt like not to hurt.

"Shall I carry you, Angel, or can you make it to the car on your own?" Luka's words breathed over me, and I shivered.

It was tempting, but I had a reputation to keep up. It was bad enough I'd passed out on the street and tossed my cookies all over the crime scene. No way was I going to let my boyfriend carry me.

Did I say boyfriend?

Ten

I heard the phone ringing, but I couldn't pull away from the dream.

In the dream I am a dancer, light and fluid, pirouetting through a garden at night. I'm drunk with the fragrance of dark blooming flowers and rich soil, with fruity liquor, and laughter, and my own youth. Spinning, a shape springs toward me, but I can't see from where.

It moves like water through air, fast and seamless, and I feel it before it touches me. For a split second I see it clearly, and together we dance for Kali, the goddess of all time, creator of beautiful monsters. He is magnificent, not quite a man, not quite a beast. With claws and teeth and rage, covered in fur and something else, something I can't comprehend. Something terrible and important and bloody.

There's screaming and then wide-open calm, a deep voice, soft and sure. A dream, just a dream, and my eyes flutter, because, no, it isn't just a dream. But it isn't a nightmare either.

Luka's green eyes search my own, my brain stumbling toward wakefulness. Three times this night I've woken wrapped in his shimmering aura. Every two hours, just like the paramedics ordered. His fingers smoothing my hair, his face bent close to mine, concerned.

"Good morning, Angel," he said this time, dropping a light kiss on my forehead. "How are you feeling?"

"Too soon to tell," I grumbled, but I was smiling. I couldn't help myself. There was something inexplicably wonderful about Luka lounging on my bed, no matter what the circumstances. As I sat up, though, I realized I wasn't wearing anything. I had a vague recollection of warm water and Luka's hands, cool and gentle, putting me to bed.

Embarrassing? Well, comparatively speaking, not really. I pressed the sheet to my chest and squirmed upright against the pillows.

"Thanks for staying with me," I offered. "I swear I'm not usually so high maintenance."

He raised one eyebrow, but didn't say a word. Smart and gorgeous, a lethal combination.

"Mmm, I heard the phone? Who called?"

"So far, your boss has called twice. He wants you to call him as soon as you're up to it. He also said not to worry. He stopped by Johnson's place and has a replacement for you. He said you would understand."

I nodded, my head throbbing just a little.

"Detective Rutledge called, too. He'll be here in an hour," Luka continued. "And a reporter from *The Observer*, who is very much looking forward to an interview with you."

"Anything else?"

"Only the reporter seemed excited to hear a man answering your phone."

"Very funny." What Mike Rutledge thought of Luka answering my phone really didn't worry me, but truly, I was thankful my mother hadn't called. The Detective and I had a working relationship, nothing else. Not that I hadn't thought about it. He was a good-looking man, tall with a strong body and a sharp mind. But I honestly hadn't thought about it much. Mike was a good cop, but he was a little too much of a boy scout for my taste.

Luka, on the other hand, was no scout. Danger thrummed around him. He made my head spin, and it wasn't just the concussion.

"I think I better jump in the shower," I said. *Better make it a cold shower,* I thought to myself. I'd barely escaped becoming the favorite flavor of an Undead assassin, had my head bashed with my own gun, and now all I could think about was sex. And coffee. Maybe coffee sounded even a little better than sex.

I swung my feet to the floor and stood in one motion, pulling the bed sheet with me. The blood rushed from my head and my balance right along with it. Once again, Luka's arms were around me, holding me steady. My face rested against his chest, my hands at his shoulders. Against the soft cotton of his shirt, my cheek warmed to the hard muscle underneath.

This close I could smell the exotic spiciness of him, and that sweet undercurrent, like jasmine. I pressed my lips to the pulse of his neck. His shoulders tensed. I held my breath.

One strong hand slid an electric path down my bare

back, loosing the sheet and pressing my body against his. His other hand smoothed the back of my neck, his fingers entwined in my hair. His power rushed through me, hot and alive.

With some rational part of my brain, I thought I heard the bedroom door pound open, and I turned my head, my reaction more than a few seconds behind Luka's. His body was between mine and the door, but that didn't stop Cole and Stacie, the red-haired coat-checking wereleopard, from gaping at us.

"Christ," she swore, shaking her head. "We thought . . ."

"Sorry, boss," Cole's eyes darted all around, pink creeping into his cheeks. "We were waiting in the kitchen and felt, uhm . . . We weren't sure what we felt, and you didn't answer when I knocked . . ."

"No problem," I said, my hand fluttering in their direction. I tried not to squirm.

"You can go now," Luka growled.

The door closed with a whoosh of air and a resounding click, but not quick enough to cover the fit of giggles that carried them away from my bedroom.

"Why are they here?" I asked, whisking the sheet from my ankles. I wrapped myself into it, blushing bright red from head to toe.

"They are Ja'Nan, Angel. Where else would they be?"

I sighed. It might have been the concussion, but I really wasn't following Luka's logic.

"Until Adrienne is contained, it isn't safe for you to be here." Luka watched my eyes as he spoke. "You need to be in a safe house before nightfall, Angel. My house."

Luka's house. *Safe?* I couldn't seem to wrap my brain around that one, either.

"So, they could feel . . . Us?" I asked, stuck on the concept. Luka's power still danced over my skin, but I couldn't believe they felt it too.

"I'm their Ra'Jahn, Angel. You know this."

"I don't understand."

"Perhaps not, but you will." He sighed and pulled me to him, gently. "The Ja'Nan are sensitive to things ordinary humans don't notice. As Ra'Jahn, I'm always in communication with them, a word, a touch, the scent of my power in the air. It's a reminder of the full moon hunt, when we feed together and share all of ourselves." I shivered, the warm rush of his breath in my hair, his hands hot on my skin. "Your magic is strong, Angel, and the power between us is like nothing else. I know you can feel it."

"I feel it," I admitted. I didn't understand half of what he'd said, but I knew exactly what he meant. "I just didn't realize they would feel it, too."

"My leopards felt only the pull of our power. To them, it was similar to my call, but different enough to raise an alarm. That's why they came. From now on, they'll recognize the feeling for what it is, and they won't be so curious."

"And what is it, exactly?"

For an answer, his mouth covered mine, tasting my lips. Softly, so softly I almost couldn't tell where his mouth began and mine ended. His tongue pressed into my mouth, and I responded, tasting him back. My breasts ached, hot against his chest. His fingers stroked the swell, raising the sensitive peaks until I could barely breathe.

It was too much and not enough at the same time. I pulled away.

This wasn't the right time, or the right place. Not with two wereleopards in my kitchen and a police detective on his way over. Besides, there was Adrienne to contend with, and Feine. And Luka still hadn't really answered my question. Not that I minded the answer I'd gotten.

"I really need that shower."

"Sounds good to me." Luka's power reached for mine. I hesitated, not ready to pull away.

"It does, but we really don't have time." I smiled, my shoulders lifting, disappointment mixed with relief. "Talk to me while I get ready?"

"I'll settle for watching you shower if I have to," he said, his hands resting on my waist, fingers circling over my hips. "But just this once."

Eleven

The closed door barred the buzz of power that permeated the air around the Ja'Nan, and suddenly my bedroom felt cold and empty. Still, it was better than the bathroom, where the lights bounced off the mirror and made everything hurt just a little more. Besides, it wasn't really cold in here. It was cozy, and the white noise of my hair dryer easily covered the feel of the Ja'Nan. I leaned forward, still-damp hair spilling over my face. Lavender scented shampoo filled my world, and I closed my eyes behind its heavy veil.

As the steady stream of superheated air fluttered through my hair, soothing the maze of sore muscles along my scalp, new aches and pains sprang to life over the rest of my body. I was in sorry shape, no doubt about it, and each new wince reminded me of the attack.

The attack reminded me of blood, and blood reminded me of half a dozen things I didn't want to think about, including the Ja'Nan. I wanted to wipe the memories from my mind, but the gods had other plans for me today. The puzzle pieces were snapping into place despite my desire for oblivion. I could see the outline of the shape within, and I wasn't sure I liked it.

From my own years of research, I knew the experts explained shapeshifting through a combination of environmental contaminants and some kind of retrovirus, though I didn't understand the finer points behind the science. The infection that activated the virus was blood-borne, and most often transmitted consensually, that much I knew. But contagion from a violent attack wasn't unheard of, either, especially not in my household.

Either way, there was plenty of blood involved, which was supposed to explain why the newly infected either shifted right away or died trying.

"Angel?" Luka knelt before me, his lips pressed into a thin line. The back of his hand rubbed the length of my leg. "You okay?"

"Hmmm." *How long had he been there?* "I was just thinking . . ." I flipped my hair back, blood rushing against gravity. Dark waves swam through my eyes.

"Careful now, don't hurt yourself." Luka's smile covered the sarcasm and threw me further off balance.

"I was thinking about shapeshifters," I said, burying my fist in the bed quilt so Luka wouldn't see it clenching. "And wondering why some people change when they're infected and some people simply die. I mean, is it the infection that kills the people who don't shift, or is it the blood loss or the shock or what?"

"Infection?" Luka sounded like I'd suggested the world was flat. "You think I'm diseased?"

"Of course not. Luka, I didn't mean . . ." *Didn't mean what?* My sentence hung there, half finished.

"I know what they say about shapeshifters, but we aren't freaks of science, Angel. And we aren't freaks of nature either."

I didn't think of Luka as diseased, or Cole, either. But the others? Maybe I did. I wasn't comfortable with shapeshifters. Maybe what had happened to me was reason enough to be leery of wereleopards, but what had the werewolves ever done to me to deserve my disfavor? Or the wereowls? Or the were-whatevers, for that matter?

"I'm sorry." My words weren't empty, but they sounded hollow, insufficient, even to my own ears.

"Don't be." Luka sat beside me, unbunched my fingers beneath the quilt. "The medical explanation is one way to look at it, but it's not the only way. The Ja'Nan are an ancient race, you know? We date back to the earliest times. The records in the Far East are the strongest, but we've been documented in cultural histories that span the ages."

"I didn't know," I admitted. "After what happened to me . . . I guess I didn't want to think about that. Looking for answers in anthropology never occurred to me."

"All kinds of shifters figure in the mythologies of one people or another. Werewolves have gotten the most press, poor bastards, but leopard lore is scattered across the globe. Well, the Indian subcontinent mostly, but we've been spotted in Africa too, even the Americas, before the Europeans arrived, of course."

My head was light, fuzzy with the words he'd spoken already and clouded with the certain knowledge of more to come, a fear that I couldn't comprehend.

"There's a myth about you, Angel." He spoke softly, a

warm lilt in my ear, his power steady around me. "Do you want to hear it?"

"No." I shook my head, stood up. "No."

"The old ones say that a new Shaman will come into the clan, a most powerful Seer who is neither Human nor Ja'Nan. The old ones know these things, Angel, have known throughout time, and have passed that knowledge into the clans through our roots."

"No," I said, backing further away from him. "It isn't me."

If Luka heard my words, he gave no indication of it. "Not all of the Ja'Nan have shaman these days. An aging human is a liability, a weakness to protect. But this clan, *my* clan—" his voice filled with strength and he stood and crossed the room in a single step. "My clan has never lost the old ways. Maybe we didn't always believe the myths, didn't think they were more than shaman's stories and legends from long ago. But not now."

"No."

His fingers danced through my hair, my whisper drowned against his chest.

"You aren't quite human, Angel, but you aren't one of us, either."

I pulled away from the tangle of him. "I'm not a shaman, Luka. I'm not even much of a witch."

He smiled, nodding to the half filled bag on my bed. "We'll talk more about this later. You need to finish getting ready."

"Luka, thank you, seriously, but no. I can't be part of your prophecy. I'm not a myth. I'm just me." I tried out a smile, but Luka only shook his head.

"It doesn't matter if you believe or if you don't believe," he said. "It only matters that it is."

Easy for him to say, I thought, and not for the first time since he'd left the room. I folded a pair of jeans and crammed them into my overnight bag, renewed irritation rushing through my veins. As I tossed in a pair of warm-ups, my eyes lingered on the sparring gloves hanging from the hook behind my door. If only I could.

Like most things that fell under the heading of "for my own good," I wasn't thrilled about this little trip to Luka's cabin in the country. Too much was happening without me, too many decisions made without my input. *Well, that's what happens when you get vamped two nights in a row,* I told myself sourly. *Time to toughen up.*

I checked the clock. Detective Rutledge would be here any minute. I smoothed my hair a few last times and tossed my brush in the bag, too. Tops, bottoms, undies—everything else I would need was already in my briefcase and stowed in the car, or waiting for me at the office. I tucked the Sig into its holster and zipped up the case.

My bare feet were decked in sporty sandals, and since none of the long sleeved shirts in my immediate view were appealing, I decided to leave my arms bare and the Sig exposed. Right now, I needed coffee more than I needed to make a fashion statement.

I needed coffee desperately.

I stalked into the kitchen, half-expecting to find it full of wereleopards. My arms wrapped my chest, surprised and not entirely pleased to find myself alone in the empty room. I peered out the window and saw Luka leaning into a long black Jaguar, talking to Cole.

Now, I'm not a Chick Who Digs Cars, but I know my way around a set of rims, and these were shiny sweet. Morning sun glinted through the windows, Cole's face serious in the bright light, warm leather soaking in the rays behind him. The Jag had Luka written all over it, and I smiled, picturing him behind the wheel, the engine racing and the moon edging over the horizon. Handing the keys to Cole must have hurt.

I poured coffee beans into the grinder, inhaling their sharp scent as the machine whirred. Once I'd started the machine brewing, I set a few mugs on the counter, spilled cream and sugar into mine, and swirled it around a few times before I added hot coffee.

Giving silent thanks to the kindred soul who'd invented Pause'N'Serve technology, I took that first tentative sip. Eyes closed, the air imbued with brewing coffee, I nearly scorched my tongue before I even tasted the richness of the blend. The second swallow was even better. This was ritual at its simplest.

I opened my eyes and found Luka staring at me and, behind him, Mike Rutledge.

"Help yourselves," I offered, gesturing to the coffee and

moving away from the counter at the same time.

A quick glance out the window told me the Jag was gone, and Mike's unmarked cop car was in its place. *How long was I in Never-Never Land?* I edged into the living room, settling into a cozy old chair. It put the tall arch-shaped windows at my back, but left me with an easy view of both the kitchen and the entryway.

A good trade, since from here I could see Luka and Mike with their heads bent close, talking in low tones. About me, no doubt.

They were remarkably similar, exuding confidence and possessiveness at the same time. Close to the same height, Mike was broad where Luka was lean, and Luka was fluid where Mike was edgy. For just a moment they seemed like two cops at a Krispy Kreme counter, and I wondered exactly who Luka Niere had been before he became the Leopard King.

I closed my eyes and tried to hear what they were saying. It was useless, though. My hearing is utterly human.

Mike cleared his throat, the proximity snapping me alert. He was sitting opposite me, close enough for me to notice concern worrying the lines around his eyes.

"You okay, Peters?" Mike asked. "If you're not up to it, we can do this later."

"What's that supposed to mean? I'm up to it." I knew I sounded defensive, but I couldn't help it. So I zoned out for a few minutes. So what? My gaze flashed to the kitchen, found Luka staring purposefully out the window. "It's just a mild concussion, Mike, and I'm low on sleep. Other than that, I'm fine."

"You always drink your coffee with your eyes closed and one hand on your weapon?"

I laughed then, the sound soft in my chest, easy. There was enough ego in the room to choke a gator, and mine was by far the most easily bruised today. Mike grinned back at me. As long as I was laughing, he'd cover this ground. We got down to business.

I came clean on the details of the shooting last night, explaining the dead vamp was an outsider, in the Triangle without Antonio's permission. I told Mike about red-shirt's confession, and how Adrienne had ordered him to scare me off the case. It explained the attack on my fire escape, though it wasn't more than a circumstantial link to the other murders. Still, I was sure Adrienne was responsible for the Double Down deaths.

Mike was used to my powers with the dead by now. After all, it was how and why we knew each other. Accepting that my visions worked with the Undead wasn't really much of a stretch. Even so, explaining Adrienne's connection to Feine was complicated. Since I'd seen her human death, I knew Feine was both the vampire who had created her, as well as the vamp I'd first seen through Anya Sorensen's eyes.

Mike was working hard to digest all this, so I smiled and made a palms-up gesture with my hands.

"Look," I said. "Sometimes I wish I couldn't see how people died, but I can. It's solved a few crimes around here and given more than a few folks at Forever Crossed comfort when they needed it most. Now we know I can use those same skills around the Undead." And then some, I thought, but kept that part to myself. "Which is a good thing, right? It could help take another murderer or two off the streets."

"I know," he said. "I'm damn glad you're on our side, Peters." He reached toward me and tucked a few strands of hair behind my ear, his fingers grazing the wound above it. The sweetness of the gesture touched me someplace it shouldn't have, and I swallowed hard, forcing myself to look away. I felt Luka tense from across the room and was grateful Mike didn't have the ability to feel it, too.

"So, what now?" I asked.

"I want you out of this, Olivia. You're too close as it is."

Wow, use of my first name. He was taking me off the case for sure. Not that I'd stay off.

"We'll put out an APB on both Adrienne and Feine, try to bring them in for questioning on the three murders. I'll request an L.V.T. and see if we can't get a warrant on what we have now. In the meantime, you need to stay out of sight for a while." He gave Luka a quick backwards glance. "If they contact you, or if you find out anything else on your own, you let me know."

I nodded and stood up. Luka's reflection in the kitchen

window glared at both of us.

"Stay safe," Mike said as we walked down the short hallway to my front door. He handed me a business card with his pager, cell, and home phone numbers written on the back. I already had the numbers somewhere, but I took the card without a word, my fingers automatically straying to the image of Saint Michael embossed on the corner.

"I'm not fooling, Olivia. This is too hot now. You need to take care of yourself, get out of town for a few days, hear?"

I closed the door behind him, listened as he waited until both locks clicked before walking down the hall. I imagined him going down the front stairs, stopping at the coffee shop across the street, window shopping the music store on the way back to his car.

I'd wanted him to see me as helpless today. I'd even used his protective instinct to make myself seem more vulnerable than I really was, hoping he wouldn't question me too closely about the shooting. *But whose idea was the attraction?* I wondered. *Had I planted that seed, too?*

I pushed the questions from my mind and meandered back to the kitchen. Luka's tension bounced around the room, assaulting me before I stepped through the archway. He appeared to be lost in thought, but my senses told me otherwise. He was focused. Leaning against the counter, hands pressed casually along the edge, Luka was a study in control.

I tried a smile, but he wasn't looking at me. He had his head turned toward the window, the tilt of his face throwing the strong musculature around his mouth into high relief. I reached past him for the coffee, and our arms brushed.

My skin burned where we'd touched, and I quickly pulled away. Who needed coffee, anyway?

"Perhaps you'd prefer to stay the next few days with the Detective? I'm sure he'd be happy to oblige."

"Mike and I work together, Luka, that's all. We're friends."

"You don't smell like friends, Angel."

"Yeah? Well, I don't have a lot of friends, Luka, so I guess I know who they are." My fingers flicked compulsively by my side, and I pressed my nails into my palm to steady myself. "He feels responsible for involving me in this, so he's protective. He doesn't know that I'm working for Antonio, remember?" I pressed my palms upward and sighed. "He's a cop," I finished, as if that explained everything.

And maybe it did.

Luka's arms wrapped around me, spun my back against his chest. There was no lightning bolt this time, just the low thrum of energy I'd come to expect. His hands roamed lazily over my bare arms, hot shivers chasing along my skin. He nuzzled the soft hollow behind my ear, the warm pressure of his lips, tasting and pulling, marking me his. I felt like a teenager, giddy and reckless, wanting to lose myself in him and never come back.

Tempting. But the power between us was tempting, too. I held on tight, drinking it in like sunshine on a cool day. When I turned in his arms, our lips just brushing, I was stronger, more alive than I'd been in days.

"Thank you." It sounded like a weird thing to say, but I meant it. "I needed that."

"I don't want anyone else protecting you," Luka admitted. "Not Cole, not Antonio, and definitely not your Detective friend."

Well, that makes two of us, I thought, mentally adding Luka to the list of men I didn't want protecting me. I could take care of myself, and if and when I couldn't, I would damn well learn how. Otherwise I'd renegotiate the sort of consulting I did for Forever Crossed, and if that didn't work, I might look into another line of work altogether. The ideas danced before me, reminding me I could change my life if I wanted to. The gods knew I'd done it before.

***

We were both quiet during the short ride to my office. I was focused on the driving, which was much more complicated than I'd expected, and I couldn't bear the sight of Luka's white knuckles for a second longer than I had to. When I finally parked the car and heard the reassuring click of the emergency brake echo in my ears, I admitted to myself that I was more than a little woozy from the concussion.

Halfway up the stairs, I realized that I wasn't really

dressed for the office. True, my khaki skirt was sleek, but it didn't feel professional. *Well, I wasn't here to work, was I?* At least the scar on my leg had faded already, an easy pink ridge that would peek out from under the hem of almost every skirt in my closet.

I dashed back to the car, grabbed the jacket out of the back. Wrinkles usually shake right out of this microfiber stuff, but I was too exhausted from the drive for more than a vigorous snap. Still, it was something.

By the time we walked through the back door, I'd nearly forgotten Luka was with me. Ellen's aura leapt with sparkles, though, and her smile told me she liked what she saw. She was talking into her headset as usual, but she waved us in and motioned for me to sit.

"Linc's in his office," Ellen said after a minute or two, "but he's taking a call. And Daniel is using your space, Olivia, since we weren't expecting you today. Linc shouldn't be too long, though. I'll let you know as soon as he hangs up." She glanced at the light flashing on her console, indicating Linc's line was still in use. "Coffee?"

"I'll get it, Ellen, but thanks." I ambled over to the coffee bar, watching Luka drape himself into one of the chairs opposite Ellen's desk. I poured a cup for each us, cream and sugar in mine, black for Luka, and artificial sweetener for Ellen.

"So why is Danny in my office and not his?" I asked, not really caring but not wanting to give Luka and Ellen too much time to chitchat.

"He brought Silkie in today, but his client isn't comfortable with dogs," Ellen explained.

Silkie was a retired Greyhound who thought she was a lap cat and had no idea how big she truly was. She'd lounge on the love seat in Danny's office all day, drowsing and dozing until someone nudged her from her spot. I couldn't picture her as a racer, but Danny insisted she was lightning on the track.

Why did I have daily freak-outs about whether or not my appearance was professional enough, when Danny brought his dog to the office without a second thought? It didn't seem fair, and I shifted uncomfortably in my chair, trying to tune back in to the conversation. Something about how you'd expect a detective to have a bloodhound, but Greyhounds couldn't track scent. Truly, I was having a hard time focusing. My fingers braided my hair as my mind wandered, and I snitched an elastic from Ellen's desk to wrap the end.

"That's bad for your hair, Olivia," Ellen chided. "You'll break the ends." Her hand appeared across the desk, and I dropped the rubber band into it, like a child spitting out gum in school.

Luka pulled a leather strip from his pocket. It looked familiar, but it definitely wasn't mine.

"It's Antonio's," he said, like it was normal for a guy to have extra hair ties in his pocket, just in case the boss might need one.

He wrapped the tie around my braid, weaving the ends through without a second thought. His fingers brushed the nape of my neck, surprisingly intimate, and I found myself hot with embarrassment, and something else, too.

Jealousy?

I was jealous of whoever had taught him this little skill. Antonio? Some past lover? It didn't matter who, not really. It didn't change the fact that I was jealous. And all of a sudden Luka's reaction to Mike made a little more sense.

Ellen cleared her throat, and I turned toward her, hoping my face didn't show my feelings. "Linc's off the phone if y'all are ready to go in."

Luka followed me, and I didn't bother wasting my breath on an argument. I could talk to Linc on my own. It was perfectly safe, but it really didn't matter. Before I opened the door to Linc's office, I looked into Luka's eyes long and hard, his body shielding us from Ellen's sight. I touched his face, soaking up a little more of his energy.

His fingers stretched beneath my jacket, seeking the raised scars across my shoulder, and I shivered, the old marks starting to throb. Luka's eyes shifted amber behind the green, and I knew he felt the leopard in me. I thought maybe I was starting to feel it, too.

I turned away just as Linc opened his office door.

"Liv, you're looking well. Considering," he added, carefully. "Mr. Niere, it's a pleasure to finally meet you."

"Finally?" I inquired.

"We've spoken on the phone," Linc answered.

"Regarding the details of your work for Antonio."

"I see," I said, and suddenly I did see. I saw there was still too much I didn't know about the Leopard King, and maybe I'd been asking the wrong questions of the wrong people all along.

I also saw Luka's eyes, guarded and careful, and I wished there was something I could do besides go over the details of last night's fiasco one more time. But there wasn't. Thankfully, Linc needed to hear the full version, because at this point I was having a hard time remembering who got which story and why.

There were details I wanted desperately to share—the feel of Cole's hands on my waist; the pounding beat separating our bodies then drawing us close again, over and over; the sheer terror of losing the Sig, alone with that nightmare in the alley; the exact color of burning vampire, and the scent, dank and rotten in my mouth. But this wasn't the time, and Linc wasn't Karen, either, not by a long shot.

As if confirming my assessment, Linc handed me another new .38 ultralight, an exact duplicate of the one I'd used last night. Luka shifted beside me, uncomfortable though I wasn't sure why.

"I picked up an ankle holster for you, but it doesn't look like you can use it today." Linc passed it across the desk to me anyway. "I figured as much, so I brought an extra rig for your waistband, too."

Linc smiled, pleased with his choices. I examined the new holsters thoughtfully, but dropped the gun into my jacket pocket. It was hard to believe such a tiny thing had taken the eternal life of a vampire last night, but it had.

No, I reminded myself, the gun hadn't killed red-shirt. I had.

"It's loaded with hydroshock silvers, of course."

Luka winced.

"Is there a problem, Mr. Niere?" Linc asked.

Luka shook his head, smiling. He crossed his legs casually, his face a pleasant mask.

"What kind of weapon do you carry?" It was idle conversation, nothing more. In Linc's world, everyone carried. What kind of self-respecting Southerner went around unarmed? None that he would associate with, that was certain.

"I think that's a conversation for another day," Luka said easily, letting his power roll across the room. It was lost on Linc, though. He wouldn't know Luka was a wereleopard unless he shifted right here in the office.

And maybe not even then.

"Thanks again," I said to Linc. "I've got my pager, so call me if anything comes up."

"When shall I have Ellen put you back on the calendar?" Linc wasn't too sensitive in the usual ways, either, but Forever Crossed was his family's livelihood, so I couldn't really blame him.

"I don't know," I told him honestly. "But if something light needs attention, I'll do what I can. Nothing serious," I stressed. "And no more homicides until this is over." I stared at Linc hard, hoping he really heard me.

Linc nodded at me and shook Luka's hand, and just like that, my schedule had been cleared and the meeting was over and I realized, suddenly, that I had nothing else to do.

As Luka and I stepped out of the building, the sun slanted into my face, a warm welcome. I took a deep breath, spring air and sunshine, and I stretched my palms toward the sky. My head still ached, and my throat was sore from all the words I hadn't spoken, but it was a gorgeous day, and it seemed a shame not to enjoy it.

I tossed Luka the car keys, biting my lip as his wrist whipped through the air lightning quick. I smiled in spite of myself, wondering when I would stop being impressed by his speed. "You mind driving?"

"Angel, I thought you'd never ask!"

Twelve

Luka piloted my little convertible like he'd been doing it all of his life, though it was a far cry from the slick sedan he'd handed off to Cole this morning.

We were headed southeast, toward Luka's place in the country. He had an apartment in the city, close to Feeling Blue and Antonio, but the bounce in his voice told me this was really his home. The afternoon light shone in his eyes, and I watched a slow smile tug at his lips. The Ja'Nan gathered here for their full moon ceremony, something that sounded mysterious and private and very much like something I didn't want to witness.

The cabin was just over an hour from the sprawling edge of the Triangle, but it seemed like another world. I'd slept for the past twenty minutes or so, which was no easy feat in the cramped passenger seat, so I must've really needed it.

"Hey," I said, smiling, "thanks for letting me sleep."

"Hey, yourself. Feeling better?"

"Much better," I admitted. I rolled my head gently around my shoulders, waiting for the pounding to start, but it didn't. No dizziness, either, and my stomach stayed right where it was supposed to be. In fact, I was hungry. "Almost like I didn't have a concussion at all."

Luka wove his fingers through my hair, searching for where the gash had been last night. This afternoon it was a tender little ridge, but even that would be gone by tomorrow.

"You're not completely healed yet, Angel." He actually looked worried. "You need to be careful."

Most people are impressed, if not a little freaked, by the rapid healing. Luka seemed disappointed.

"If it had been you who was injured last night," I asked, "how long would it take you to heal?"

"I wouldn't have been injured so easily." He sounded smug, like he was boasting.

I glared at him. *Easily?* Most humans wouldn't have survived what I'd been through, but I didn't say a word.

"I wouldn't have a concussion, either," he added. "But my body would completely heal a cut like that one in a few hours. No trace of the injury, nothing to indicate that I'd been wounded. You won't be so lucky, Angel. You're going to have a scar."

"Yeah? Well, I have a nice collection." A thin white line hiding in my hair was nothing compared to the rest of them, but he didn't have to point it out, either. It had taken me years, but I'd come to think of my scars as a history of sorts, like time, written on my body for later remembrances. "Anyway, as scars from a vampire attack go, I'll take this one without a whole lot of complaining. It could have been much worse . . ."

My voice trailed off. I didn't really want to talk about this, but I didn't know how to ask about the things I really did want to talk about. Like who else would be at the cabin, for starters. And what would happen in five days, when the moon was full and the Ja'Nan gathered?

Luka gave me a sharp look, as if he'd read my thoughts. I sent silent thanks to all the gods that he couldn't. His senses were sharper than a human's, but he wasn't psychic. No more than the rest of us, anyway. I turned in my seat so that I faced him and tried to keep my expression casual.

"I haven't spent much time in the country since I was little," I said, remembering long ago summers with my Nana. Memories of her washed through me in a sweet grass wave. She was so clear I could almost smell the flowers in her hair, see her smile as I scooted through the branches of the tall oak in her backyard, her fingers stained with the warm red juice of fresh berries picked on our morning walk. I was a city girl now, no doubt about it, but that hadn't always been the case. New memories waited for me in the country, and I was anxious to meet them. "Tell me about it?"

As smooth roads turned to gravel and then hard-packed dirt, the world sliding by my window transformed. The gray cityscape dwindled, became lush and green. Where buildings had clouded the landscape, now the spaces stretched wide, dotted by tractors and goats. Stonewalled edges lined the road, and long drives meandered toward hidden houses. The magic of Luka's voice wrapped around me, and though he was talking facts and figures, county politics and rural economics, had he been speaking in another language, I would have thought it was poetry.

I wasn't too sure about the plan though, which was to lay low until Antonio had taken care of Adrienne. It didn't sound like much, and I had mixed feelings about tracking Feine without using Adrienne as bait, but when Luka said he figured he'd be driving me home in three days or so, I let my worries about the strategy go. *Woo Hoo!* No full moon with the wereleopards for me.

Neat rows of green plantings and grazing fields gave way to thick stands of old pine and wide tracts grown over with blooms and weeds. Drawn into the scenery, my eyes rested in the distance, settling on a craggy windblown tree. It stood by itself, the only tree in the middle of a field grown wild. I felt pulled to it, as though I'd known this tree all my life and before, long before, forever.

Maybe I wasn't over the concussion after all.

When the world outside my window came to a sudden halt, it took a few seconds before I realized we'd reached Luka's cabin.

"That tree? It's special?" I asked, hoping I didn't sound like an idiot. It was a tree, how could it be special? Of course I sounded like an idiot.

"Yes, it is. Special." His voice was thick, raspier than it had been. "Let's go inside, Angel. I'll show you the rest later." He grabbed my bags from the back seat and got out of the car, a blur of fluid motion I could only envy.

I didn't see the Jaguar anywhere, so I was guessing Cole and Stacie weren't here yet. I swallowed hard, reluctant to go inside. The idea of being trapped in a cabin with unknown wereleopards prickled up my spine.

I took a deep breath and smiled. My mother had devoted years ingraining the finer points of social etiquette deep within my soul. I could hear her listen-to-me-young-lady-I-know-about-these-things voice clearly in my mind, "A pretty smile goes a long way in diminishing one's flaws, Olivia."

Well, Mother, I thought. *How far does a pretty smile go when the nice people can smell one's flaws?* Just imagining the look on my mother's face in response was enough to make my smile a little brighter.

***

From the front, Luka's cabin looked just like I expected. Rustic and dated and, well, like a country cabin. But a quick peak around the corner told me years of updating were hidden behind the façade. Calling this place a cabin was an understatement. It was more like a private lodge than anything else.

The interior was modern, open and airy, with inside angles opening to cozy nooks, and skylights flooding the entire space with light. There was a deep loft bedroom, which was where the Ja'Nan were now, and I imagined they were watching my every move with suspicion. I felt like an intruder in their territory.

As Luka walked me through, he pointed out the kitchen, the bathrooms, a few closets, and finally crossed through an actual doorway and into a private bedroom. The opposite wall was mostly glass, sliding doors leading out to a large deck. From here I could see the tree, with its rounded, windswept shape, and I thought how peaceful it would be to wake up to this view.

"This is it," Luka said, setting my bags on a chair beside the bed. The room was small, and the bed with its antique-looking brass frame took up most of the space. All of the furnishings looked old, a marked contrast to the sleek modern feel of the rest of the house.

"The Ja'Nan have the run of the place, for the most part, but this is more or less my personal space. They know you'll be here for a few days." He shrugged, and I wondered what I wasn't getting, because there was obviously something.

Luka pulled the slider open, and we stepped onto the deck. The air smelled clean, like rich soil and green things growing in the sun. Luka pointed out a wooden enclosure that turned out to be an open-air shower, but a smile paraded across his face as though he'd just shown me his most prized possession. I must have looked skeptical, since he assured me there was also a full bath inside.

"This isn't what I expected," I admitted. "But it's really wonderful. I guess I thought there might not be electricity, you know, this far out."

He shook his head, laughing about city folk. How he managed to fit in here so perfectly with his tailored clothes and Italian loafers, I couldn't explain. But he did.

"C'mon," he said, giving my arm a tug. "Cole and Stacie are bringing lunch from town. Besides, I want you to meet the others, and I need to check on Jayne."

"Jayne?"

"She's still recovering from the vampire attack." His voice was tense, stilted. "She shouldn't have been at Anya's in the first place."

My jaw dropped, and I winced as it clicked back into place. I assumed the injured wereleopard was male, and as I recalled the feel of the crime scene, my impressions remained the same. Hmmm. Maybe the forewarned wereleopard simply felt like a protector, a rescuer of some kind? And maybe I identified those qualities with men? I didn't think so, all things considered, but either way, my interest in Jayne was piqued.

"She should have healed by now," Luka admitted. "And I don't know why she hasn't. I'm worried. Without Anya, I'm a little lost."

"I don't follow," I said, trailing behind him as we crossed the deck and reentered the cabin. Inside, the presence of the other wereleopards clung like dense fog, and I turned back to focus on the view. I strained to hear the tree calling me, to feel the sun's dappled light across my skin. But the sound of my own fear was an endless echo, crowding out everything else.

"They don't want me here," I whispered, hoping the Ja'Nan couldn't hear me.

"I am Ra'Jahn, and you are my guest. This is my home, Angel." His green eyes were smoky, almost gray with emotion. "If I say you are welcome, then you are."

"I don't want to cause a problem for you."

"You misunderstand." He shook his head. "It's not that they don't want you here, they just don't know *why* you're here. Which is my fault, and I'll correct it." He sighed, wrapping his arms around me. His voice filtered through his chest, mixing with his heartbeat in a way that made it hard to pay attention. "They've been edgy since Anya's death. Our shaman meant a lot to us, and we miss her. Anya was our healer, our spiritual center. She was the grounding energy of the Ja'Nan."

Some Bereavement Specialist I am, huh?

"Luka, I'm sorry. I'm not trying to be insensitive. You're

right. Once I meet them, it will be easier."

***

I followed him across the room and up the stairs to the loft. I focused on projecting calm. Recalling Anya's chant for protection, I kept its rhythm in my mind, let it stretch out in swirling tendrils until it filled the space around me and beyond.

I waited at the top of the stairs while Luka spoke to his leopards, all the while filling the loft with the protective rhythm that was part Anya's, part mine. I hoped they would feel it as familiar, reassuring even.

They didn't, and I couldn't stop the gasp before it caught tight in my throat. One of them spun toward me, teeth bared, his power crashing across the room and forcing me to take a step back.

He was angry, that much was clear, but confused and sad, too, underneath the rest of it. He made a show of sniffing the air around me. "You might smell like our Ra'Jahn, witchling, but you aren't one of us." His lip curled. "You don't belong here."

"Back off, Andrew," Luka warned.

I looked at Luka and shook my head. I know grief when I see it, and I could handle this on my own.

"I'm actually not a witch," I said. "And maybe I don't belong here, but since I *am* here, maybe I can help? I'm not your shaman, but I know a few things about healing. I might be able to do something for your friend." I gestured to the figure that lay prone on the bed.

"No." Luka's voice was firm, too quick.

No? I glared at him from across the room. *Why the hell not?*

"Olivia, you can't. It's too soon."

If I could help Jayne, then the rest of them might see I wasn't here to steal their Ra'Jahn. True, I happened to need protection from a couple of ambition-crazed vampires at this particular moment, and it was unfortunate timing that I was here seeking their help while they were still mourning Anya's loss. Still, this was something I could do to help them.

"You aren't completely healed yourself," Luka insisted. "It's too dangerous."

"Doesn't look like she's hurt from here," Andrew

snarled. I took it as a compliment, seeing as he didn't mention the obvious damage to my leg. Also, it was proof that the scar didn't look as nasty as it might have, certainly not a mere two days old.

"Not that it matters," he added, defiance shining in his eyes. "She couldn't help even if the Ra'Jahn allowed it. If his blood won't heal Jayne, there's nothing she can do."

"What does he mean?" I asked Luka, nervousness twitching my fingers against the hem of my skirt. "What about your blood?"

"Aww, look, I've scared the little human!" Andrew snickered, and someone laughed, though I didn't look to see who. "Maybe you should run now, witchling. Run while you still can."

He was right, I *was* scared, and I hated him for that. Scared of what I didn't understand, scared of these people who were so much like me and yet nothing like me at all.

I tightened the muscles along my spine and focused on the protection spell I'd started earlier, adding the words for healing to it, making it more mine, less Anya's. I held the new energy inside, weaving it tightly and not letting it spill out. My gaze was locked on Luka, watching his face, waiting for him to answer me.

"I am Ra'Jahn, Olivia. I feed the clan in many ways." His eyes were like flat green glass, perfect reflections of the weariness in his voice.

Obviously, this was a line he hadn't wanted to cross, though I couldn't imagine why. It hardly seemed possible that he was afraid I would leave, but as soon as my mind touched on the thought, I knew it was true. He didn't know I couldn't turn my back on him now, wouldn't turn from the Ja'Nan and run away like Andrew's taunts dared me to do.

I moved closer to him, blocking the others out, never taking my eyes from his. "I can do this, Luka. I want to do this." I rested my hand against his face, searching his eyes for a sign. "I guess I need your permission, but I'd rather have your support."

He turned away from me, knelt by the bedside and whispered something to Jayne. A low wounded sound rose from the bed, drawing my attention to the prone figure I'd offered to heal. Despite her pain, the Ja'Nan laid hands on her body, and I watched as a thin layer of Luka's energy buzzed over her, intersected with other colorful strands. The Ja'Nan were pouring their strength into her, and I knew without their touch she wouldn't have made it this long.

Her body was draped lightly in a white sheet, her right leg left bare, exposing the open wound that ran from her calf to her thigh and maybe beyond. Her arms were covered in deep gashes, defensive wounds, I noted, and her face was bruised and swollen. I could only imagine what I would find under the sheet.

All of the cuts were clean, without the slightest trace of infection. *Licked clean,* I thought, forming a mental picture in an instant. I shrugged, not sure why the idea sounded so right to me, but knowing that it did. My eyes darted over them, wondering who had sent me the image before I realized I'd conjured it myself. Besides, they were shapeshifters, not vampires, and except for Jayne they were very much alive.

I touched Luka's shoulder, visualizing the glowing sphere of protection I had created moments ago. I let it expand slowly and sent it outward, through Luka and beyond. Once again, the air in the loft billowed with my spell.

Luka pulled me aside. Worry creased his brow, made me think twice about what I was attempting. Before this moment, I hadn't imagined Luka as anything but solid strength and power.

"Angel, I appreciate what you're trying to do, but it's too risky. If you fail, and Jayne doesn't improve, they'll blame you. Do you understand? It isn't the right time for you to come into the clan. Not yet, not like this."

"No, I don't understand." I shook my head. There was so much I didn't understand these days, I almost wished I hadn't said it. "I'm not one of you and I'm not trying to be. I'm not a witch, and I'm not a shaman, and I only know as much about healing as I learned from my grandmother . . ." My voice trailed off. I wasn't making a very convincing argument. "Look. I don't know how I know, but I do know I can help her."

"Jayne is dying, Olivia." He looked away, sighing. "Her

wounds shouldn't have been fatal, not to one of us. She won't survive the full moon, and we will mourn two of the clan instead of one." Luka's mouth was soft, more pink than red, and I could only begin to fathom the searing pain in his eyes. "You can't fix this, and I can't risk losing you, too. Not now."

Someone coughed, pulling my attention away from Luka. One of the wereleopards edged closer. She was small, maybe five foot five, with short blonde hair and a roundish figure. I liked her, for no reason other than she hadn't attacked me yet, I guess, since I ordinarily don't like short women right off the bat.

"You've got to let her try, Luka," she said, looking up at him with determined brown eyes.

See? I knew I liked her.

"Leah, I can't."

"You can. Even Andrew thinks so." She waited a beat and when Luka didn't say anything, she went for it. "I know this is a decision the whole clan should be here for, but we can't wait. You're our Ra'Jahn, and we'll back you, if it comes to that. If she succeeds," Leah's hand jutted out in my direction, "then Jayne will back you, too. But the Ja'Nan won't question you, Luka. I know they won't."

The prickle of Andrew's energy reached me from across the room. "Decide Ra'Jahn," he said, his voice booming in the open space. "One way or the other, it's time for you to decide."

Thirteen

I rummaged through Luka's kitchen, looking for the items I imagined a real healer would have on hand for this sort of thing. Unfortunately, my imagination had dulled to a filmy paste in recent days. Who needed a fantasy world when wereleopards romped through your reality?

But I'd managed to locate the basics. I sent Andrew upstairs with two bowls of steaming water and had Leah search the linen closet for clean towels and fresh candles. In the pantry I found last summer's herbs drying upside down, tied at their stems with a rough snaky twine. I pinched a few leaves of sage and peppermint, and a bit of rosemary, too. A jar of local honey, a bottle of red wine, and a stack of small glass bowls lined the counter now—a meager offering, but it was the best I could do.

I heard Luka's voice in the hallway, then Cole's in quick response, and although I couldn't hear what they were saying, I had a pretty good guess. After a few minutes, Cole slipped into the kitchen and set the crinkly bags of whatever he and Stacie had picked up for lunch carefully into the fridge. He gave my arm a quick squeeze and carried the stack of items I'd gathered to the loft. Stacie shook her head at me, but followed Cole upstairs without a word, leaving me alone with Luka.

Doubt hung between us, palpable, and I couldn't think of anything to say that might disperse it. The truth was, I didn't know a thing about healing shapeshifters. Hell, I didn't know all that much about healing humans, either, since my body almost always healed itself. What I did know was that I probably shouldn't have volunteered for this, and when Luka said *No!* I should have listened. But I hadn't. And I wouldn't back out now.

For the second time since I'd met her, Leah stood beside me clearing her throat. Not that she was interrupting. In fact, I was grateful for the distraction.

"These are the only candles I could find," she said, holding up a box of brightly colored birthday candles.

My face lit with renewed inspiration. "These are perfect!" I wouldn't have sought them out, but there was something about those little candles with their swirling colors that I just couldn't resist. I wasn't alone either. A broad grin flashed Leah's straight white teeth, and even Luka cracked a smile before he turned away from us and headed up to the loft.

I went back to the pantry and filled one of the small glass bowls with coarse salt and carried it up the stairs, allowing the energy in the loft to spread over me. The wereleopards radiated power, and I reminded myself not to shut them out.

At least I knew enough about rituals from my work at Forever Crossed to put on a damn good show. But if I was going to heal Jayne, not only did I need every scrap of ritual knowledge I'd ever learned and long forgotten, I'd need whatever threads of strength the Ja'Nan would lend me, too.

They hovered around Jayne, soft words and softer touches filling the space around her. A slow ache beat in my chest, an usher, coaxing me to begin. I took the three purple candles from the box and stuck them upright in the bowl of salt, smiling at the symbolism. This was a birthday, all right. Maybe not what the manufacturer had in mind, but quite an occasion nonetheless.

I lit the first candle, the whisper of the flame sweet in my ears. Spindly stalks of dried rosemary crumbled between my fingers, the bits falling easily into the rounded spoon I held over the flame. The herb's sharp scent filled the room, nurturing the protection spell I'd cast earlier and cleansing the remnants of fear and anger from the air. Breathing deeply, I crushed the peppermint leaves into one of the bowls of hot water and, for good measure, dropped a few dried sprigs of rosemary in there, too.

Next I poured a small amount of the red wine, added honey and crushed sage, and a good amount of clear steaming water from the second bowl. This was a healing tonic I'd used on myself with some success, with the addition of the red wine. Ordinarily the blood from whichever of my wounds needed attention was enough, but Jayne's wounds weren't bloody anymore, and I wasn't about to ask for donations. Not if I didn't have to, anyway.

I began my chant, using Anya's protection spell as a building block. My voice was quiet, searching for its own level in the rhythm of the words. I soaked one of the towels in the peppermint water and used it to wash my hands and arms. The muscles along my spine and down my arms stretched tight. Power pooled in my chest, a liquid swirl.

I lit a second candle and visualized my energy as a glowing indigo sphere. As I walked around the bed, I felt the wereleopards back away, making room for me. With the third candle lit, I carried the warmed wine to Jayne's bedside and cast my energy in a clean circle around us.

Kneeling over Jayne's still body, I took a sip of the wine. A flick of my wrist set the suspended sage in motion, and I used my fingers to drip the mixture into her mouth.

I stretched outward with my power, forcing away my fears and searching the room. I swallowed my doubts, sure the Ja'Nan scented my uncertainty, certain they would reject me outright. The first tentative wisps of my power brushed over their roiling energy. I felt Cole and Luka, cool in the charged atmosphere, and the others beside them, surprised but steady.

As the connections stabilized between us, I focused my power on Jayne. I handed off the bowl, and one of the leopards continued dripping wine into her mouth. For a fraction of a second I hoped whoever it was had washed their hands, and then I let that go, too.

Jayne's body warmed beneath mine, and I stretched my hands just above her skin, pressing through her mottled aura. I found the wound along her leg, mentally stitching the flesh together. I pressed my hands closer, hovering over her chest but not touching her. Memories of Nana spilled through me then—her warm hands roaming around childhood injuries, coaxing and culling, making everything all right. *You can do this, Livvie,* I coached. *Just keep going.*

In my mind's eye, I pushed through Jayne's rib cage. My hands pulsed around her heart, steadying the beat and warming it into a strong rhythm. My clothes clung to me, damp, and I worked hard to maintain my presence in the healing state.

Above her body, my hands continued to search her aura for injury. When I visualized her ribs, I found the broken one and fused the shattered edges. I listened only to her breathing until I heard the air leaking from her lungs. Gently, I located the puncture and squeezed it back together. Her aura steered my hands, and I focused a steady flow of energy through it, trusting it to feed her organs enough for them to heal.

She was starting to come around now, and I knew that once she regained consciousness, the pain would be intense. I didn't know how to dull those feelings, and I was sorry for that, but at least she would survive. I refocused and tried to close the last gash in her shoulder as quickly as I could.

My own strength ebbed, but I wasn't about to stop now. I reached for the Ja'Nan, felt their strength like a lifeline in the rushing tide. Luka's energy coursed along my skin, cool and tingly, and again I smoothed my hands over Jayne's aura. I had healed her wounds, or started the process anyway, but what crippled her wasn't entirely physical. Something tugged at her subconscious, something dark and secret, and I reached for that black echo with the last of my power.

Jayne's grief flooded through me, and with the loss came an overwhelming sense of guilt. Of course! She blamed herself for not getting there in time, for not being able to save Anya from the flames. In her heart of hearts, she felt responsible for Anya's death.

In this state, there was no way for me to comfort her, to tell her it wasn't her fault. Instead, I stretched as close to the Ja'Nan as I could, their energy pooling in my body and flowing out to Jayne's. It was all I could do, and I hoped it would be enough.

My knees ached from crouching on the bed, and every muscle in my body sang with the strain of the ritual. I eased myself upright, stumbled back to the dresser. I soaked a fresh towel in the warm herb-water and washed my face and hands again. Salt buried the flame of the first candle in the bowl, purple wax crusted around the well like wet sand at sunrise.

I crushed the rest of the sage into the water bowl, and added a good bit of honey, too. It would be sticky, but it would do the trick. I soaked two more towels, and laid them gently across Jayne's leg and shoulder.

The work I did internally would save her, but her skin wasn't completely healed and her muscles would be more than a little sore. I didn't know what else to do.

The second candle sputtered into the salt. With the final flame, I filled the room with the cleansing scent of rosemary, until it, too, burned out in the bowl. I used the salt to close the healing circle I'd opened, and worked hard for a few moments to slow my breathing.

Still, I was buzzing with borrowed power. I looked into Luka's eyes, reached for his body to ground my own.

It was a mistake.

Skin to skin, the power between us sparked through me in an electric shock that sent me reeling away. I shook my head, wanting to explain but not trusting myself to find the right words. Like a prism dangling in the sun, energy bounced through my body, stabbing and sparkling and wreaking havoc with my nervous system.

With that bit of distance between us, my power grasped the network of mental connections I'd created earlier. I took a deep breath, and as I released it, I visualized the prism bursting, sending spirals of power back to the Ja'Nan.

Andrew swore under his breath, Stacie and Leah rubbed each other's arms. I leaned back, grateful for the wall behind me. Since this was a loft, I guess I was lucky I wasn't on the other side of the room. Cole stood beside me, not touching, just smiling like there was no tomorrow.

"You're the real thing, all right," Cole said.

I nodded, even though I wasn't sure what he meant. "I think Jayne will be okay," I said, hoping it was the right response.

"Unbelievable," Leah said, or was it Stacie? I couldn't tell.

"Believe it," Cole responded.

Cole was full of energy—they all were, like they'd had their batteries charged. Maybe they had.

When I reversed the energy flow, I'd wanted the surplus power to reach them, wanted to give them something back for the strength they'd lent me. How and why the power shifted from healing in nature to whatever this was, I didn't know, and I didn't have the strength to care, either.

"As long as it was good for you guys," I joked, "that's the important thing." Maybe I didn't know much about the Ja'Nan, but I knew I wasn't about to give up my sense of humor. They'd either accept me or they wouldn't, and there wasn't much else I could do about it either way.

My eyes sought Luka. I wasn't sure what I was looking for, but I know I didn't find it. He sat beside Jayne, talking quietly and holding her hand. Cole followed my gaze. He mouthed *Ra'Jahn* and gave me a shrug.

"Let's eat," he said out loud, taking my arm and directing me down the stairs and into the kitchen.

"I'm not very hungry," I protested.

"Too bad, little witch," Andrew said, surprising me with a casual touch on my arm while he spoke. "You'll eat anyway. You look like you need it."

***

The years I'd spent separating myself from the wereleopards crashed over me in a flood of regret. I was starting to see the Ja'Nan like a new kind of family, joking and jostling with each other in the kitchen, handing around beers from the fridge. Just at this moment, I was comfortable with them, and comfortable with myself around them, despite the questions nagging in the back of my mind.

I might not be one of them, and I certainly wasn't Anya, but I had saved their friend and that was enough. At least for now. The magic I'd used was on the outside edge of even my own comprehension, but the Ja'Nan seemed to take it in stride. Maybe it was normal for them. Maybe their Shaman had performed similar rituals in the past? Maybe, though I had the feeling the energy surge that followed the healing wasn't part of their usual fare.

I'd said I wasn't all that hungry, and it was true, I wasn't. But since lunch had come from my favorite deli south of the Mason-Dixon Line, I managed a few bites. When Cole leaned over and asked me if I was going to eat my food or just play with it, I gladly handed over my plate for him to finish.

Half-listening to their conversation, I wondered if there would be trouble with the rest of the Ja'Nan when they learned what I'd done today. Leah didn't think so, but Stacie and Andrew weren't so sure.

Talk drifted to more personal matters, discussion of the merits of being in or out of the shapeshifting closet, and who else was expected at the cabin and when. As interested as I was, my eyelids drooped and my head weighed heavily in my hand.

I listened mostly for mention of Luka's name, strained to hear the rhythm of his voice. My body ached for him, but he still hadn't come down from the loft.

Whatever, I thought, trying not to care so much. He was Ra'Jahn, and if Jayne needed him, by her side is where he'd be. And me? Well, right now I just needed some sleep. Everything else I'd deal with in the morning.

I sighed, and Cole's arm wrapped around my shoulders, so warm, and so right, and I smiled to myself, thinking maybe, just maybe, I needed more than sleep after all.

Fourteen

I woke slowly, unaware that I'd been sleeping, unsure where my dreamworld ended and where reality began. In the dim light of early evening, I shivered and moved closer to the warm body next to mine. Strong arms wrapped around my waist and pulled me close. Even half asleep I knew it was just comfort—there was no spark in the heat.

So it was Cole's face I would see when I finally opened my eyes. Cole, with his sun-streaked hair and easy smile, the sandy scent of the Crystal Coast clinging to him like a second skin. Cole. Not Luka.

Maybe I could coax sleep into returning?

But no. I was awake now, and the world of dreams elusive. I sighed, enjoying the closeness for another minute or two before I inched away.

"Why are you here?" I looked into Cole's eyes, wanting to understand.

"Disappointed, are you?"

Not exactly. I covered a yawn and snuggled back into the comforting circle of Cole's arms. "More like confused. What happened?"

"You fell asleep out there," he said, inclining his head toward the door, "and I carried you in here. You don't remember?" I shook my head since he seemed to be waiting for an answer. "Anyway, Luka was still upstairs with Jayne, and I didn't think you should be alone when everyone else went outside to play, so here we are."

I didn't like the way he said Luka was with Jayne, but I didn't want to ask him about it, either. Instead I asked the other obvious question. "Play what?"

"Play wereleopard, of course! They're out there now, running through the fields, stalking prey, feeling the night unfold from the limbs of a favorite tree . . ."

I shivered again, and not from the cold.

"I'm just kidding, Liv. They are outside, and I don't doubt they're running around, but with a Frisbee or a football or something. They aren't *changed.*" He wound his fingers through my hair, playing with the long strands. "How can you still be so afraid of us, after what you did for Jayne?"

"I don't know," I answered. "One thing has nothing to do with the other, I guess. I healed Jayne because I couldn't let her suffer when I knew I could help. That's who I am. It has nothing to do with who you are."

"But we still scare you?"

"Maybe." Cole's shirt was soft against my cheek, his chest hard and smooth beneath the fabric. "I don't know."

Neither one of us said anything for a while. I soaked in the country quiet that wasn't quiet at all, full of cricket songs and insect chatter, laced through wind and woods and other sounds I couldn't quite identify. Even now that I was listening for them, I could hardly hear the Ja'Nan over the rest of it.

"So, yeah," Cole said. "That's why Luka is with Jayne, and I'm here."

My lousy human hearing hardly seemed like much of a reason, but I guess it was as good as any. On the other hand, maybe I'd misunderstood. "Again, please?"

"I said, that's why Luka is with Jayne, and I'm here with you," he repeated slowly.

"Explain."

"After you'd healed Jayne, Luka touched you, remember? You pushed him away. You weren't just scared, Liv, you were terrified. It only lasted a second, but it was there. We all felt it."

"No." The denial wasn't enough, but it was all I could manage. "No."

He sighed, sounding again like he was explaining something very simple to a small child. "That's why Luka didn't join the rest of us downstairs, and why he's still with Jayne. He won't force himself on you, and Jayne is more than happy for his company."

"No," I said again, rising up on my elbow and locking my eyes with his. "There was too much power building inside me. I was afraid I wouldn't be able to control it. When I touched Luka, the contact intensified everything. I had to break the connection." I swallowed hard, my voice filling with emotions I couldn't explain. "I was *not* afraid of Luka."

"It didn't feel that way to him, Liv. And it didn't feel that way to me, either."

"Well, that's the way it was." I felt like a balloon with

a slow leak. Everything around these people prickled and poked, and I couldn't seem to put my finger on why. "Even if that explains why Luka is with Jayne, which it doesn't, how could it possibly explain what you are doing in my bed?"

"Technically, this is Luka's bed."

I just looked at him. In my opinion, that only made it worse.

"Luka isn't like me, Liv." He exhaled slowly, twirls of my hair falling from his fingers. "I wanted to be here when you woke up, even if you didn't want me here. It just feels right to me. *You* feel right to me."

I wanted to say something, something sweet and true, but his lips brushed my forehead and my heart filled, whisking my would-be words away.

"I know who you are, Olivia. I know the legends as well as Luka does."

I had to let that sink in for a minute. I couldn't accept that I was part of some ancient mythology, and it bothered me that the Ja'Nan thought I was something other than what I was. Considering my recent activities, though, I wasn't doing a very good job of convincing them otherwise.

"Does everybody know?"

"Well, it's probably obvious to them how I feel about you."

None of this was Cole's fault, which didn't make it any easier. I swallowed hard and asked my question again. "I meant, does everybody think I'm part of this prophecy?"

"Oh, that," he replied easily, settling my head back down on his chest. "No, they don't know. I spent a lot of time with Anya, so I know more about the old ways than some of the others. When Luka sent me to protect you that first night, he made it clear that you were important, but he didn't say why. When I saw the bullet wound, and your leg healing around it, I put two and two together."

This night, I realized, wasn't unlike that one.

Cole's voice, soft and soothing in the semidarkness, doing for Luka what the Ra'Jahn couldn't do for himself. Tonight Cole's words were warm in my hair, his hands hot against my skin. I listened to his heart beat, inhaled the salty scent of him, and I knew I should move away, get up from the bed now and find something else to do besides what I was doing. The truth was, I didn't know how to handle his feelings for me, but I wasn't entirely uncomfortable with them either.

I was attracted to Cole, although it was nothing like my attraction for Luka. Cole was more like a good friend, someone I might get cozy with, but not someone I could get passionate about. He was familiar. In fact, he was exactly the kind of guy I normally went for. Good looking, strong, warm, fun to be around. But Luka had changed my expectations. Now I wanted more, sparks and chemistry, fireworks.

So unfair, I sulked to myself, hating it, because sparks and chemistry were exactly why I was wrapped in Cole's arms now, and Luka was upstairs with Jayne.

Fifteen

Cole propped himself up on one arm, watching me inch further and further away. Already, I missed his body next to mine, and part of me wanted to hide in here forever, safe.

"You should go," I told him, wrapping my arms around my chest.

The Ja'Nan were inside now, their laughter filtering through the closed door. I didn't like it.

"Olivia, I know you want me to stay."

Hovering on the edge of the bed, my back to him, I could still feel the heat of his body, the thrill of his hand meandering along my spine.

"Even so." I hopped up, started pacing. Of course I wanted him to stay, but the Ja'Nan had my attention now, too. Were they talking about me? About me and Cole? As much as I wanted him to stay, he had to go. Now. "I need to think, and I can't think with you here."

Cole slid to the door. "Careful, Livvie. Flattery will get you everywhere." Laughter danced in his clear blue eyes, the light behind them visible even in the shadows by the door. His lips brushed my cheek, and then he was gone, the door snicking closed behind him.

I leaned against it, the pane-carved wood cool on my back, listening. *Wimp,* I admonished myself. *You should be out there, too!* But I wasn't ready for total Ja'Nan immersion again. Not so soon.

I heard their voices rise to greet Cole, and above them, Andrew's nasty tone. "You smell like the witch, brother."

Cole's lighthearted laughter echoed my earlier words, reminding Andrew that I wasn't a witch. I winced, my throat aching with the need to speak. But I stood silent, waiting for him to explain how we'd spent the last few hours. Sleeping. But he didn't. He just laughed some more, and though I knew Cole damn sure didn't smell like sex, I wished someone would have taken a minute to point that out, too. If Luka was within earshot, I hoped he could hear everything that had been left unsaid.

Without turning on the light, I searched my bags for my cell phone. If I could talk to Karen for a few minutes, maybe I could get a grip on some of this. My eyes drifted over the dresser, the night stand, the chair. No phone in sight. Maybe I'd left it in the car?

A sudden surge of adrenaline spun me into motion. I needed fresh air and room to breathe it. I avoided the wereleopards by slipping through the sliding doors in the bedroom and following the deck around the back of the cabin.

I lounged in my car for a few minutes, waiting for my breathing to slow, savoring the solitude and feeling the night pulse through the air. Once my pulse dropped to a level close to normal, I rummaged through the glove box. Service receipts and maintenance manuals, hair ties and half-melted lipsticks, but my cell phone wasn't among them. I checked under the seats, just for good measure. The carpet fuzz-bunnies that called my car home were not pleased to be disturbed, and they crept between my searching fingers, damp and itchy.

Finally, my hand slipped over a cool plastic lump. I snatched the phone, whipping my arm out from under the seat. I nicked my knuckles on something sharp, and the next thing I knew, the seat flew forward, crushing me into the dash. *Damn, damn, damn!* I'd made so much noise Antonio probably heard me back in the city. To top it all off, the phone's LED flashed "Out Of Area" in mocking, boldface type.

Global Services, my ass! I chucked the useless blob of black plastic into the glove box and snarled up at the heavens. Millions of distant suns blinked their dying light at me, then hundreds of millions. My depth perception deepened in the dark, and the constellations seemed to multiply. More stars twinkled in the crowded country sky than I had seen in years.

Humbled, I crept back to the bedroom, weathered wood warm beneath my bare feet. For a moment I forgot that I was anxious to put some distance between myself and the Ja'Nan, forgot that I was desperate to talk to Karen, that I had problems that needed dissecting.

The empty place beside me where Luka should have been seemed to pulse and shimmer, taunting me with a low ache and a restless bolting energy. I needed to calm down, clear my head. Karen would have told me I needed to meditate, but even under ideal circumstances, I couldn't get into staring at blank walls, becoming the emptiness or whatever.

Its motion that clears my mind, which is why I thanked all the gods I'd stumbled into Tai Chi early on. I forced myself through the first form of practice, still seething inside and unable to focus. Midway through the second form, I could hear the swishing sounds of my body moving through space. And by the time I reached the end of third form, I had gotten past my fight or flight reflex, and the loose threads of my anxiety had stitched themselves into a far less daunting pattern.

I had unfinished business all over this cabin, and I hadn't even been here a full day yet. Andrew, Cole, Luka. Most of it I wasn't ready to touch, but I could wipe the slate clean between Jayne and myself. I could do that tonight.

I told myself that I wanted to see how she was feeling, let her know that I was here if she wanted to talk. We had both been witnesses to the haunting images of Anya's death, and I needed to be certain the messages I'd sent her during our healing session had gotten through. Anya had chosen her death, and it was important that Jayne understood the choice. Important for Jayne, for the clan, and for Anya's transitioning soul as well.

Right. And when I finally admitted to myself that I also had an ulterior motive for visiting the injured wereleopard, I opened the bedroom door.

With what I hoped was a pleasant smile, I approached the loft and lifted a quick hand to the wereleopards in the living room. I took the stairs two at a time, determined to focus on Jayne and ignore Luka. I needn't have bothered. The Ra'Jahn was nowhere to be seen, and Jayne was sprawled across the bed, sleeping soundly and oblivious to my presence.

Probably just as well. I sank into a sturdy chair someone had pulled to the foot of the bed. Jayne's aura was warm and full, her breathing even. It was hard to picture her as she had been just a few hours ago.

Images of Anya's death flickered through my mind, and I tried to imagine the Shaman as she must have been in life. I couldn't help wondering how she had come to this clan of wereleopards, and what she'd meant to them, exactly.

"You're not Anya," Jayne said, rubbing the sleep from her eyes. "With my eyes closed, you feel a little like her."

"I'm Olivia Peters," I said, feeling oddly pleased with myself. Honestly, I couldn't believe I'd healed her. I had help, true, but it was mostly my doing. "You had everyone really worried for a while there, but I think you're gonna be fine now."

"Thank you." She didn't sound shy or awkward, like I imagined I would have, just grateful. Her eyes were clear, still touched by loss, but no longer consumed by it.

"You're welcome." As soon as I said it, I found that I meant it. Regardless of who she was or what her relationship with Luka might be, I was happy I'd been able to help.

"Would you like to talk about it? About Anya?" I asked. It would be good for her to open up, but I also had my own agenda. I wanted information on the Shaman more than I wanted information about her death, but the truth was, I needed both.

"I'll always wish I could have saved her," Jayne admitted, "but I know it wasn't my fault."

"That's good to hear," I said, touching her hand for just a moment.

Jayne smiled. "Sit with me for a while?"

"Sure." I was comfortable in the loft. The space felt peaceful now, not charged and chaotic as it had been this afternoon.

"She was a beautiful person, even though it sounds clichéd to say it . . . You could tell her anything. She was a great listener, you know?"

I murmured my agreement, hoping my own listening skills would measure up.

"She was always encouraging us to be who we were, to allow ourselves to be individuals as well as clan members, not to hide behind either identity but to be fully both."

"That's a tall order," I said.

"Yeah, but when you were with her, it didn't seem like it."

I nodded and made encouraging sounds as she spoke,

letting her wander around and get out what she wanted to.

"Anya was married once, a long time ago," Jayne confided. "Her husband died of some horrible disease, and she never remarried. She traveled the world instead, went to all the places they talked about going to together."

"Lovely . . ."

"When Anya went to India she stayed there for years. Australia, too. She said if she lived forever she would never learn all the spirits those lands could teach. She always wanted to go back, but once she came to us, she didn't want to leave, you know?"

"Came to you?"

"Shaman find the clan, not the other way around. You didn't know?" The corners of her mouth tugged toward her eyes. "There's a whole ritual for it, and the applicant must be found worthy before being accepted into the clan. I wasn't here for Anya's welcome ceremony. I was just a kid then, still living with my parents." She sniffled, rubbing her face.

"Thank you for this." She gestured down the length of her body. "Without your help, I wouldn't be well enough to say good-bye, either."

"I couldn't have done otherwise."

"Maybe," but Jayne's pause stretched on, and for a moment I thought she might have dozed off. Then her eyes flashed open, boring into mine, and I nearly fell off my chair.

"You're not old enough to be our Shaman," she said, making it sound like an accusation. "Besides, shaman are mostly men, anyway. Fewer ties to their lives before the clan, I guess. And they aren't supposed to have mates, either."

"Interesting," I said. That made Anya unusual on several counts.

"You think?" Jayne's tone rose, a confrontation in the making. "Sometimes they live with the clan, sometimes they don't, but they're *never* romantically involved with any of the Ja'Nan. Never. It isn't done."

My eyebrow arched and I swallowed hard. I offered a prayer to Sige, the Goddess of Silence, but my tongue continued to twitch.

"Besides, you're way too young."

I knew it wasn't unusual for the bereaved to have torn loyalties, especially in a situation like this one, where Anya's role would almost certainly be filled by another. But not by me, and Jayne needed to know that, too.

"Yes, I am too young," I acknowledged. "Also, I'm not applying for the job."

"Okay," she said, settling back against the pillows once again.

"Okay," I repeated, relieved. Silence is a grief counselor's best friend, yes, but it isn't our only one. "How about some hot tea?"

When I returned with two mugs of a spicy tea I'd found in the kitchen, both laced with honey and steaming, Jayne was propped upright and glaring at me again. I stopped short, rattled by her intensity.

"How do you know Luka?" she demanded.

"I'm working for Antonio at the moment. I'm a Bereavement Specialist." I set one of the mugs on the night table, held on to the other. I hadn't answered her question, but the tightness around her eyes softened and she sank back into the pillows.

"Luka isn't in the habit of bringing stray humans home, you know." She took a tentative sip of the hot tea.

Like I was in the habit of hitching rides with random wereleopards? *As if.* "I guess you could say I'm just hiding out here for a few days. Apparently, I need more protection than I can get in the city." I looked her in the eye as I said it, hoping she would see the truth of my words. "It has to do with Antonio," I added, trying to stick as close to the truth as possible.

"Since when does Antonio need a Bereavement Specialist?" Jayne asked, stifling a yawn. It was a rhetorical question and one I couldn't have answered, even if it wasn't. "Or maybe he's just hired himself a witch, eh?"

"I'm not a witch." The words were thick on my tongue, little more than a mumble.

Jayne laughed. "You might want to consider giving that one up. Seriously. The magic's obviously in your blood."

"I'm not Wiccan," I said a little louder. "I'm a Faithologist, now. But my Nana was a witch and a healer, too. That's where the magic comes from."

It wasn't any of her business, but it wasn't a secret, either. "After she married my grandfather, he forced her to convert. He wanted his children raised Christian, didn't want any little Pagan babies sprouting along his family tree. After he died, she started practicing again." I smiled, remembering her. "I'm pretty sure she never really gave it up, no matter what my grandfather said. She was too proud for that. Her magic was too strong to be denied."

"And yours isn't?"

Ouch.

Jayne was good, yes, but I'm a professional.

"I'm glad we had a chance to talk," I said, working my way to the top of the stairs. "You should rest though. Enjoy the tea, it will help you sleep."

***

I didn't want to sit around watching TV with Cole and the rest of the Ja'Nan, even though I could hear the Hurricanes skating hard. Truth be told, I liked them all a little bit better for being hockey fans, which probably wasn't rational. But, hey, a girl's got to have some kind of standards.

Once the announcers slipped in the score, I snuck out through the bedroom again. The night sky illuminated the fields, and I followed my instincts to the tree that had called to me earlier.

Tall grass licked my calves, making me glad I'd changed into my warm-ups, despite the pull of cotton across my wounded thigh. Between the cool breeze and the hungry insects, I hardly noticed the little .38 pressed snugly against my ankle, but I felt better knowing it was there.

Owls hollered from the tree limbs, and barn swallows, too, swooping and screeching, scattering field mice in every direction. Deer eyes peered at me in the distance, reflective holes in the fabric of the night. Harmless, of course, but my fingers flicked against my leg, and my ribs ached where the Sig usually rested.

So, lately I find the idea of being well-armed more than a little bit comforting. So what?

As I got closer to the tree my power stretched itself out in curling tendrils, touching and tasting everything around me—the earth, the air, and the strong remains of other people's magic. I recognized Anya's power here, and others as well—too many to count. They were the Shaman of the clan, stretching back through time, before records and memories, back to the beginning.

Overwhelmed, I dropped to my knees. The warmth of their magic enveloped me, coaxing and cajoling until I brushed cool tears from my cheeks. I wasn't worthy of this trust. Their magic protected this tree, a sacred place of parting rituals and welcoming ceremonies, where the clan had gathered on every full moon and every important occasion for longer than anyone could remember.

The magic invited me in, encouraged me to loosen my own power and let it flow with theirs. Slowly, I walked around the tree, following a spiral path until I leaned against the trunk. Death had no hold here, despite the spirits that remained. Freed from its link with souls in transition, my power sank roots and spread its wings, if only for a moment.

I stopped short, realizing that a full three days had passed since Anya's death. Her soul had left this plane of existence, but still her power lived on. At least it did here, in this place. And within me, too.

I could feel her because I was part of this somehow, a link in a chain I hadn't even known existed before today. This tree was the resting place of the clan's Shaman, which explained Luka's reaction when I asked him if it was special. It would have been special to his Shaman, and now it was special to me. I let that sink in, not questioning for once, just letting myself get used to the idea that one way or another, I was part of this.

Sixteen

"You shouldn't be out here alone," Luka said, looming over me in the shadows of the tree.

I hadn't heard him approach, but I wasn't startled, either. I wanted to tell him that I wasn't alone, that I had Shaman keeping me company, but instead I held the silence.

"Antonio hasn't been able to locate Adrienne."

That got my attention. If Adrienne was on the loose, it could be dangerous for us. Along with the danger, and the continuing threat of Feine, I needed Antonio to find her in a hurry for reasons of my own. Maybe I was starting to feel my connection to the Ja'Nan, but I wasn't ready to witness their full moon ceremony.

Besides, they were a long way from accepting a new Shaman, and they were even further away from accepting me. For now, it was enough that I knew I belonged here, at least in part. Enough that Luka and Cole and maybe a few of the others knew it, too.

I sighed, and Luka knelt in the grass beside me.

"So, what's the plan?" I asked.

"Nothing's changed. Not yet, anyway."

Easy for him to say.

"We'll stay here and let Antonio handle Adrienne. He'll contact me again before dawn. If he hasn't made any progress, we'll meet tomorrow night to figure it all out."

"I'd like to speak with Antonio directly," I said, mustering as much authority as I could. "I won't have the two of you making decisions for me as if I were a child."

His eyes snapped wide, two green orbs in the night. "You were unconscious last time."

"Even so . . ." I was irritated, but I couldn't keep the sound of a smile from tugging at my lips and creeping into my voice. Despite the layers of confusion between us, my body responded to his presence. Not just physically, but emotionally, too. When he was nearby, I felt happier than when he wasn't, lighter, more at ease with my self.

"Angel, I—" Luka started, but I couldn't let him finish.

"After the healing," I interrupted, "I didn't mean to pull away from you. There was just too much power and

I . . . I couldn't control it." I wasn't explaining myself very well, but my heart was in the right place, and that had to count for something.

"I know."

My eyes narrowed.

"Now, I know," he corrected. "I spoke with Cole. I'm sorry. I should have understood earlier, but I didn't."

"It's okay." I shook my head, denying the words even as I spoke them. "It doesn't matter."

Of course it mattered. It had mattered very much. But right at this moment, none of it seemed important. Luka rose in one fluid motion, and I stretched my hand out to him, letting him pull me up.

Suddenly, I was itching to move away from the tree. Being there with Luka felt ill-timed, as if it shouldn't be happening, shouldn't be happening *yet.* "Let's go back."

We walked slowly, holding hands. The moon was bright, not quite full, but close to it. I could feel the play of moonlight over my skin, and I wondered how much more intense the sensation was for Luka. We spoke lightly, unconcerned with symmetry.

"I'm surprised Cole told you . . ." I said, letting the sentence trail off without needing to finish it.

"I'm Ra'Jahn."

"Yes, so I've heard."

"I asked. He answered. We have no secrets, Angel." He stopped walking and turned to look at me. "I can smell his desire for you."

I appreciated that he left the rest of it unsaid. "Cole has been a good friend to me, Luka."

"Is that all he's been?"

"Yes." I answered truthfully and started walking again.

"Do all of your friends find you so attractive?" he asked, squeezing my hand a little tighter. "Or just the ones I've met so far?"

"All of them, I imagine."

Luka laughed and pulled me closer. Wrapped in the sounds of the night and the rich echo of Luka's laughter fading in the distance, I wanted to leave well enough alone, but I couldn't.

"Jayne's doing better," I said.

"Yes."

"Tomorrow she ought to spend some time meditating," I suggested. "Outside, by the tree."

"Why?" I felt Luka tense, felt it right through his fingers as his power pulled away from mine. The heat rolling off his body made me shiver.

"She needs to reconnect with Anya," I said. "Guilt is a powerful force. It isn't going to disappear on its own."

"The Ja'Nan will gather at the tree when the moon is full, Angel. We will heal together."

"Well, you're Ra'Jahn," I said. "You know best."

I'd spoken the words evenly enough, but a deaf man could have heard my doubts. Luka *did not* know best, not in this case. I wasn't a wereleopard. I couldn't sniff the air and know the details of the moment like they could, but I was part of this clan now, for better or worse.

The Shaman had drawn me into their fold, and I wasn't about to throw that gift away. If that meant I knew things Luka might never know, about Jayne and how she'd been healed, about the magic and spirits that made the tree their home, then so be it. Luka would have to learn to deal with me as I was, not as he thought I should be.

***

Inside, the Ja'Nan were spread across the furniture, a jumble of bodies that reminded me vaguely of my college dorm days, somehow both innocent and not. They were comfortable with each other, more like littermates raised all at once than strangers drawn together by random biology.

Jayne was with them, dozing against Stacie's chest. Andrew had his arm around Cole's shoulder and Leah was stretched out with her head in Andrew's lap. There were two new bodies in the mix that I didn't recognize, and I closed my eyes for a moment, picturing Luka with them, completing the image.

He was Ra'Jahn. These were his people.

It took me a minute to realize the stabbing pain in my chest was envy. Whatever else I might be, I was human. I would never be one of them.

Leah sat up and scooted closer to Cole, making room for me in the press. I appreciated the gesture even though I didn't take her up on it.

"Who won?" I asked, still standing, and was met with

a chorus of blank stares. "The game? The Canes were up when I left. Did they finish strong?"

"Nah," Andrew replied.

"They choked in the third," added one of the newcomers. He was brown-skinned and bald-headed, and he flashed very straight, very white, teeth in my direction. I thought he was starting to look familiar, maybe from my adventure at the Double Down, or maybe from a magazine ad, I couldn't tell which. "No endgame. As usual," he said.

"Too true," I commiserated.

"Well, Sports Fans," Jayne said, stretching and stifling a yawn, "I'm going back to bed."

Andrew lifted her gently, as if she were a little girl. She hardly protested, although she did ask if someone would bring her tea. Since no one else did, I drifted into the kitchen and set the kettle to boil.

It must be wonderful not to worry that your boyfriend wouldn't be able to lift you, I mused, a relief to know that you would never be too strong or too heavy. Not that I thought Jayne and Andrew were involved, not exactly. Familiarity lingered in the air around all of them, making them feel like lovers while they acted liked friends. Good friends, to be sure, but friends nonetheless.

"I can take that to Jayne," the other newcomer said, rousing me from my thoughts. "I'm Sue Ann, by the way."

Sue Ann was tall, like me, with short corn silk hair, light brown eyes and lots of freckles. I had a vision of her in coveralls and gingham, and wondered if it was just the name or if she really was a farm girl.

"I heard what you did for Jayne," she said, laying her hand on my arm. "I couldn't, I mean, we couldn't heal her ourselves. We owe you her life."

I shook my head in protest, but Sue Ann persisted. "It's true. You won't hear it often, and maybe not ever from some of them, so let me say it, okay? Thank you."

She gave me a quick hug and took the tea upstairs. I felt warm and fuzzy all over, and I knew that for a while at least, a few of the wereleopards were on my side.

***

I could barely keep my eyes open, lounging in the living room beside Luka, but the Ja'Nan were just warming up. The later it got, the more my eyes stayed closed, and the more the wereleopards opened up. Finally, I leaned my head on Luka's shoulder and slowed my breathing. I was drowsy, but not asleep. They talked, and I listened.

Hey, I'm a private investigator as well as a grief counselor, and this was an eavesdropping opportunity I couldn't afford to pass up. Besides, who would?

"Antonio's risking all of our lives," Andrew fumed. "He's too ambitious for his own damn good."

"He knows what he's doing," Cole said, though he didn't sound convinced. "Besides, what would you do in his shoes? Let someone else take your territory?"

Luka's arm around me tensed, waiting for his leopards to answer. Unbidden, my hand slid over the lean muscles of his chest, fingers splayed. My palm covered his beating heart, my pulse matching his and filling my ears. *Like an echo,* I thought sleepily, *or a shield.*

"All I'm saying is," Andrew continued, caught up in his own train of thought, "Antonio is too powerful for this. He doesn't need this human's help to track a rogue vampire, and he doesn't need the humans' laws to bring Feine to justice, either."

Even with my eyes closed and my senses dulled by exhaustion, I knew he'd spoken the truth. A shiver worked it's way around the room as the twin concepts of Antonio's power and Antonio's justice touched each of them, and I was sure they'd felt the simple truth in Andrew's words, too.

So, Antonio didn't really need me to solve his Feine problem, that much was obvious. And he was terrifying—I already knew that, too. I hadn't expected the Ja'Nan to find him shiver-worthy, but in a weird way it made me feel a little more secure knowing that they did.

"Oh, get off your soapbox," Leah said, laughing. "Antonio's a big old softie, and you know it. He's put a lot of effort into making things better for shifters, too, not just for his own kind."

When she reminded him that Antonio had helped fund the election campaigns of human politicians active in the New Civil Rights Movement, Luka's heartbeat slowed. He moved, repositioning me, and beneath my cheek his shoulder seemed to stretch, muscles striating, pulling me closer. Apparently, Antonio had bought himself a few significant enemies with his politicking, though I had the impression Luka didn't want to go down that road tonight. Feine and Adrienne might be Antonio's most pressing problems, but by no means were they his only ones.

"Yeah, yeah, yeah," Andrew said. "He's Mr. Politically Active. I know all about it. Politicians! Damn snakes." This was clearly one of his regular rants. "He's more trouble than he's worth, if you ask me. Making enemies all over the place."

"Hey now! Go easy with that," Cole jumped in. "He's complicated, but he's worth it. Antonio has his share of enemies, but the last thing we need around here is a new Ruler and you know it. Antonio is good for us."

So maybe he was terrifying, but he also treated his people with respect. And whether they liked it or not, the Ja'Nan were his people.

I still wasn't exactly clear on Antonio's link to the wereleopards, but I'd heard enough tonight to make an educated guess. It was common knowledge, or at least it was established urban myth, that in the old days the Ruling Undead could take the shape of different animals. I smiled, thinking about B-movie bats and pale-faced Draculas, with their dark capes and slicked-back hair, so different from Antonio.

I'd never truly believed those stories, but as I shifted against Luka's shoulder, his thick muscles spreading to make room for me, none of my doubts seemed real anymore. If vampires lost their shape-changing ability centuries ago, but their link to the animal form remained, that would certainly explain Antonio's connection to the Ja'Nan.

"He doesn't ask for much, Andrew," I heard Stacie say, something in her tone grabbing my attention. I'd been fading in and out of the conversation, the dreamworld pulling me closer than I wanted to go just yet. "It's only blood, for god's own sake. It's no big deal."

"Yeah, well, you'd donate just for the thrill of it, even if he didn't demand it from us. So your opinion doesn't really count."

"He has a point, Stacie." Cole's voice was soft, and I could almost see him reaching out to her, stroking her arm, touching her hair.

"No, he doesn't have a point," she responded, but the fight was gone from her voice. She sounded tired, older than she was. "He has a lousy attitude, and I'm sick of it."

Again, Luka's muscles bunched beneath mine. He was so still and so quiet I would have thought he was asleep, too, but already I knew better. He was awake. Wide awake.

Andrew was worked up now, despite Stacie's resolve. "It's a goddamn blood price, and we shouldn't have to pay it," he growled, his voice deep and resonating.

Old fears leapt to my throat, and I bit the inside of my lip to keep them from flying free. Andrew seemed massive behind the cloak of my eyelids, his frustration monstrous in the darkness. My heart slammed in my chest. Feverish and damp, I could hardly keep still. Luka's arms held me close, his power cool and light, seeping calm through my pores.

"I'm working on it, Andrew," Luka said finally, sounding calm and sleepy even though I knew he wasn't. "Give it time. Change doesn't come easily for the Undead, but Antonio's coming around."

Luka's heartbeat was steady, which was more than I could say for mine. Any of the leopards who cared to listen would surely hear the panic in my pulse. But Andrew's anger had awakened memories I wasn't ready for, reminding me how much I didn't know, how much I didn't want to know.

Besides, I had assumed that giving blood was a pleasurable experience, and that it was a voluntary one as well. Now I knew the latter wasn't exactly true. Antonio required the Ja'Nan to donate as proof of their loyalty.

I couldn't be sure how much of this I was dreaming and how much was real, since I didn't have much of a framework for most of their conversation. Until recently, I'd never really known a vampire. Now my best friend was dating the Undead, and I was working for the local Ruler, whose past I'd seen in full-color flashes over drinks in Luka's bar.

I thought I'd heard enough for one night, truly, but I couldn't tear myself away. Vampire magic was legendary, and the Ja'Nan made sharing blood sound like sex the way you always dreamed sex could be, the way it was in the romance novels I read at the beach and abandoned on airplanes.

Even the wereleopards who didn't like donating admitted it was more the principle of the thing that bothered them than the act itself. That they would enjoy it despite their objections only added fuel to the fire. In a small way, I understood their dilemma. My body responded to Luka even when my mind rebelled, and it made me more empathetic than I might have been if that hadn't been the case.

I wished I had a blanket to hide beneath, like someone's little sister, staying up late and listening to the big kids talk about things she didn't quite understand. My eyelashes weighed against my cheeks and my lips parted, and I figured I was sleeping more than I was staying awake.

"What's with the witch?" Andrew's voice sliced through the fog, making me wonder if I'd been snoring, or drooling, or something else equally embarrassing.

"Give her a break," Leah said. "What she did for Jayne today would have drained any of us. I'm surprised she lasted this long."

"Yeah," Stacie said, more to defy Andrew than out of any loyalty to me, I supposed. "She's only human."

My breath caught in my throat, waiting for someone to contradict her. I exhaled slowly when no one did.

"Y'all don't know the half of it," Cole added.

Again, I held my breath.

"In the past couple days she's been shot, attacked by a vamp, and seen the wrong side of a concussion. Seriously."

There was a chorus of doubt, which I took as my cue to open my eyes, if only for a moment.

"I'm sitting right here, you know." But even as I said it, I stifled a yawn.

Seventeen

I woke to a beautiful sunrise and an empty bed. The sheets were still warm where Luka's body had been, and his spicy scent lingered on the pillow. He'd crept into bed hours after I had, silent, though I'd felt his body wrap around mine and warm me through the night. I'd slept in blissful quiet, the dreamworld held at bay by unseen forces, and I snuggled back under the covers, trying to recapture the feeling.

When I opened my eyes again, I expected to see the sun rising over the empty field and shining through the limbs of the shaman tree. Instead I saw Luka, a dark green towel wrapped loosely around his waist, staring at me through the sliding glass doors that were supposed to keep the wild things out of the cabin.

He smiled, and suddenly I was wide awake. I slipped out of bed, snuggling into the shirt he'd discarded by the bedside last night. I didn't bother to button it, just held it loosely around my middle and stepped out onto the deck.

The morning air was cool and damp. I shivered, goose bumps galloping over my skin, and stepped closer to the heat radiating from Luka's body.

"Good morning, Angel."

"It's starting to look that way." I smiled. "The sun's usually a little warmer when I leave the house, though." I snuggled against him, tracing my jaw along his collar bone. "What time is it?"

"Six thirty."

"Are you crazy?"

His mouth covered mine, and I swallowed my protests. So I hadn't been up this early since I was a teenager. So what? I hadn't felt this way in that many years, either.

His power reached out to mine, sending a new wave of shivers through my body. I tensed against him, feeling one strong arm wrap around my hips and pull me closer, long fingers tangling in the hair at the base of my neck.

My hands pressed into strong shoulders, slid down smooth ribs, teased the sensitive hollow of his lower back. His skin was perfect, no bumps or bruises, not a single mark exposed beneath my fingers. In comparison, the collection of scars that peppered my own body seemed immense, each one throbbing its own response to Luka's demands. He pulled his mouth from mine, leaving my lips swollen and full, his tongue tracing a hot path down the claw marks that started on my shoulder. My breasts burned against him, responding to his mouth even before it reached the first sensitive peak.

My leg slid behind his, wrapping around him, exploring. The towel wedged from his waist, fell in a soft heap at our feet. There was nothing between us now, and I could feel him hard against me. He groaned, slipping his hand lower and separating our bodies.

His fingers circled lightly, teasing, until the breath caught in my throat and I was gasping for air. He pressed his fingers to my lips. I tasted myself, his skin, the swell of his knuckles as they grazed my teeth. I wanted this man, wanted him inside me, wanted to be part of him in a way I had never wanted anything before.

He reached behind me and I heard a latch give way. The outdoor shower. Luka adjusted the water temperature without letting me go, never taking his mouth from mine. Steam billowed around us, Luka's power wrapped into it until it was the warm mist, dancing a delicate ballet through the early morning chill.

But I didn't want to step under the hot spray, didn't want to feel anything against my skin but him.

And then I knew.

"Angel," he whispered into my ear, biting it lightly. "Angel, I can't. It's too complicated."

I kissed his neck, his chest.

"You don't understand," he said gently.

My teeth scraped his skin, the slam of his heartbeat pulsed in my mouth.

"We can't." His tone wasn't all that gentle any more.

I stepped into the water, feeling it run down my back, over my shoulders. I tilted my head, exposing my neck and letting the hot water soak through my hair. My fingers played across the soft skin of my throat, my belly, my breasts. My power flowed into his, drawing him closer, drenching us both.

I found his soap, spicy and dark, and rubbed a rich lather over his chest, his back, his hips. I reached lower, slipping my soapy hands around him, teasing him as he'd teased me earlier. I rubbed against him, my nipples burning hot lines across his chest.

The groan in his throat turned to a growl, his fingers digging into my skin, sharp and clawlike. My head snapped up, and I looked deep into his eyes. I saw him in there, buried in the pools of iridescent green and fighting to stay in control. I covered his mouth with mine, wanting to taste the leopard separately from the man, feeling the bones in his jaw changing, slipping, and changing back.

Somewhere close, a car door slammed.

"Hey! Wait!" Stacie's voice carried through the open windows in the loft.

The front door banged open.

"No! You don't understand!" she shouted.

Really, her words were more for us than the approaching Ja'Nan. They wouldn't heed her warning. How could they? They would only feel their Ra'Jahn's power, laid bare and mixed with my own. And me . . . Well, they didn't know me from Eve.

Heavy footsteps bounded across the deck, and I heard Stacie's voice once more. "Stop!" The wince in her voice was audible, even above the rest.

Three skulking wereleopards paced on the other side of the deck, tense and swearing. Stacie's voice again, hushing the giggling Ja'Nan in the loft, and then Leah's, calling the newcomers inside.

"Maybe we can't," I whispered in Luka's ear, feeling the laughter ripple through his chest before I heard it, warm and rich with promise.

***

For a long time afterwards, I stayed in the shower alone, letting the hot water rinse away my doubts.

I knew I'd been reckless, carried away by a passion I couldn't even begin to understand. I knew I should be relieved or anxious or even grateful we'd been interrupted. I knew I should feel something other than the thrill, something other than the cool absence of guilt. Something responsible. But I'd given up the nice girl routine back when I gave up ballet. I'd given it up with a vengeance, and I'd never looked back.

And now, wrapped in a thick towel and my hair dryer

blaring hot and loud in my ears, the warm ripples of Luka's laughter still danced over my skin. I flipped my hair over one shoulder and looked toward the door half a second before Luka burst through it. His energy crackled in the air, amusement written all over his face.

My body reacted to him, to the feel of his power, to his presence in the room. My blood surged, the corners of my eyes crinkled. This wasn't like vampire magic, or any other magic that I knew of. It was deeper, more personal.

Luka's power had a purpose. He was Ra'Jahn. He was meant to influence the clan. Why the effect should be this intense between us was something I didn't really want to think about, not too much, anyway. Not yet.

"Get dressed, Angel," Luka said, pulling me to my feet and planting a playful kiss on my lips. "Let's get out of here for a few hours."

"If there's coffee involved, I'm all for it."

His good mood was contagious. I tossed my towel at him and crossed the room to my overnight bag, stark naked and warm. But the moment I turned away from him, his energy changed behind me.

"What is it?" I asked, pulling a clean white top over my head. "Luka, what's wrong?"

"I hurt you." His voice sounded thin, almost hollow, like a whisper on an empty night. "Angel, I'm so sorry."

"Luka, I'm not hurt," I said, feeling his power pull further and further away, cooling my skin, leaving it dull, lifeless.

"I don't know what you think you did, but I promise you, I'm fine." I couldn't breathe. My fingers were icicles, the back of my neck damp and sticky.

"Luka, please. I'm not hurt," I said again, crossing the room, needing to be closer to him.

"Your skin is *marked.*"

Without touching me, his fingers traced a path from the middle of my thighs up to my lower back, and the thin, raised wounds began to tingle. I tried to turn my head enough to see them, feeling like a cat chasing her tail.

The sharp crescents covering my skin were nothing to be alarmed about; most of them were already healed over. But there was no doubt about what they were or where they'd come from. "Hmmm," I said, kissing him lightly. "I hadn't noticed. And in another twenty minutes or so, neither would you. They'll disappear. I promise."

It was true, mostly, although it would be closer to an hour before the marks vanished entirely. Of course, now that he had drawn my attention to them, I recalled the feel of his hands *changing* in the shower, and my body's response to their demands. I flushed all over just thinking about it.

"Do I seem hurt to you?" I rubbed my cheek against his, feeling the tension drain out of his jaw. "So. Tell me where we're going," I insisted, pulling on a pair of jeans. "And is there coffee involved or isn't there?"

"Angel, this is serious." He hesitated. "I shouldn't have . . . I know better, damn it. This close to the full moon, it's too risky. You're too important to us, just the way you are."

"Are you telling me that I have to wait almost a week to finish what we started this morning?" I tried to look serious. I knew he was telling me something and it was important that I understand, but I ended up laughing out loud. "Now that hurts!"

Eighteen

Luka and I wandered through the rest of the morning in the little town that shared a zip code with Luka's cabin. Fancy trim work outlined the old buildings here, their doors freshly painted and bright in the morning light. It was perfect, like a bed-and-breakfast picture book.

I don't know why it surprised me that everyone seemed to know Luka, but it did. They all had a "Hey there, Luka" or "Mornin', Mr. Niere" ready for him, and an easy smile for me, too. I'd assumed he would have put more effort into not being noticed, thinking small town people have a way of making a big deal out of nothing. And the Ja'Nan were definitely not nothing.

"Nice neighbors," I commented.

"Yes. They are."

"Do you know them well?"

"I don't spend as much time out here as I'd like," Luka said. "But when I'm here, I try to get into town every day."

I looked back at the General Store we'd just been in, its bulletin board littered with colorful notices and weather beaten slips, all push-pinned into aging cork. The heart of the town, this store combined hardware and apothecary, had a post office thrown into the back, and grocery items, too. They served steaming teas and sweet thick coffee, and the clerk had warned us to be careful with the foam cups and their tricky plastic lids. I took a tentative sip from mine, grateful for the caffeine, and turned to look around.

Flowers bloomed in pots on porches and storefront stoops. Dogwoods lined the center green, new leaves shiny in the morning light, still waxy in the wake of their recent blossoms. When the breeze picked up, it lifted a sea of petals from the walks, freshly fallen and still sweet, swirling around our ankles.

A dusting of pine pollen tinged the town in grainy sunshine, and the scent of magnolias filled the air, their teacup flowers bright pink and flashy on spindly limbs.

It was beautiful, peaceful, the perfect shade of Southern spring with all the promise of a sweltering summer yet to come. I loved it already, looked forward to lazy Saturdays and morning walks just like this one. But truly, how much time could a person spend in this town? Especially if that person happened to be the Ra'Jahn of the local wereleopard clan?

Luka grinned, answering my unspoken question. "Honestly, I guess I spend more money than time around here."

"On what?" I laughed, pulling petals from my hair.

"Well, the furniture in my room came mostly from Swanson's Antiques. And there's a potter's studio around the corner that way." He gestured into the distance, and I recalled the warm mugs and well-shaped bowls in his kitchen. "There's a farmer's market every Saturday that I try not to miss when I'm here. And . . ."

"Enough!" I laughed, but the crinkles at the corners of his eyes smoothed over and his smile caught across his teeth. "Luka?"

"The Ja'Nan have been safe here for longer then I can remember. We've never had any trouble, and I wouldn't want to start any now."

"You take good care of them," I said.

"I try." He sounded tired all of the sudden, the weight of his rank thick in his voice. "I'm Ra'Jahn."

"You're more than that, Luka."

He turned to look at me, his fingers snaking over my wrist. "That's where you're wrong, Angel. I am Ra'Jahn. All of me. Always."

Tears sprang to my eyes, and I blinked furiously, irritated by the wave of emotion. "I don't understand."

"Are you sure you want to?" He wound his fingers through mine again, warm and pulsing.

"Yes," I whispered, a softened exhale, a shadow of itself. I wasn't sure, not at all. But if he would tell me, then I would listen. Luka's arm wrapped around my waist, and he touched my face quickly, just a trace of his knuckles beside my ear.

"When I came into the clan, I knew I would be Ra'Jahn. It's what brought me here."

"How?" I shook my head. I knew the majority of shifters weren't brought over involuntarily, but Luka made it sound like a career fair. "How could you choose this, Luka? How did you know?"

"It chose me. I didn't know until later, but Vince knew all along." Luka's voice caught on the name, and I watched the memories flicker through his eyes.

"Vince?"

"Vince brought me into the clan, made sure I found my way to Antonio."

I shivered, and Luka's eyes flashed in the midmorning sun, his smile tempered by the stubborn angle of his jaw.

"I might not understand, but that doesn't mean I don't care," I said, unsure where to go from here. "I don't report back to Antonio, and I have no interest in Ja'Nan politics, either."

Luka grinned, and I breathed a sigh of relief.

"People tell me I'm a pretty good listener, too. They say it's in my blood."

"I know, Angel." Luka's lips brushed over my cheek. "I know all about your blood."

His whispered words echoed in my ear, a warm tickle, dazzling. But he didn't say anything else, not about Vince, and not about himself, and I still didn't understand.

We walked around for a while longer, peering in windows and watching our reflections laugh back at us as we circled around to the car. The sun was warm in my hair, and my Calvin's felt sticky, rough against the tender scar on my thigh. But they concealed the snub-nosed .38 tucked into my ankle holster, and that was worth a little extra heat.

"Days like this," I said, spreading my arms wide and turning my face to the sky, "I thank all the gods for seeing fit to grant me a convertible."

Luka opened the passenger's side door and I slid inside, laughing as his broad smile flared back at me, a prayer in its own right, and another reason to offer thanks.

***

"You really do need a safer vehicle, Angel." We were stopped at a roadside stand, hovering beneath the hand-painted sign advertising hot boiled peanuts and farm fresh fruit.

"What? I love this car!"

"The top half is canvas at best, open-air at worst. It's not safe enough for you."

"And you'd suggest what? A Volvo, maybe? Or

something from the Brinks line?" It was hard to be serious, trying not to spill salty water from the peanut shells all over ourselves.

"Laugh all you want, Angel. I just don't want anything to happen to you."

I knew it was true. He wanted to protect me, and it was easier to focus on my car than on the rest of it. But the fact was, my world hadn't been all that dangerous before I stepped onto Anya Sorensen's back porch just a few mornings ago.

Working at Forever Crossed isn't for the squeamish, and the life of a Bereavement Specialist, or a P.I. for that matter, isn't something I'd recommend for just any-ole-gal, but until recently I'd never needed more protection than the Sig could offer. And I'd only needed that when I was on duty.

"As long as we're on the safety subject, have you heard from Antonio yet?" I had to ask, boiled peanuts or not. Luka was right, we were in a serious situation and pretending we weren't wouldn't make it go away.

"Three little messengers arrived with news early this morning, or have you forgotten already?"

"No!" How could I forget? I flushed all over remembering. But I'd been so focused on their arrival, I hadn't thought about where they'd come from, or why.

Laughing, I hopped back into the car and we started toward the cabin again. I was adjusting to Luka's moodiness, though I wasn't sure if I'd ever get used to it.

"You know what? I think I recognized one of the Ja'Nan this morning. The dark-haired one. He's close to Antonio, isn't he? I think I saw him in Antonio's mind . . ." I paused, letting the green fields distract me for a moment. "Is he from Italy? I think Antonio called him *dolce micetto*. That's Italian, right?"

"That's not an expression you should use, Angel." Luka frowned, his eyes cloudy and tight.

"Why? What does it mean, exactly?"

"Exactly? It means *sweet, nice kitten*. Most of the Ja'Nan don't like it." He looked uncertain, his brows pulled together and his arms stiff at the wheel. "And yes, James and Antonio are close. And no, he doesn't object to the term."

"Do you? Mind it, I mean." I kept my eyes focused on his face when I asked, knowing he could interpret my question in two ways.

"No. But like anything, it depends on the circumstances. If I were you, I wouldn't use it."

It was a well-worded answer. As usual.

Luka drove slowly on the winding country roads, goats and farmers marking our progress. I could smell the flat of fresh strawberries warming in the back seat sun, the richness of freshly turned soil, and the green of emerging seedlings. I slid my fingers through Luka's hair, adding his sweet-spicy scent to the air. The tension drained from his face, wordless but not silent, and for a minute or two nothing else mattered.

"Antonio's network of spies delivered four of their own vamps last night," Luka said, back to business. "They confessed their betrayal and admitted Adrienne is working with Feine to take over the Triangle."

"That's fantastic!"

"It's a start. He didn't get Adrienne, and the traitors don't know where she is. Or how to find Feine."

"Is Antonio sure?"

"Angel, whatever they knew, believe me, they told Antonio." Luka looked me in the eye for a few seconds before turning his attention back to the road. "They aren't keeping any secrets."

I swallowed hard, staring into the distance, letting the greens and yellows blur. I didn't want to know how Antonio got his information. I really didn't.

"Adrienne's not one to accept defeat," Luka continued. "We're pretty sure she'll turn up tonight, looking for a fight. She'll have Feine's reinforcements with her, whoever's left. Hell, Feine might even show his face."

"So this could be it." The wave of relief nearly pulled me from my seat.

"Could be."

"You sound disappointed," I said, feeling a little guilty.

"It's going to be one hell of a fight."

My muscles tensed, like my body knew what was coming before my brain did. "Do you mind missing it?"

"Oh, I'm not going to miss it, Angel."

"We're going, then?"

"Not we. Me. You're staying at the cabin."

I stared daggers at him, but he wouldn't meet my eyes.

"I'll leave a few of the Ja'Nan behind. You won't be alone."

As if that's what bothered me.

Not that I'd been looking forward to a death match between a couple of crazy vampires, but I liked to think of myself as an asset, not a liability. Getting left behind with the baby sitters was the vilest sort of insult. I had weapons, magic, police backup even!

And a concussion, I reminded myself, a bullet wound, and a slower reaction time than anyone else in the ring.

Damn.

Sometimes being human was such a total let down. In Luka's world, it would always mean helpless, and I'd never been good at helpless. If he imagined *breakable* tattooed across my body in a million interlocking patterns, there wasn't a whole lot more I could do to change his mind. I would never be one of the Ja'Nan, but I was damn sure more than some mangled refraction of what might have been. Wasn't I?

I pulled a pair of sunglasses from above my visor and popped in an unlabelled CD, the first gravelly notes a welcome surprise. I reached into the back seat for a handful of sun-warm berries, pressed a perfect red teardrop to Luka's lips. His teeth sank into the ripe fruit, the juice catching in the corner of his mouth. Desire pulsed deep in my belly, and I swallowed hard, determined.

As long as I focused on the moment and didn't think about tonight, there was no reason we couldn't enjoy the rest of the afternoon. Tomorrow I'd be in the driver's seat, steering my little convertible in the opposite direction.

And tomorrow, I would be alone.

Nineteen

I stood in Luka's kitchen, heating milk for my coffee and feeling lamer with every passing second.

All of the cool kids got dressed up and went out to play at Antonio's, while I was stuck here feeling sorry for myself. Cole and Jayne had been left behind, too, not that they seemed especially upset about it. Cole, who had the most to gripe about since he was actually healthy, seemed the least put out.

"I fight my share of Antonio's battles," Cole said when I asked him if he minded baby sitting duty. "Luka's too, if you want the truth. I don't mind missing out on this one."

"He's got a point," Jayne said, popping a spoonful of chocolate ice cream into her mouth.

"Aren't you worried about them?" I asked, knowing it was an irrational question. Of course they were worried. "I'd rather be there, in the thick of it. I hate having to wonder what's happening."

"Well, Olivia's got a point, too," Jayne said, this time around a mouthful of fresh strawberries.

I paced through the open spaces, coffee in hand, fuming. Flipping light switches off as I went, I marked my steps, waiting for the sliding glass doors to disappear in the darkness. Finally there was only a pool of light in the center of the room, and the rest of the cabin faded into the night. I wanted to step into that warm glow, but the restless energy building inside me wouldn't let me. Not just yet.

"You might as well put your feet up and relax, Liv. Nothing's going to happen for hours yet." Cole's legs were stretched across the couch, waiting for Jayne's ice cream bowl to vacate her lap.

How could he be so damned reasonable?

"They won't be home until dawn, you know," Jayne said. "And Luka may even be later than that." She sounded sort of nastier than was called for, like she didn't think I had any right to my feelings for Luka.

"You know what, Jayne?" I asked, stepping into the light. I let the question hang there, unanswered, until she met my eyes. "You're right."

I smiled, watching as surprise worked its way from her eyes down to her open mouth.

When I was small and pouting over some childhood slight or imagined injustice, my Nana would ask me, *Do you want to be right, Livvie, or do you want to be happy?* I was too young to really understand the question before she crossed over, but it's one of those things that always comes back to me whenever I need it most.

I wanted to clear the air now, but I didn't want to make the situation any worse. I forced myself to stop pacing and looked for a spot close enough to Jayne to be friendly, but not close enough to present a threat. I settled on the floor instead of the couch, leaning against the soft cushions, reminding myself to breathe.

Before I knew it, I was unbraiding my hair, pulling at invisible knots with my fingers as I went. Long hair is like built-in stress relief. There's always something to do, something to keep my hands occupied while my brain switches gears.

"Your hair is amazing," Jayne admitted, taking a handful from the pile on the futon, stretching it out across the fabric. In the quiet light all the colors seemed to separate, shining bronze and toasty, glints of red and a darkish green that I normally didn't notice.

For Jayne this was a natural response, like reading body language or watching someone's eyes to gauge a reaction. But for me it was complicated. I didn't like the idea of it, the sensation of being groomed by a stranger, the assumption of closeness. On the other hand, the wereleopards' senses were a much more evolved communication network than my own, and this simple act might tell her more about me than hours of girl-talk ever could.

My hair slipped through her fingers, and I wondered what she was thinking. "Have you ever let yours grow?" I asked.

"It's too much hassle," she said, scrubbing a hand through her own short-cropped hair. "I'm more of a wash-n-go kind of gal."

"Oh, me too," Cole joked, executing a hair flip with his own streaky blonde locks.

Jayne threw a pillow at him. Laughter caught in my

throat as he jumped to avoid the missile. He moved in a blur of speed that I could never hope to match, reminding me of my own limitations and why I was here with them instead of out with Luka.

"So." I was taking a pretty big chance since Jayne's fingers were back in my hair again. "I get the feeling you don't want to like me, Jayne, but you just can't help yourself."

"Humphf," was her only response.

Cole sat down beside her, his hand automatically rubbing her shoulder, the tension around us tangible. He clearly didn't want to be trapped in this conversation, loyal to Jayne and protective of me at the same time.

I didn't drop my gaze, though. I wanted to know what this was all about.

"It's not you," Cole said. "It's Luka."

"What about Luka?" With a practiced sweep I twisted my hair and secured it in a messy knot, well beyond the reach of angry fingers.

"He's Ra'Jahn," Jayne said, as if I didn't know.

"Yes. And?"

"He shouldn't be involved with you," she said. "You're going to hurt him, and then the pain will pull him away from us, and it's really just not fair."

I was shocked by the plain emotion in her voice, not to mention her assumption that I would be the one to hurt Luka, instead of the reverse. When I looked at Cole, concern narrowed his eyes, and I knew that it wasn't for Luka, or even for me. He was worried about Jayne.

"What makes you think Luka will be hurt?" I asked the question, but I suspected Luka didn't have much to do with this.

"You're a Shaman. It's just not done. I already told you that!"

"I'm not a Shaman, Jayne, and I've already told you that." Even to my own ears, it sounded too familiar, and I remembered how many times I'd said *I'm not a witch* without ever convincing anybody of that, either.

"Maybe not today, but you will be, and then you'll leave him."

Tears slid down her face. Cole looked at me accusingly, like this was all my fault. Maybe it was, but I had to press on. I'd stopped this once already because it was uncomfortable, and the situation had only gotten worse.

"You will leave him," she repeated, forcing the words at me, trying to make them true.

"Like Anya left you?" It was a stab in the dark, but she winced, proving my guess had found its mark. Her energy pulled away from mine, folded in on itself. I pressed anyway. "Is that what you think?"

"Yes." She was crying now, her face buried in Cole's shoulder, and I wasn't sure if she'd spoken or simply exhaled.

Sometimes I hate it when I'm right.

Jayne loved Anya. It was as simple as that. Maybe her love was unrequited, maybe it wasn't. It didn't matter now.

"Anya's death had nothing to do with your love." My voice was steady, soft but firm. "I swear to you, it didn't."

"She didn't want me there, didn't want to be saved."

"That's not true," I said, reaching across the cushions to touch her. Once again I recalled the images and sensations of Anya's death, wrapped my own power in the feel of hers. "She warned the Ja'Nan away to keep you safe. All of you."

This wasn't working.

"C'mon," I said, standing up and taking one of her hands and one of Cole's. "We need to go outside for a while."

Luka could holler at me later for bringing the Ja'Nan to the tree without him, but Jayne needed to reconnect with Anya's spirit. She couldn't do that cooped up in the cabin.

While Cole coaxed Jayne from the couch, I slipped into the bedroom to gear up. Maybe it was as safe as houses out here in the country, but I'd feel a hell of a lot better with both guns loaded and my broken bracelet rigged around my wrist.

***

We weren't halfway to the tree when I felt the first sharp stabs of warning. The Shaman filled my head with words of protection, and I spoke them aloud without a thought, reaching for Cole and Jayne instinctively.

For a split second, I thought maybe I was breaking the rules after all, that Luka was right, and the Ja'Nan shouldn't be here until the full moon ceremony. Then I felt the Shamans' energy pressing toward me, their collective spirits wrapping the three of us in a darkness so complete we might have lost each other if we weren't already touching.

"What's happening?" Jayne whispered.

We formed a tight triangle, close enough that I could feel short bursts of breath on my skin, hot and loud in the surrounding night.

"It looks like we're not going to miss out on the action after all," I said. "They can't see us yet, thanks to the Shaman, but—"

"What?" Cole interrupted.

"I'll explain later. For now, just try to remember how Anya's magic felt, all the ways she protected the clan when she was alive." I squeezed their hands, a silent plea to give it a try. "You should be able to feel her now. She's part of the spell keeping us hidden."

Jayne squeezed my hand back. I had a feeling that if I could see her, she would have tears streaming down her face again.

"I don't know if this is Adrienne or Feine or what, but I know whoever it is, they're close." A cool splay of hostile energy pressed against the darkness. Three separate energies were closing in, probing in the night, looking for us. "Damn close. And there's three of them," I said. "What are our chances?"

"Not great," Cole admitted. "If Jayne and I change now, we could do some damage. You think you're up to it, Jaynie?"

If she nodded I couldn't see it, but I felt her tense and then relax, felt her hand go soft in mine before she let it drop.

"Try to make it back to the cabin, Liv." It wasn't a request. Cole's eyes were iridescent pools looming just in front me, and I struggled to fill in the outline of his face around them. "Run as soon as the darkness breaks. You can make it."

"Yeah, I can make it." I probably couldn't, but I wasn't about to try, either. Our borrowed cover was already eroding around the edges, and I knew if we split up, none of us would survive.

"As soon as you're ready," I told them, "I'm going to shatter this spell."

With the Sig in my right hand, I took a deep steadying breath. "Watch your eyes," I warned. "It's going to be bright."

Eyes closed, the Shaman's energy surging around me, I concentrated all of my power in one sharp point of light.

"They're directly in front of us, three across, and about twenty feet away." I had no idea if the wereleopards could see through the blackness that surrounded us. I couldn't, but I could feel the evil coming.

Weaving my voice into the Shamans' voices, I focused on the white light in my mind. It was just a pinprick now, but it was growing in intensity with every breath. When Cole's hand released mine, I pulled the cross from my neck and held it straight out in front of me. I drew the point of light in my mind toward the cross, pulling the circle of darkness tighter as I did.

Then I offered a small prayer for forgiveness to whatever gods were listening. I don't know why, exactly, but it felt right.

The ball of light in my mind approached the cross, and the cross began to glow. The metal warmed in my hand, tingled and pricked. *Now or never.* With a final quick breath I connected the light and the cross.

Sparks flew like fireworks in the night, snapping my eyes open in time to see Adrienne not ten feet away, her face twisting into a rabid snarl. The other two vamps cowered behind her, shielding themselves from the light.

And then it happened.

Time froze around us. I couldn't move, couldn't fire my weapon or let go of the cross sizzling in my hand. In front of me, Adrienne struggled forward. She and I were stuck in the moment, like dragonflies in amber, unable to break away. From the corner of my eye, I saw two forms dashing through the light, leaping at the vampires in the background.

I forced myself to breathe, to hold the magic in place with Adrienne straining against it, fangs bared and eyes seething.

A high-pitched scream cut through the haze, unidentifiable but not human, filled with terror and anger and suffering, and something else—something familiar and true. And again, only lower, more feral. There was nothing else. No other sound. No other feeling. Only that desperate cry filling the night.

In that instant, that moment of pure horror, time regained its momentum, and thrust me forward without warning.

I found myself squeezing the trigger even before I blinked. With Adrienne closing the distance between us, the white hot cross slipped from my fingers, its light extinguished before it hit the ground. The two bullets I'd fired into her shoulder were gaping red holes, pinching closed even as she knocked the 9mm from my hand.

Her fingers gripped my throat, lifting me until my feet dangled above the ground. My breath caught in my chest, and I fought every instinct to struggle away from the sharp-faced terror holding me in her grasp.

"Bitch," she hissed. "Who are you to take the eternal life from one of my own precious glories?"

I gasped, trying to squeeze oxygen past her vice-like fingers. Against all good judgment, I reached for the arm that held my throat, forcing my wrist closer and closer to the vampire's flesh.

"Do you think me a fool? Your silly charms won't save you tonight!" She laughed, a terrible, soulless sound, while very, very slowly twisting my arm, pulling it backwards until it separated from my shoulder at the joint.

Pain, hot and jagged, tore the last of the breath from my lungs. Blood pounded against my eardrums. My head drooped against my shoulder, the broken bracelet dangling from my wrist, useless, just like she said. I struggled to breathe, fighting just to stay alive.

"Am I talking to myself?" she intoned. "Answer me! Who are you?"

"Can't," I croaked, trying again. "Can't breathe."

She pulled me closer, until my mouth was biting distance from her ear. "Air," I gasped.

She relaxed her grip on my throat, and for six full heartbeats I drew breath enough to clear the buzzing from my head. I could feel Cole still fighting hard. Jayne's energy was weaker but she was still alive.

"You're important to Antonio," Adrienne said, snapping

my head around to face her. "Before I kill you, I want to know why."

I stretched my power toward the Shaman, but instead of their comforting thrum I felt only fresh, sharp pain.

My own.

Adrienne's finger tore into the soft skin just below my collar bone and drove everything else from my mind.

Her magic swirled toward me when our eyes met, the pain from my wasted arm dulling to a throb. "I'm asking you for the last time, mortal. Who are you?"

"Olivia Peters," I told her. "I'm Olivia Peters."

What was I supposed to say? *I'm your worst nightmare?*

For the first time in my life I wanted to fall into the vampire magic, rather than run away from it. I didn't know how much of that was Adrienne's doing and how much was simply the pain, slick-sharp and burning, loose skin fanning around the wound, blood already congealing between my breasts.

Her magic should have taken my will right along with my pain, leaving me helpless under her gaze. It should have, but it didn't.

"Don't play games with me, Olivia Peters." She dug a second finger into my chest, and the coppery smell of my own blood filled the air between us.

She relaxed her grip on my throat, coaxing the skin away from the wounds she'd opened.

"I'm nobody." I made an effort to keep my voice toneless. "Antonio is just using me to get to Feine."

"Yes, my sweet. You are nobody. Tell me why Antonio chose you, and I might just keep you for myself. I might just make you somebody."

Cole's energy pulled closer, a blur of motion in the moonlight. Adrienne's face twisted into a gruesome mask, but I basked in that dark light as if she were the most beautiful woman I'd ever laid eyes on.

"Why you, Olivia? Why you, of all the little nobodies in the Triangle?"

Licking the blood she'd drawn, she slid her teeth across my skin. Panic flooded through me. Cold sweat played across my face. My heart soared out of control. Blood pumped from the wounds she'd opened, the surge drawing her fangs like the moon drawing the tides.

She curled her magic away from me, still drinking from the fountain of my chest. Her horrible laugh caught in her throat and set every one of my shattered nerves on fire. She was beyond caring about Antonio or even the fledgling that I'd killed. Beyond everything but the blood and the terror and the desperation that seeped from my skin in place of the power that had been there before.

Here, on edge of consciousness, only the scent of my own blood called out to me. I breathed in its power, tasting it strong and metallic in my mouth, feeling its energy spill between my breasts and seep into my lungs. Blood magic, and I forced the last breath from my lungs in a howl that shook the night.

Adrienne's eyes whipped around to meet mine, but a mass of fur and teeth that could only be Cole crashed through the darkness, sending us both sprawling to the ground. His power melted into mine, a low roar rumbling through his throat.

They battled for position, Adrienne ripping through the spotted fur of his shoulder, Cole's powerful jaws tearing into undead flesh. The grate of teeth on bone fueled my struggle through the blood-soaked grass as I clawed my way out of their reach.

Twenty

I fumbled for the .38 at my ankle, right hand sweat-slick on the cold metal, gaze fixed on Cole. I could feel Jayne, close, but not strong enough to help him. My left arm dangled uselessly, every movement shooting tremors through my body.

Steadying the gun in my shaky hand wasn't my only problem. Adrienne was a blur of streaky motion and Cole a tangle of fur and blood. They were too damned fast! My heart slammed in my chest, pounded against my ribs. Gun drawn, I struggled to stay in sync, letting the tiny muscles of my eyes direct the rest of my body. Without the visual rhythm of the fight, my reflexes wouldn't be fast enough to respond.

Jayne crept closer, clumsy in human form, the slick grass matting in her wake. I could hear her breathing, as ragged as my own, maybe more so, and feel the heat of her body next to mine. The scent of rotting vampire hung around her, and I knew the corpses of Adrienne's helpers were nearby, returning to the earth at long last. I wanted to look, to make sure, but I kept my eyes on Adrienne.

"The Ja'Nan are coming," Jayne croaked through bruised lips. "Can you feel them?"

I shook my head, cursing myself for the movement that took my attention away from the fight. I knew I was only going to get one shot.

"How close?" Maybe they would get here in time. Maybe I wouldn't have to shoot at all.

"Close." She hesitated. "But take the shot if you get it. Don't wait."

Their bodies clashed and separated, fur and bone, teeth and fangs, and I knew I couldn't wait. Cole's strength faded even as the Ja'Nan approached, their energy coursing through the night, reaching out to us. It was all they could do.

I raised myself to one knee, desperate for a clear shot. Jayne slid behind me, solid now, balanced. Skin to skin, every ache in her body pulsed through mine, every ounce of her determination wound alongside the pain and pressed itself into me, too.

She wasn't about to lose Cole. Not to a vamp. Not tonight.

Lethal and lightning quick, Adrienne slammed into Cole, her legs digging into his belly, her hands crushing his face and neck. Blood scented the air, and even with the thrum of collective power getting closer, I knew I had to do it.

I stared down the too-short barrel of the .38, trying to focus on where I thought Adrienne's head would be by the time the bullet reached her. I closed my eyes and pulled the trigger.

My aim was off, but not by much.

The force of the impact knocked Adrienne off balance, sent them both sprawling. Adrienne's wounds were closing over already, and Cole lay beside her in the sodden field, stunned. Before I could fire again, she was flying toward me, Cole's body grasped across her chest, knowing I wouldn't risk him.

Jayne threw her own vamp-battered body in front of mine, an extra moment's protection, an offering. Rage poured from my throat, primal and inarticulate. A curse, tearing the fabric of the night.

Time edged forward, carrying Adrienne's warped face closer and closer. Cole's body twisted against hers, tail thrusting for balance, heedless of her fingers sinking through his flesh as his body coiled and bucked.

At the last moment, Adrienne threw the wereleopard aside and tensed for the strike. She wouldn't waste time playing with me now, not an extra second, not even if I begged. My jaw convulsed, magic ripping through time, piercing the night.

Power snapped sharp against my skin, and a massive wereleopard leapt from the darkness, shining dark gold in the moonlight. Adrienne crashed to the ground, broken by the force of the blow. The leopard ripped into her throat with a storm of blood and power so fierce and so familiar that I knew it was Luka even before I saw his eyes.

The Ja'Nan closed around them, fur flying and claws extended, pouncing inward to lend their bodies to the press. Mesmerized, I struggled to my feet, the .38 still clutched in my hand.

The wereleopards circled. Lithe bodies, taut with power

and muscle, filled the air with hot sharp scent. Terrifying and beautiful, impossible. Again and again, my eyes were drawn to Luka. Blood matted his fur deep russet, blending the spots and blurring my vision.

With his jaws sunk in Adrienne's shoulder, his body weighing hers into the muddy ground, Luka's power saturated the night. A flood of relief, dazzling and sweet, washed over me, my heart beating a strange new rhythm against my ribs. These were my people. I was safe.

More leopards joined the fray, tearing into Adrienne with teeth and claws, letting the Undead flesh reform over and over. *How much could she take?* Thick blood oozed between fingers of flapping skin, raw ragged breaths shook her chest.

With her lips stretched taut across dull white fangs, her mouth froze in a silent scream. Claws raked into her, deliberate and vicious. Shredded flesh squirmed toward itself, leaking blood into the ground before meshing into her body and reforming. How much of that precious fluid belonged to me? To Cole?

My fingers fluttered over the slices in my own chest, tender-soft and burning, still open to the night. Would she beg for release? I wondered, and I really thought she might. I almost hoped she would, because Luka would never give in, and he would never let her go. She might never go anywhere again. I wanted to care, but I didn't.

The Ja'Nan stalked through the field, low rumbles and high-pitched calls filling the air. They rubbed against each other, scenting the night and marking their territory. Leopards in the wild might be solitary animals, but the Ja'Nan were most definitely not. Hovering around the injured, licking Cole's wounds and pressing their bodies against Jayne's legs, they offered comfort and assurance wherever it was needed.

Finally, I tucked my gun into the holster at my ankle. I was done with it, and I really needed the free hand to keep my other arm from moving too much. Popping the joint back into place was going to hurt like hell, and it wasn't something I could do by myself regardless, so holding it still was really the best I could do. Jayne was the only other person in human form at the moment, and despite everything, I couldn't bring myself to ask her for anything else tonight. When I tried to thank her for what she'd done, she shrugged and brushed me off. I guess we were even now.

I found a spot to rest beside Cole, offering what energy I could while I more or less tried to stay out of the way. His breathing was uneven, more from exhaustion than from any serious damage, and the coarse tongues of the Ja'Nan were already helping him heal. I soothed his face with soft strokes, wishing there was more I could do.

I closed my eyes, and Cole was just Cole, hurt and weakened, not a wereleopard, not the image from my nightmares, not at all. Surrounded by the Ja'Nan, I'd never felt safer in my life. And when I opened my eyes, my fingers deep in soft wet fur, I saw only my friend.

Funny, but even when I closed my eyes Luka wasn't just Luka anymore. He was so much more than that now. He was the being I'd been hearing so much about these last few days. He was the Ra'Jahn.

***

I couldn't be sure how long I'd been sitting with Cole, half-tranced in the lingering afterglow of adrenaline, but my jeans were grass-damp and bloodied, and my hands were starting to shake again. When I opened my eyes, I found Andrew standing beside me, in human form at last, one hand outstretched to help me up.

"You did good, little witch," he said, and it sounded so sweet to my ears that I bit my lip to keep it still.

"I didn't, not really." My tongue felt thick, and my throat ached. "Cole and Jayne saved my life, not the other way around."

"I know what I know." His voice dared me to look away. "And I know that two wereleopards and one human shouldn't have survived this attack."

I shrugged. "Now what?"

"Now we're going to take care of your shoulder." My eyes flashed wide, staring into his. "It's dislocated, isn't it?"

I considered pretending that my arm was fine, but I had the feeling he would make me prove it. Making a run for it was out, too. I looked around for help, and while my attention wandered, Andrew grabbed my good arm.

"Still don't trust me, witchling?"

I raised an eyebrow, watching him raise one back.

"Not to worry. Sue Ann's a pediatric nurse. I'm just hired muscle." He laughed, and I had the distinct impression he was going to enjoy keeping me still while Sue Ann popped my arm back into joint.

I let myself be steered away from the open field, and as we made our way to the cabin, the Shaman tugged quietly on my consciousness. Their energy had given me the strength and the will to fight tonight, but it was their acceptance that flooded through me now, stinging my eyes and making me shiver.

I wasn't a Shaman, not exactly, not fully, but I belonged here nonetheless. The phrase *Kaluu Ja'Naa* echoed in my mind, and though I couldn't remember where I'd heard it or what it meant, I knew I liked the sound of it. Soft and strong, *Kaluu Ja'Naa.* I paused for a moment, wove a spell of gratitude and unity, and released it into the night.

Twenty-one

My whole body ached. Again.

I eased myself into Luka's oversized tub, Cole and Jayne keeping me company and soaking their own pains away as well. We didn't speak. We listened to the foaming rush of water and inhaled the calming scent of lavender. When Sue Ann came in to check on us, we murmured our well being and then returned to our soaking. Eyes closed, mouths open, only the hot water existed.

There's something about bathing that is so simple and so intimate that it's the only real comfort for life's truly complicated hurts. Maybe because you're vulnerable, maybe because it's womblike, I really don't know. But when Sue Ann came back through the door, ordering us out of the bath and leaving an assortment of ice packs, I yearned to stay behind and soak reality away for a little while longer.

Reality, of course, had other plans.

Reality wondered why had the Ja'Nan let Adrienne live when they could have just as easily not. It was more work to guard her until Antonio arrived than it would have been to tear her limb from limb. They'd wanted to, but they hadn't. Luka hadn't let them.

The image of Adrienne's twisted face looming over my own battled for position with the feel of the torture I'd glimpsed in Antonio's mind. That meeting at Feeling Blue seemed like ages ago, not days. I shook my head, pushing the images away, and reached for the robe hanging on the back of the door. Soft, sweet-smelling cotton, Luka's spice still clinging to the fabric.

Adrienne was Antonio's problem now, not mine, and that was reality, too. He'd said it himself, right? There are fates worse than death for the Undead, and the truth was, I wished them both well in their endeavors.

***

Antonio's power, a jumble of seething emotions, announced his presence in the cabin. I felt him approach, felt the shifts in his energy as he moved among the Ja'Nan, and I pulled my robe tighter, but I didn't move. I couldn't, not yet.

Cole leaned beside me on Luka's bed, half-dressed, heat radiating from his bare chest. "Antonio will want to speak with you," Cole said, his fingers dancing over the scar on my thigh.

"I'm not ready."

"Okay. He'll be out there for at least twenty minutes, anyway." Cole sighed, letting his fingers trail across my leg. "You were amazing tonight, Olivia. If you'd gone with Luka, Jayne and I would have been toast."

"If I'd gone with Luka, Adrienne probably wouldn't have come out here in the first place. Besides, you two were incredible!" I swallowed hard. "You all were."

"Jealous?" he teased, a smile pulling at his lips.

"A little," I whispered. "Maybe."

Cole's voice was playful, but I was serious. I looked into his eyes, touching the new skin along his jaw line. He'd been battle-worn and beaten bloody not more than a few hours earlier, but I couldn't tell by looking at him. Not in this light, anyway.

"You're doing all right on your own," he said, his words fluttering softly in my hair.

His fingers played along the opening of my robe, exposing the twin wounds just beginning to heal above my breast. I closed my eyes, and the feel of Cole's body so close to mine was enticing. I reached for him, his lips capturing mine, the surge of desire welling between us a comfort we both needed tonight.

The knock on the door caught us off guard, spun us into motion. "That's Antonio," I murmured, wishing the Undead Ruler would go away but grateful for the distraction all the same.

Cole nodded, smiling. He crossed the room to Luka's dresser and slipped into a t-shirt snagged from the middle drawer. He ran his fingers through his hair, eyes steady on the door. I smiled, too, noticing he left the borrowed shirt untucked.

"Will you be okay alone with him?" Cole asked.

I nodded, pulling the robe close around me. I tied the belt in a tight knot and tousled my hair, wishing I'd gotten dressed when I had the chance.

Cole kissed me again, softly this time, his lips like sweet cream. "Get dressed, Livvie. I'll talk to Antonio for a few minutes."

I grabbed clean clothes and locked myself in the bathroom, but I still heard Cole open the door for Antonio, felt the vacuum fill as air from the other room rushed in. They exchanged greetings, and then their voices dropped too low for my ears to pick up the remainder of the conversation.

I dressed quickly. Hands on the doorframe, I said a prayer to Cardea, the goddess of thresholds, before stepping from my sanctuary. Cole's voice trailed off as both men turned toward me.

"Olivia." Antonio's power brushed my own, thin tendrils like curious antennae, searching for answers.

Cole winked at me and slipped out of the room, closing the bedroom door behind him. I smiled after him, taking a few extra moments before drawing my gaze back to Antonio. I was suddenly weary beyond words, the air in the bedroom already cloudy with exhaustion.

"Do you mind?" I asked, gesturing toward the sliding doors and the wide wooden deck hidden in the darkness behind them.

"Not at all."

I blinked, and fresh cool air washed into the room. Antonio's footsteps sounded on the deck.

"Showoff." I walked past him to lean on the railing, picking the spot Luka favored for watching me sleep.

"I didn't intend for you to become quite so involved in my affairs, Olivia." When I met Antonio's eyes, I couldn't help but believe him. He seemed worn around the edges, tense in a way I hadn't expected. "Adrienne took the loss of her fledgling personally, I'm afraid. I think she may be quite mad."

"Does that happen to your kind often?" I asked. "Madness, I mean."

"Yes, it does." A shadow flickered in his eyes, made them seem almost black. "Certain bloodlines are more susceptible than others. Most perish quickly, a decade or two, sometimes less. It is rare for the madness to take someone as old as Adrienne, though many in her line have succumbed."

Wistfulness tugged at his lips, memory shading reality, and his voice slipped into a whisper. Images of another time flashed through my mind. A much younger Antonio, startling in his innocence, cavorting through a moonlit night with Adrienne by his side, their lips scarlet and fangs gleaming white.

"What will happen to her now?" I asked.

"She will tell me where Feine is hiding."

He seemed certain that she would. More certain than I was entirely comfortable with.

"And then?"

His magic swirled towards me, glanced over the surface of my mind, assuring me everything was going to be all right.

"And then?" I asked again, my teeth clenching with the effort. I had to know.

"Ahh . . ." he breathed, a wave of assurances, a whisper of confidence. "Olivia, my dear, there are some things you should not want to know."

My eyes narrowed. Maybe, but it wasn't a decision I wanted Antonio to make for me.

"When I have decided what to do with Adrienne," he finally conceded, "I promise to inform you of her fate."

"I don't know why I care," I said. And it was true, I didn't know. She was a murdering sadist, and she deserved whatever Antonio had in store for her.

His expression softened, and he felt rounder to me, like a regular guy with everyday problems. *Neat trick*, I thought. I'd have to remember to ask him about it someday.

He laid a cool hand against my aching shoulder, kindness overwhelming my instinct to back away. "I can help you, Olivia. Let me take the pain. It is a small magic, nothing more. You shouldn't suffer from my lack of foresight."

"No, thank you."

"Yes, I think so." He smiled, ignoring me completely. His magic was a gentle pressure against the automatic barrier I sent up, and then that barrier weakened.

"Relax, Olivia. Close your eyes."

I surprised myself by doing just that. The tension drained from my shoulders, taking the pain with it, until there was only a dull ache surrounded by icy fingers.

I could feel those fingers on my skin long after I opened

my eyes, unsure exactly when Antonio had disappeared.

***

It was nearly dawn before I saw Luka again. He moved among the Ja'Nan effortlessly, with a touch, a word, a moment for each of them. I tried to compare the man I saw now with the beautiful beast tearing through the night and the lover I knew yesterday.

Images of him spun off in every direction, wrapping around each other and separating again. Man, wereleopard, Ra'Jahn. Powerful, stubborn, intense. How can you compare a person to himself?

When he didn't come to me, didn't have a word or a soft touch for me, it probably shouldn't have bothered me. But it did. It bothered me a lot. His energy reached for mine, the force of his body pulled on my own, but determination set his jaw in stone. When he finally crossed the room and stood before me, tension radiated around us.

"You should be resting, Olivia."

"I wanted to see you first. I was hoping . . ." My voice trailed off, the rest of my words vanishing into the void.

Luka's silence offered me nothing.

"You saved my life tonight," I started again, hands hanging awkwardly at my sides. I itched to feel the texture of him, needing to understand. "I thought you deserved a thank you."

Green eyes flashed broken-bottle sharp, anger boiling around him. "Are you mocking me?" he demanded, just this side of a teeth-bared growl.

Mocking him? What the hell was he talking about? His power burned in the empty space between us, flaring against my skin, reminding me of the feel of his body curled around mine in sleep, blankets tangled at our feet. Maybe my expectations were unrealistic, but I'd thought even if things had somehow changed between us, the least he would offer me was the same kindness he'd shown the rest of the clan. I held his gaze for another moment, seeing nothing but my own reflection in his eyes—a broken human, reflected over and over, like a mirror with a crack. Tears spilled over my cheeks, slick and salty on my lips before I noticed they were there.

I spun on my heel, a move that left me lightheaded,

and closed the distance to the bedroom before I had a chance to reconsider. Swiping my keys from the dresser where Luka had tossed them yesterday, I looked around the room for any of my things that may have scattered to the corners. I didn't want to leave anything behind if I could help it.

Both bags slung over my good shoulder, I tucked the Sig into the back of my jeans and the .38 into the pocket of my jacket. In Luka's world, I would always be the human who didn't understand. I would always be fragile. I would never be enough.

And I would never get over it.

I was already in the car, stashing the Sig in the glove box when I felt Cole's eyes on me.

"You can't just leave, Olivia." His voice was thin, like a sleepy child's, and as much as I wanted to make him right, I wouldn't. Because I could *just leave*, and I was going to.

"Please don't do this." I touched his face, careful around the seven shades of bruise blooming in the sunrise. "Please, Cole. I can't stay here."

"I'll come with you," he offered, stone still and quiet.

I wanted to say yes. I wanted to take him home with me, wrap myself in the comfort he was offering and forget about the rest of it. I wanted to, but I scrubbed my hands over my face instead, glimpsing the pale moon, almost full, still hanging in the morning sky. He followed my gaze.

"Get in," I told him, adding silently, *before I change my mind.*

He pushed the hair from his face, white teeth smiling bright. "Nah," he said quietly, complexities I wasn't likely to understand any time soon racing through his eyes. "You go ahead. I'll take care of Luka."

"See you?" I asked, looking over my shoulder, ready.

"Yeah," he said. "Soon."

I needed the drive now. The pure physicality of it, the constant motion, revolution after revolution, like a prayer to all the gods. My fingers reached for the radio, sliding the volume louder and louder the further I got from the cabin, until the only things left of any substance at all were the music and the road.

The morning sun was warm against my skin, soft and aching in a way I couldn't fully ignore, and I pulled into the lot of the first Circle K on my route. Pretending to stretch my legs, I walked a small circle of my own. My hair fell free from its twist, and I raked through it, gathering dozens of loose strands. Fingers toward the sky, I let the wind take my small offering where it would.

Inside, the clerk was flipping through a magazine, steam rising from a full cup of coffee by his hand.

"Coming or going?" I asked.

"Shift ends at seven," he answered, glancing at the clock on the far wall.

I paid for a large coffee and a small box of Krispy Kreme doughnuts, a driver's breakfast if ever there was one.

"Do you have real cream for this?" I asked, lifting my coffee toward him, careful not to spill.

"Supposed to use the powder," he said, shrugging. "But you can grab some of the good stuff from the dairy case if you want."

"Thanks," I said, opening the tiny paper carton. "It makes all the difference."

"Sure enough," he said. "The gods are in the details, eh?"

"Yes," I said, pushing the door open, letting the morning air rush into the convenience store. A playful leaf danced in the breeze, drawing my eyes to my convertible. I could hear the road now, calling me back to the city, the birdsong fading in the distance.

"Yes," I said again. "They certainly are."

Twenty-two

"I'm fine, Mom. Really. I spent a few days in the country with a friend."

According to my answering machine, my mother had called seven times since I'd left for the cabin. Her messages had grown progressively terse, each one more concerned than the last. A mother's intuition? Maybe. Or maybe there was more magic in my family than she cared to admit. *As if.* My eyes rolled of their own accord, and I tried hard not to sigh. "It was nothing, Mom. Sort of a getaway, like a long weekend."

"If you want to get away, Olivia, you know you can always come home."

Of course I knew. She reminded me every time we spoke, her voice edgy with the tiny frown lines pulling at her eyes.

"Your father would love to spend some time with you."

Ahh, the sweet sound of guilt.

"And it would be good for Rose to have her sister closer. Those two little boys are running her ragged!"

Here it comes, I thought, stretching against the tightness building in my shoulders. *Might as well open the gates myself.*

"So what's new with my nephews?" There. I'd done it, and while my mother enthused about the amazing adventures of her unruly grandsons, I hauled my bags into the bedroom and started unpacking.

The scent of dried blood and stale magic billowed around me, earmarking the clothes I'd brought back from the cabin for the laundry. Worn or unworn, I'd drop them all off at Lares Laundries tomorrow, and when I retrieved them in a day or two, they would be neatly folded or perched on proper hangers, smelling of fresh soap and a hot iron. My life might be a tangled mess at the moment, but a steamy shower for me and a trip to the cleaners for my clothes would go a long way toward making everything just a little bit better.

I shrugged into my robe and padded barefoot through the apartment, half-listening to my mother, my fingers trailing along chair backs and windowsills as I went. The rooms seemed different somehow, insubstantial in my absence. I paused in the entryway, careful to cross my shoes left over right behind the door, comforted by the simplicity of the offering.

On the other end of the phone, my mother went on and on, just as I'd known she would. If she noticed my lack of enthusiasm for the subject, she didn't let it bother her. I did my part for the conversation through a smattering of interjections. "Really!" and "No!" and "Already?" had become my only defenses against the familiar onslaught.

I had no idea what my mother told her friends about me, but I doubted my life got much airtime in her social circle. Which was fine by me, really. Truth be told, I did my best to shelter my family from the details of my day-to-day activities. They were uncomfortable with the paranormal world, and I'd learned a long time ago that we were better off not discussing it.

As it was, I was well into my second cup of coffee and nibbling the edges of a graham cracker, when I heard the telltale shift in my mother's tone that spurred me into action.

"Mom, I've got to run," I said, interrupting when she paused for a breath. I couldn't take the time-for-you-to-settle-down-and-have-children-of-your-own speech this morning, and oh yeah, it was definitely coming. "I'm not dressed yet, and I have to work today."

"Not dressed?" My mother was appalled. I could almost see her brows rising in perfect twin arches, her lips pursed in displeasure. "Olivia, it's nine in the morning already!"

"I know what time it is, Mom, that's why I have to go. Give Daddy a kiss for me, okay?"

As usual, this chitchat reminded me why I kept my work life and my family life as separate as humanly possible. If my mother knew what it was really like around here—the mismatched colors, the late hours, the sheer volume of grime—she would pass out cold. Seriously.

***

So I wouldn't have to hang my head in shame for lying to my mother outright, I called the office to check in with Linc. Ellen answered, of course, and her cheery voice tugged at my heartstrings, though it did nothing to dispel my foul mood.

"Is Linc around?" I asked.

"He's indisposed at the moment. Would you like his voice mail or would you prefer to hold?"

Despite myself, I smiled at Ellen's formality. She must have clients in the office. "I'll hold," I said.

"May I make an inquiry?" she asked, again her voice warm and professional.

"Go for it, Ellen."

She paused, no doubt composing the question with an ear toward the clients who might overhear. "If you have a moment to spare following your conversation with Mr. Anderson, might we discuss the details of your most recent business association?"

"If you're asking about Luka, I'm afraid the answer is no. Unfortunately, there's nothing to discuss."

"I'm sorry to hear that," she said, pausing a moment before completing her thought. "I must admit I'm quite surprised by this turn of events."

"You and me both, Ellen. You and me both."

"Hmmm. Perhaps we can continue our conversation this afternoon? Mr. Anderson is available now, I'll put you right through."

Linc got right down to business, not bothering with the same sort of pleasantries Ellen and I exchanged. He'd never expressed an interest in my personal life, and as long as it didn't interfere with my work, I expected it would stay that way. Even so, I knew he cared.

"You comfortable with the .38 yet?" he asked.

"Like I've had it forever," I answered. "The ankle rig was a good idea. Thanks again."

"If you're carrying today, why don't you try the waistband holster?"

"Meaning, make sure I'm dressed appropriately if I'm coming in to the office?" Sheesh! First my mother, now Linc. I looked at the neat line of identical dresses hanging in my closet and the heap of cabin clothes piled in the laundry basket. My wardrobe had Bereavement Specialist written all over it.

"Not to worry, Linc, I'll look the part. But I still don't want to see any clients. I'm in no shape for Meet-and-Greets today," I said.

"Right. No clients."

"I'm serious, Linc."

"Just get your butt in here, Olivia. There's plenty of paper for you to push around."

He was right, and I didn't have anything better to do, anyway. After a few hours with the stack of paperwork on my desk, maybe I'd feel more like myself.

Private investigation, even for a funeral home, is mostly grunt work. Tons of phone calls, endless searches for documents and files in government offices that nobody pays much attention to, typical needle-in-a-haystack type stuff. Even if the nature of the case files with my name printed across the top tended not to involve as much of this sort of thing, the administration of grief counseling was no thrill ride, either. But for once I didn't mind.

I was too exhausted to sleep, and the work kept me from worrying too much about my hasty retreat from the cabin. Just when I was starting to feel comfortable around the Ja'Nan, just when I'd started to think dating the local Ra'Jahn might not be so strange after all, Luka went and threw me for one hell of a loop. And I still wasn't sure why he'd reacted the way he did.

So he was a wereleopard. So what? I could handle the shapeshifting, or at least I thought I could, and I damn sure respected the sense of responsibility that soared around him. But did he really have to interpret everything I said as some sort of threat or misguided challenge? What kind of alpha-male crap was that? Maybe I just didn't have enough testosterone to understand.

Lucky for me, Mike Rutledge's voice, deep and musical, interrupted my brooding. "Hey! Peters? You in there?"

"Detective," I said with a smile, enjoying our standard greeting more than I usually did.

"What are you doing in the office today?"

"I might ask you the same question," I answered.

"Tell you about it over lunch?"

"Hmmmm." I pretended to consider. "You buying?"

"Of course." He looked wounded, offended by the question. In this part of the South men still opened doors for women, held their coats at the perfect height, and always, always, picked up the tab.

Someone please explain to me how on earth my own

mother thought I'd be happier if I moved back home?

***

The pile of Luka-linked paperwork I couldn't bring myself to deal with at the office was now stacked on my coffee table, a bland manila tower adrift on a sea of glossy magazines. I didn't want to think about the case anymore. The vamps who betrayed Antonio were dead, and Adrienne was out of the picture, so Feine didn't have much support left. He'd probably slither down whatever hole he'd crawled out of and leave the rest of us be.

But Mike had made it plain over lunch that he wasn't convinced any such thing would happen, which was why I brought the files home with me. It was also why a black-and-white was parked in my back lot. When I told Mike I'd be fine on my own, he struggled with a half-smile that he eventually managed to control. I waited for a sharp comment about Luka, but if he had one, he kept it to himself. Instead, he'd arranged as much police protection for me as the department could spare.

I stared glassy-eyed at the files, trying to feel something other than dread. I couldn't think, I wouldn't sleep, and I wasn't hungry. The only bright spot in my foreseeable future was ESPN Classic's rebroadcast of an old Stanley Cup match, and even that wasn't on for another few hours.

When the phone rang I was grateful for the distraction, determined to take my frustrations out on whichever telemarketer had the misfortune of dialing my number today.

"Liv, it's Karen." I think she'd started talking before I even picked up. "I was sure I was going to get your machine again!"

"No such luck." I stretched out on the couch, dark velvet rubbing whispers against my skin. "I'm in a lousy mood, and I don't really want to talk about it. What's up?"

"Umm, I thought you might want to come over and watch the game with me tonight?"

"What! You're home?"

"No, but that's what I was thinking, and isn't it the thought that counts?"

It wasn't funny, but I started laughing anyway, and pretty soon I couldn't stop. That's the way it was with Karen, and right now she was exactly what I needed. Before

I knew it, I was telling her everything, despite the fact that I hadn't wanted to talk about it.

I sighed. "Whenever I'm around him, I feel all tangled up, and I have no idea why or how to change it."

"Are you sure you want to change it, Liv?"

"Yes." The answer breezed across my lips before my brain could stop it.

"So let me get this straight," she said. "You meet a man, the local Ra'Jahn no less, and it's so hot that sparks literally fly between you. Then you tease each other for a few days, sleep in the same bed but don't have sex, and now you're wondering why he's moody?"

"That's one way to look it," I conceded.

"You have the strangest problems, Liv."

"Me?" I said. "You're the one dating a vampire. Tell me that's not strange!"

"Strange it is, Livvie, I'll give you that. But Davis is really cool!"

I winced at her word choice, but I let it go. It was too easy, and if he made her happy, who was I to judge?

"Hey, Liv? Can I ask you something?"

"You can ask me anything, you know that."

She hesitated. "I want to ask you something about time."

"Time?" My fingers flicked slow swishes on the sofa, deep purple trenches in the early evening light. "And?"

"And vampires."

Already I didn't like where this was going. The sight of Adrienne's leopard-torn flesh flashed in my eyes, and I remembered slow motion bullets slicing the air, bodies suspended mid-flight. I remembered the fury unleashed in my voice and ripping through my throat, and the feel of Antonio's cool hands lingering on my skin long after he'd gone.

"What about time and vampires, Karen?"

I wasn't sure, but I thought I heard her laughing, way down low.

"Have you noticed how time doesn't feel the same around them?" she asked.

"Well, yes. But I thought it was me."

"It's not you, honey, it's them. Most people aren't sensitive enough to feel it. But trust me, it has all sorts of fabulous possibilities . . ."

***

When we finally hung up, my side hurt from laughing so hard, and all of a sudden, I was starving. I called out for a pizza, and even the fifty-five minute wait for delivery didn't bother me. I had time.

I opened my kitchen window wide, leaned halfway out and waved to the rookie on surveillance duty. The least I could do was feed the poor cop who'd been putting in extra hours to score a few points with Mike.

"Hey down there!" I shouted. "If you don't hassle the Pizza Guy there's a few slices in it for you!"

I almost fell over the sill when Detective Rutledge himself stepped out of the cruiser, a slow smile spreading across his face.

"Is it Lilly's pizza?" Mike asked, the fire escape clanging under his heavy shoes.

"What do you think?"

Everybody with any taste at all knows Lilly's is the only place to get a pizza in this city. The crust is just right, not too thick and not too thin, and sweet and doughy in all the right places.

Mulling over the details of the murders with Mike, an empty pizza box perched on our knees and greasy paper napkins littering the coffee table, I knew he wouldn't be able to walk away from this case. It bothered him, and it would keep bothering him until it was resolved. His way.

Mike wanted someone to pay, and he wanted The Law to be the ultimate authority. From what I'd seen, vampire justice was no walk in the park, but that didn't make much difference to Mike. He was a cop, plain and simple. He wouldn't rest easy until Feine was in custody.

"You think that's crazy, Peters?"

"No, not crazy. Predictable."

He wiped the back of his hand across his mouth and leaned forward. "What do you mean?"

"You can bet Antonio's counting on you not to give up." I smirked, thinking about how disappointed Antonio would be if he knew I'd spent most of the day hoping Feine would slink off into somebody else's night. "He wants Feine caught and publicly trounced. That's why he hired me."

"Is that so?" Mike laughed, but it was a gritty, angry

sound that felt out place in the air around him. "Is he going to get what he paid for, Peters?"

"I don't know, Mike."

Our eyes locked, neither of us sure this was a road we wanted to travel down tonight. There's a fine line between what's fair and what's just, between law and reality. Part of what makes a Bereavement Specialist worth her salt is knowing when to cross that line, and when to back away from it. Usually, I'm worth my weight in gold. But not tonight. Tonight, I just didn't know.

"No? Well, I *do* know," Mike said. "Feine is going down, hard, and I'm not going anywhere until it's done."

"Is that so?" I repeated, not quite ready to let the moment go. Mike nodded, eyes narrow, waiting. "In that case, Detective, I'm really glad you're here."

Twenty-three

Two full days had passed since I'd driven away from the cabin, leaving Luka and the Ja'Nan behind, and both had been so terribly ordinary that I wanted to do nothing more than slip back into bed and dream it all away. I was feeling awkward and lonely, uncomfortable in my own skin.

Sleep was my only refuge, a respite from lackluster work nights in which I visited clients, the scent of death and hospital sickrooms hanging thickly in the air. I filed reports in triplicate whenever necessary, hiding behind the mountain of paperwork that had become Forever Crossed.

Those times when I couldn't sleep, I huddled under the covers anyway, hoping. My sheets still smelled vaguely of Luka, and I clung to his sweet-spicy scent as if it held all the answers. Like a child with her nub-furred bear, I would keep this small comfort as long as I could.

Meetings with the city's Undead were something I looked forward to now. I'd become accustomed to the stream of images from Antonio's colleagues, and even filtering out the death scenes didn't take much effort anymore. After all, they weren't really dead. They were swarming across the Carolinas, night after night, alive and breathing.

Well, Undead and breathing. But still.

My link with Antonio, on the other hand, was more disturbing than ever. I had so many unanswered questions that I hardly knew where to start, and they were becoming harder and harder to ignore. The link was just too easy with Antonio. Even blocking him from my mind wasn't much trouble, and I wondered if it had something to do with the leopard in me. I wondered if he could call me, like he called the Ja'Nan. I wondered if he even wanted to.

As scary as my questions were, truth be told, they weren't at the heart of what was bothering me. At least not at the moment. Just now my irritation focused on my own physical limitations. I wasn't used to being the weakest link, the smallest kid, the last picked. And I didn't like the sensation one bit.

For the better part of a decade I'd been the fastest, the strongest, the best at whatever sport or game I played. I'd toned it down, not played as hard as I could, made sure I didn't win all the time. Now I was fighting for my life against beings that were superhuman in almost every sense of the word. And it wasn't just the vampires, it was the Ja'Nan, too, and really, that part was almost worse.

Everything about my days with the wereleopards hit an emotional trigger. My skin felt dull from lack of touch, and I missed the constant play of energy in the air whenever they were around. Even my apartment seemed different. I used to cherish my time alone, but after spending a few days with the Ja'Nan this space felt empty, too big for one person, and it hurt. From the moment I'd first walked into this apartment, dust motes dancing up from the wood floors, sparkly in the filtered afternoon light, I'd known this would be my home. And now it wasn't.

So, damn Luka for not calling. And damn Antonio, too! Who did they think they were, dragging me into this mess, using me to get to Adrienne, and then leaving me out here dangling in the wind with my shoulder aching and doubt pulling at my soul? Only Mike Rutledge cared enough to make sure that I was safe, and he had the worst chance of surviving an encounter with Feine than the rest of us. He was a damn fine cop, no *ifs* or *ands* about it, but when you came right down to it, facts were facts, and Mike was only human.

My fuming was interrupted by the phone, the sound of which made me sneer, then smile, in such rapid succession that even I was confused.

Maybe it was Luka. Maybe it was Luka!

See what I mean?

"Olivia Peters," I said, throwing my legs over the edge of the bed.

"Must you answer the phone in that manner?" My mother's voice was distinctly agitated.

I made a mental note to call BellSouth and sign up for Caller ID first thing tomorrow.

"Olivia? Are you there?"

Maybe if I didn't say anything, she would take pity on me and simply hang up?

"Olivia?"

"I'm here, Mom." I pulled the phone away from my mouth, allowing myself a dramatic sigh. "What's wrong?"

"Nothing's wrong. Can't a mother call her daughter

without something being wrong?"

"We just spoke the other day." I rubbed my eyes, made an effort to lighten up a little. "Are you all right?"

"No, Olivia, I'm not all right. I'm worried about you."

"I'm fine, Mom, really. There's nothing for you to worry about. I'm just tired."

"Tired? You're never tired. You haven't been tired in years!"

She had a point, but I was stunned that she'd given voice to it. My family rarely spoke of my differentness. My strength, my stamina, my body's ability to heal itself—these were all subjects of considerable taboo. But my mother covered this breach of conduct with a nervous laugh. I joined her, both of us hiding behind this simple façade.

"You sound blue, Olivia, and you know what beats the blues every time?" Her voice rose, a little shaky, and I couldn't stop the smile spreading across my face.

"A new lipstick?" I asked, with all the seriousness I could muster.

"Exactly! Now go put on something fabulous and get yourself to Nieman's this minute."

Not that the idea wasn't appealing, but I needed something a bit more challenging than a trip to the mall. I considered going for a long run, but rejected the idea almost immediately. It would be good for my body, sure, but I was too emotional today. I needed something to ground me, something that would slow my thoughts down, not blur them beyond recognition.

Two solid hours, split between the punching bag and the ropes, plus one deep tissue massage later, I left the gym. I was feeling more balanced than I had in days, sore muscles soothed to compliance, and nothing on my mind except my mother's advice. And why not? This particular bit of wisdom had been passed down from generation to generation in my family. Besides, I needed a new lipstick as much as the next gal, and I had nothing better to do until sundown.

***

Sunset, moonrise, nightfall—all three held enormous significance tonight.

When the moon rose it would hang in the darkened sky, round and brilliant, illuminating the Ja'Nan and their hunt, shining its stark light on my loneliness.

When the sun set the Undead would rise, stretching their powers into the night, waiting for the cover of darkness. At night's full depth the city would swell with Vampires, newly released from the sun's light and free to bathe in the warmth of the full moon.

For Antonio Vesci, Undead Ruler of the Carolinas, this night held both peril and jeopardy, marking it a night of uncertainty unlike any other. The pull of the full moon was more powerful than his hold on the wereleopards, so on this night they were released from his service. On this night, he would defend his territory without them.

If Feine was still in the city, and as the afternoon pressed on I was more and more certain that he was, he would certainly strike tonight. Whether he would continue his assault on the human population, casting doubt on Antonio's ability to control the Undead, or whether he would attack Antonio directly and attempt to seize power over the Ruler's rotting corpse, I couldn't begin to guess.

And since neither Antonio nor anyone else saw fit to let me in on the big secret, I planned to spend the night holed up in my apartment, alone, armed to the teeth and ready to pounce. What else could I do?

In theory, I had no reason to believe Feine would come after me. Sure, Adrienne was a nightmare bitch with a grudge, but Feine just wanted power and position, neither of which he could get from me. Then again, theory had never been my strong suit, and I couldn't quite shake the feeling that something more was amiss tonight.

And believe me, it had nothing to do with the fact that I'd just spent a small fortune on lipstick.

I emptied my bag of goodies into the woven basket on my dresser. Miniature-sized beauty products spilled over the edge, tinkling across the glass top like hard candies or ancient coins. I had dozens of these colorful wonders: age-defying creams I wouldn't use and designer scents I wouldn't wear, powders and potions in various hues, not one of them quite my shade.

So I couldn't resist the call of "bonus-time" at the cosmetics counters. So what?

As I stripped out of my shopping clothes and pulled on an old pair of Calvin's and a comfy cotton sweater, I was glad I hadn't tried. The basket of baubles on my dresser meant something to me, something special and silly at the same time. It was a bounty of tiny talismans, to be sure, but if it was also a link to my mother, a guilty pleasure we both could share, then to me it meant that much more.

I gave my hair a quick brushing, then climbed over my bed and peered through the far window. The parking lot was empty—no cop car, no bad guys, no one at all. None that I could see, anyway.

Nobody here but us chickens, I thought, and a little bit of a snicker caught in my throat. I shivered, nervousness creeping over me like hunger, and suddenly I realized that I was ravenous, nearly delirious, and that it had been at least a day since my last meal.

I marched into the kitchen, opened cupboards and closed them again, muttering in disgust. I hadn't been to the grocery in weeks—even my bottled water supply was running low—and the shelves were close to bare. A box of dried pasta and a tin of fragrant olive oil held the most promise, and that wasn't much.

I glanced out the small window over the sink, eyeing the tenants' garden with suspicion. The blue Carolina sky hinted at shades of sunset, but I dashed out the back door and down the fire escape anyway, kitchen shears in my hand and the Sig tucked in the back of my jeans.

Through the weeds that threatened to crowd our planned plants from the plot, I snipped a handful of basil and a few sprigs of parsley, a stalk of rosemary. After I traced a shaky spiral in the hard red dirt, I sprinted back up the stairs, my rumbling stomach louder than my fear. Safe inside, I slammed the dead bolts home and leaned my back against the warm wood door.

The small symbol scratched in the garden wasn't much of an offering, but the sinking sun painted the night, and it was all I had time for. Still, I made a silent vow to spend a few hours this weekend getting to know the local weeds a little bit better.

I moved around the kitchen, reminding myself of childhood evenings at my Nana's, her friends gathered to prepare holiday meals or celebration cakes. Or so I'd thought. Now I wondered which holidays they were celebrating, and what types of preparation had gone into those meals.

Whatever else might have been true, Nana was an amazing cook, and my memories of her kitchen were richly scented—yeasty warmth and tangy herbs, simmering sauces and baking breads, the hum of conversation low in the background.

I'm not nearly the cook she was, but even I can toss pasta into boiling water and stir. I rinsed and chopped the fresh herbs, crushed the few cloves of garlic withering on my windowsill, mixed in a bit of olive oil, salt and black pepper. And, voila! Sauce!

While the water for the pasta boiled, I made a quick call to Mike's voice-mail, as promised, letting him know I was locked in for the night. The city couldn't spare the manpower this evening for the surveillance team I'd started to get used to, but Mike and I had a plan. I would page him if I needed to leave the building after dark or if anything spooked me, and he'd check in with me when he could. Simple, but the best plans often are.

I drained the pasta a few seconds before it turned to mush and stirred the crushed herbs, garlic and more olive oil into the pot to keep it from sticking all together. With grated Parmesan smothering my plate and fragrant steam filling the air, I caught myself wondering why I didn't cook more often.

Truth be told, most of my dinner hours are spent working, or at the gym, or even in Tai Chi practice, and it's just easier to eat out or pick something up on my way home. Besides, cooking for one is a drag and a half, no matter what the magazine features say.

I ate slowly, surveying the weapons I'd gathered for tonight. A motley bunch of holy objects, silver bullets and two wooden stakes that had been garden markers in their previous lives. I had to laugh. My vow to pass this evening armed to the teeth seemed more than a little silly with the cold light of reality reflecting off my limited resources.

Still, I had two stunning new lipsticks that promised to stay fresh all day and all night, so at the very least, my worries about facing Feine with faded lip color were laid to rest.

Twenty-four

In the dream I am eleven.

My grandmother is rocking me, murmuring soft words about gypsies and pretty girls and flowers. Only she isn't, not really. She can't be, because she's dead. I know this because my mother told me, and my mother wouldn't lie. I know this, too, because my father is crying. I've never seen my father cry, and it's a vision so alien to me, that at first I don't believe it's him.

I want to tell him, *"Just close your eyes and breathe."* When I do this, I can feel Nana with me still, the sharp scent of rosemary in her hair, the taste of her garden in my mouth. But the words catch in my throat, and I don't say anything at all.

Nana is smiling at me, wanting to tell me everything, wanting to tell me so much more, to keep me with her a little longer, but she can't. She has to go. She is telling me something, something terrible and important, something that I must do. Now. This now. And then she's gone.

But I am not.

I realize, panicking, that I'm neither awake nor asleep. I'm trapped in the dark nothingness between these worlds, neither here and now, nor there and then. It's dizzying, this floating, and I want it to stop.

I search for an anchor, something to ground me in this space, but there is only terror here. I'm surrounded by a darkness so complete that the only word that comes close to describing it is eternal. Once I've got that word in my head though, I can't get it out. Eternal darkness, over and over, an endless loop. And then it hits me.

Vampire Magic.

There is no other explanation. The feel of Feine's power has haunted me from the moment I stepped onto Anya Sorensen's back porch, unshakable, and now I know why. His magic is deafening. All consuming. A black hole.

My encounter with Anya's death left his imprint in my mind, and encountering him again feels like a recurring nightmare. I remember Anya's swirling descent into his magic, and I know that with nothing to grab hold of, I will drown in the absolute emptiness of his mind. Anya had survived long enough to summon the fire that took her life, but Anya was a powerful Shaman, with years of wisdom and experience on her side.

And I am just me, not a Shaman, and not all that wise, either. Unsure what else to do, I open myself to the emptiness, my fear seeping through the feathery cracks. I have the vague sensation that something is burning, and I focus my efforts into strengthening that sense.

What I'm attempting is not much more than a parlor trick, hardly my first choice for battling a power like Feine's, but it's all I have. Thin wisps of smoke swim against the pitch. It's a start, but what I really need is full-fledged fire. The rest is so much window dressing.

The hard part is, I don't know that much about fire. But Karen does, and I know Karen. I can almost hear her voice now, feel the heaviness of her firefighter's gear. There's a certain light in her eyes, and her face shines, animated in the aftermath of another battle won.

Beginning with the intensity of the heat and the myriad colors, I give life to the flames. Sweat trickles down my back, cool and wet against my skin. Elemental, fire both cleanses and destroys, a perfect melding of beauty and terror.

The sound is inescapable. Flames burning through wood, through metal, through brick and steel, burning with a ferocity that would never be extinguished.

I open my eyes to see a small bundle of yellow-orange flames hovering just above my palm. Hardly the inferno I imagined, but enough to throw shadows into the void. The shadows are gray areas, lurching and flickering, letting me know I have Feine's attention. He can't maintain the blackout, and he won't get close enough to douse the fire. It might be smoke and mirrors, but it's working.

In the back of my mind, I'm vaguely aware of my body sprawled across the couch. I must have dozed off while on the lookout for bad guys. *Damn carb-laden pasta,* I grumble, searching for more, but my living room is dark and I can't see Feine, although I know he must be in the apartment somewhere.

Why me? I wonder, but even as I hear the faint sound of a telephone springing to distant life, I know why.

I've got connections.

I fan the flames in my mind, imagine sparks dancing through the pitch like butterflies on a warm afternoon. The fire glows, smoke billows around me, and the illusion of heat is convincing enough that I start to sweat. Yet Feine remains resolutely beyond my grasp. He's lurking in the corners, sealing off the dream world and preventing me from waking.

Still, my body is helpless and alone, and he could kill me anytime. I wipe my brow, wonder what he is waiting for. Whatever it is, I get the feeling he won't be waiting long.

I collect all of the images I have of Feine—his attack on Anya, Adrienne's death, his own human demise so many years ago. I consider them carefully, like cards fallen from a loose deck, looking for significance in the drop. Although it's not as spectacular as the first two, the image of his own death is by far the most surprising, something he definitely won't be expecting.

Seeking Feine in the darkest part of the void, I feel my way through the smoke, flames burning cold blue and throwing the darkest shadows into high relief. I'm getting closer.

I wrap the image in smoke and tie it with snapshots of Antonio, bright red ribbons floating through the thick gray haze. I force my pretty little package against the emptiness of his mind, letting the flames lick the edges of the bait. I only need a moment. Two moments, really, but I'll take what I can get.

The instant Feine senses Antonio, he's furious. His power rushes through me, wiping out everything else. I throw myself into it, tumbling in the zero gravity tide of Feine's anger. By the time he's torn through the smoke, watching his own death unfold before him, I'm following the flames through the chinks in his armor, disappearing in the brightest white light I've ever seen.

I'm falling, free form and weightless. Falling, faster and faster. Falling forever, until I slam into my body with a force that knocks it clear off the couch. I land with a bounce on the cold wood floor, wedged under the coffee table and gasping for air.

Chin to the ground and breathing hard, time coalesces around me, the wake of the dream world shimmering through normal space. Solid.

Without a second thought, I gripped the Sig with both hands, arms stiff and bent slightly at the elbow. There's a vampire here somewhere, but where?

Fortunately, I heard Feine before I saw him, heard his howl so fierce my bones ached from the sound of it. Then a blur of motion streaked toward me, Feine's black coat flying behind him, like a trail of death in his wake.

The Sig was heavy in my hands, thirteen bullets begging to be released into the Undead monster hurling closer. I squeezed the trigger, watching each bullet cut through the air in super-slo-mo before knocking him back a few feet, then a few more, but not fast enough to stop him.

I aimed for his chest, hoping to put enough bullets into vital organs before he sealed the gap between us, but I didn't have much of a chance. I'd seen the inside of his mind. He wasn't psychotic. He wouldn't feed from my desperation as Adrienne would have, and he wasn't trying to scare me, either. He didn't have any use for my fear.

He wanted only power.

Need drove his ambition, and my power would do until he got to Antonio. I could see it in his eyes. Feel it in the pulse throbbing at my neck. Hear it as the seconds ticked away in time with the beating of my heart.

He hadn't chosen me for my symbolic usefulness or my connections or any of the other reasons I'd guessed at. He'd chosen me for my blood, as simple as that. He was a power hungry vampire, and he wanted my blood. Every drop. Nothing more and nothing less.

And he would have it. I couldn't stop him, and I couldn't count on Luka to leap in and rescue me, not this time. Not tonight.

And maybe not ever. Moonlight poured through the windows, prickling my skin even through the horror, reminding me of who I was, and who I would never be.

Feine stretched through the air, his arm closing around my waist like a steel band, pulling me to him until his breath beat cool against my throat. My fingers squeezed the trigger of the Sig, empty and useless, a reflex I couldn't stop.

Thirteen silver bullets, most of them direct hits. And

still he breathed. Even now I could feel the warm wet ooze seeping from his chest, but I knew it wouldn't stop him.

In my mind's eye I pictured Antonio as I'd seen him at the cabin. His energy in constant motion, a deliberate weave among the Ja'Nan. He marked them over and over, until the scent of his power mingled with theirs, effortless. I recalled the sensation of his hand, cool against my aching shoulder and the soft look in his eyes when he spoke to me. He'd marked me then, too, marked me as one of his own without me even realizing it. I reached out to him now, focusing my terror as Feine loomed over me, hoping our link was strong enough for this to work.

Tricks and trinkets, I thought, remembering Adrienne's words.

I had nothing else.

Twenty-five

The thick wood of my front door splintered, fragmenting into empty seconds before Antonio burst into the room.

Feine tensed against me, muscle and bone rippling beneath his skin.

"Release her!" Antonio's words shook with control.

Feine's face twisted in a fang-filled grin. "So, young one, you've come at last. We've been waiting for you." His voice, rough and breathy, made my skin crawl. Everything about him was ancient and nightmarish, as different from Antonio as night from day.

"You have hunted in my territory for the last time, rogue." Antonio radiated rage and power, an impossible aura, luminescent.

"You have always cared too much for the simple beasts, Antonio. Including them in your protectorate as if they were your own."

"Release her. Now."

"Can you hear the power singing in her blood, young one? Ah, of course you can." Feine's tongue scraped across his lips, his breath cool against my throat. "She's an extraordinary little hybrid, but even she isn't worth your trouble."

"Let her go."

"And if I don't? Will you end this damned existence of mine?" Feine's mouth twitched at the corners. "I don't think you will."

"Do you think I'll let you live?" Antonio's voice edged closer, the chill of his anger stabbed through air. "Do you imagine I care so little for what is mine?"

Feine threw his head back, laughter seeping from his wide open mouth. The sound made my bones itch, and I squeezed my eyes against it, forced my body into action. My fingers closed around the warm metal of the Sig, and I slammed the barrel into Feine's exposed throat. I froze in the sudden silence, as if Feine might actually choke on his own foul mirth.

A mistake.

He flung my body against the wall, a feral howl rent

from his throat, and my right foot crashed through window glass, shards raining over the floor and tinkling against the pavement below. The sound distracted me from the hot blood dripping down my leg, sliced flesh, sharp and burning.

I huddled beneath the gaping window, unable to move. In front of me the two vampires clashed and separated, moving in blurs of speed so fast I couldn't distinguish one body from the other until a rush of cool blood splashed across my face. Antonio fell to his knees, clutching his arm against the red stain blooming over his chest.

Feine flew toward him. Antonio's feet shot out, cracked into Feine's kneecaps. A distinctive pop echoed in my ears as I watched Feine's body spiraling out of control. He landed hard against the wall, the impact shaking the rest of the glass free of the broken window frame.

Pieces of my coffee table scattered across the room, the wood snapping like matchsticks as Feine bounded over it, his body undamaged by Antonio's blow. My stash of hydroshock silvers rolled into each other, bouncing back across the floor. I inched my way toward the closest one, ignoring the tiny bits of glass poking through my skin, keeping my eyes glued to the action.

Antonio and Feine landed blows with untiring accuracy, fists and feet flying, teeth bared. Dizzied by their speed, my own injuries still largely unheeded, a bloody smear marked my path through the debris. I reached for the nearest bullet, shaky fingers finding the chamber.

The vampires separated finally, circling, a wary stalk. They didn't gasp for breath, didn't press their palms into their bodies or wipe the sweat from their eyes. They didn't need to.

"You would risk the Council's wrath for her?" Feine spat the words at Antonio, not bothering to look my way.

"You risk the same should you succeed in killing me."

Their hands didn't shake or twitch, nerves strung out and twisted. No, that was me. They were steady. Steeped in vengeance. Deadly.

"Your territory will be mine, Antonio, and since you've been so kind as to take care of Adrienne for me, I won't even have to share it. You've made my reward so much more worth the risk."

"Never," Antonio growled. "My territory will never be yours!"

His fist pounded through Feine's ribs, the snap of breaking bones distinct in the sudden stillness. Antonio shook his hand free of the shattered cage, pulling bone and thick tissue with it, Feine's blood spilling over the jagged wound as he dropped.

"I will tear you apart, piece by murdering piece." Antonio hovered above Feine, pinning him to the floor with his legs.

Sirens screeched into the parking lot below, drowning out Antonio's words, illuminating every move in rhythmic flashes of red and blue.

"Do it!" Feine taunted. "Kill me if you can."

"No," I said, surprising myself as I leveled the gun at Feine's head. "He's not worth it, Antonio."

I moved in, closer than I meant to, taking dead aim at the monster sprawled on my living room floor. "Let the police take him, just like we planned."

I was near enough to see the bones knitting themselves together in Feine's chest, to hear the wet gurgles of blood and air filtering through the wound. We were all three covered in gore and glass, the blood-reek almost enough to knock me out. How Antonio controlled himself, I couldn't begin to fathom.

I didn't move a muscle. Didn't lower the 9mm. Didn't so much as take a clean breath until I saw the Triangle's finest, decked out in riot gear and crashing through my broken door. Even then, I only moved enough to shield Antonio, just in case some rookie was hyped for action and overzealous with his Uzi.

My lungs burned, and my eyes watered. I would have fallen over if Antonio wasn't behind me, but I didn't move until the deep voice barking orders demanded my attention.

"Police! Drop your weapon!"

I half-heard him, my brain responding to the command.

"My name is Olivia Peters," I said slowly, the Sig easing to my side, eyes still glued to Feine. "I'm working with Detective Michael Rutledge. He should be here. Call him, please. Now."

I didn't tear my gaze away from Feine until Antonio's grip around my waist tightened, his nails pressing into me like sharpened claws. His other arm stretched out, fingers pointing at the yellow letters running across the broad back of the cop who seemed to be in charge. *L.V.T.* So this one wasn't a cop after all, he was a Licensed Vampire Terminator.

Relief flooded through me at about the same rate anxiety gripped Antonio, and I realized he was more afraid of the L.V.T. than he'd been of Feine. If he'd died battling Feine, he would have known why, would have agreed to the risk beforehand. The L.V.T. was another matter entirely, an unknown threat in a government issue flak jacket, a vague warrant in his hand and an ambitious judge in his back pocket.

As if on cue, the L.V.T. turned his back on Feine and took a step toward us. Menacing eyes flicked over my body before their attention focused on Antonio. This man enjoyed his work. I read that much in the cursory glance he gave me, in the set of his jaw and the sharp-edged feel of the energy that vibrated around him.

My own power flared to life, weaving into Antonio's like a cocoon, and I wondered what kind of person would enjoy the kind of work he did.

"State your business here, Night Walker." The L.V.T.'s voice was deep, the statement mechanical.

"He rules this city's Undead, and he is here by my invitation," I answered, still gripping the Sig in my right hand. I don't know what bothered me more, that he'd taken his eyes off of Feine or that he was questioning Antonio.

"What kind of invitation?"

Was he leering at me? It sounded like it, but I couldn't tell for certain. I was watching Feine's breathing slow, his chest rise in regular rhythms. The wheeze that marked his shattered rib cage all but gone.

"Is this what you've come here for?" Antonio asked. "To harass Ms. Peters? Shouldn't you be seeing to your quarry?"

"I'm speaking to the lady, Night Walker, and I'm still waiting for an answer."

"You're insulting us both," I said, keeping my voice even and my eyes on Feine. "That one," I jutted my chin towards Feine. "That one is the rogue who's been terrorizing the city. He attacked me tonight, and if Antonio hadn't gotten here when he did, I wouldn't be alive to tell you about it."

"Secure the prisoner," the L.V.T. boomed, and the officers sprang into action, pent up energy finding an outlet at last.

The L.V.T. watched the officers move into position, then walked a slow circle around Antonio. As soon as his back was turned, a slow smile spread across Feine's face.

I raised the Sig, steady.

Three officers surrounded Feine, two holding his arms and the third behind him, ready to lock the metal wrist shackles behind his back.

The L.V.T.'s equipment was enchanted, of course. It was one of the dirty little secrets that had recently been exposed by the media, but it was true enough. The government employed a handful of the most talented spellbinders in the world, and they focused much of their energy on L.V.T. weaponry. They had to. If the equipment wasn't enchanted, there would be nothing to stop captured vampires from breaking free.

Enchanted or not, the bindings would have zero effect on me, but watching them gather Feine into their trap, I felt as if I was paralyzed, too. Lungs empty and muscles protesting, agonizing seconds ticked forward while I waited to hear the first lock snap around his wrists. I was sure I would hear it, even over the blood pounding in my ears and black dots swimming before my eyes.

I should have known better.

Feine whipped his arms across his chest, throwing the officers in opposite directions. Still, I didn't move until the third man screamed, Feine's teeth piercing his neck. I couldn't see Antonio or the L.V.T., but I knew they were there, moving, taking up offensive positions. Neither one of them was willing to let Feine walk out of here.

Sharp gasps filled my lungs, desperate, like liquid fire. The oxygen cleared my vision, threw my body into motion. I dropped to the floor, rolled once, glass and blood clinging to me, bits of debris scattering like demented marbles. I came up on one knee, using both hands to keep the Sig leveled at the back of Feine's head.

The only bullet I had was already in the chamber, my finger moist and cold against the trigger. What was the L.V.T. waiting for? I risked a sideways glance, found his gun trained on Antonio instead of Feine. The two cops in full gear were on their feet again, Uzis vacillating between the two vamps. The third had become a writhing shield in front of Feine.

"Drop the hostage. Now!" The L.V.T.'s voice barked into the silence, like a command that couldn't be ignored. But Feine only smiled, his teeth shining pink and wet around the fresh blood in his mouth.

"He's not a hostage, you imbecile." Antonio's words hissed against my skin, bridging the distance between us. "He's fuel."

"That's Willy he's got," one of the cops behind me pleaded. "Give the order, Sir. I've got a clean shot."

"Do something or I will!" I shouted, sweat pooling in every bend of my body.

I didn't have the training for this, the will to stay calm as I watched a man's life slowly drain away. Even if the cop survived Feine's feeding, he was headed straight for a holy water shower, and that was no joke. Vampires left behind enough of themselves when they fed that an open wound would smoke and fizz like an acid burn when the holy water touched it.

It wouldn't be pretty, but it was better than the alternative.

The alternative was living with that bit of vamp DNA embedded in his body, fast food advertising on the Undead Interstate. Which wasn't a bad thing if you were into it, I guess, but I was willing to bet that this guy wasn't.

His eyes fluttered open, dull and brown. "Help me," he whispered. "Please."

A room full of cops trained to take down vampires and other assorted predators, sworn to protect the rest of us, and not one of them moved. They were waiting for orders I knew in my gut the L.V.T. would never give.

Antonio's power reached out to mine, warm and strong. Was this the order I'd been waiting for? I didn't know, and at that moment, I simply didn't care. I adjusted my aim and pulled the trigger, the lone silver bullet burrowing through the air.

Feine's body jerked twice in rapid succession, once on impact and once when the bullet exploded in his brain. Bone and gray matter rained over the rest of us as his wasted body pitched forward in a bloody heap.

Twenty-six

For the second time in as many weeks I turned my weapon over to the police. Only this time there were several witnesses to the shooting, and I couldn't claim self-defense. This time it could get messy.

Mike Rutledge loomed large, concern and anger chasing each other across his face. I forced myself to meet his eyes, the inch or so he had on me seeming like a lot more.

"Damn it to hell, Olivia! What were you thinking?"

"Feine was going to kill that cop, Mike, and the L.V.T. wasn't doing a fucking thing about it!" I scrubbed my hands across my face. "Corrupt bastard," I mumbled into my palms, more of a curse than a complete thought.

"What did you say?" His tone was riding the edge of civility, sharp and caustic.

I paused, trying to connect the dots, failing. "Nothing. I didn't say anything, Mike."

I closed my eyes, replaying the scene in my head. Only twenty-five minutes had passed since the L.V.T. squad first reported their arrival on the scene. It seemed like hours. Mike's hand brushed over my cheek. His skin was rough, the feel of long hours and hard work seeping into me, a comfort.

"I could hear him dying, Mike."

"Are any of the witnesses going to corroborate your story?" His voice was tense, resignation filling in around the edges.

"I imagine the victim will," I answered, sending a silent prayer to all the gods that the injured cop would be strong enough to give a statement tonight.

"Anybody else?"

"Antonio will. And your boys should, too, depending on how loyal they are to the L.V.T."

"This isn't about loyalty." Mike actually sounded like he believed that, like the Blue Wall was a phenomenon created by the media to jump-start ratings or to make the police look bad—or both. "The L.V.T.s are federal issue, Olivia, you know that. We've only got one of them attached to our squad and, gods be damned, I'm under orders to make sure he's happy here. My boys are walking a tightrope, and you know that, too. Don't make this about something that it's not."

"Sure thing, Mike." I jammed my hands into my pockets to keep them still. "I need to make a phone call, okay?"

He waved me away, muttering a reminder not to leave the building.

I found Antonio leaning against the wall, as far from Feine's rotting corpse as he could get and still keep his eyes on me. He had the phone in one hand, and a sticky note in the other.

"Is that what I think it is?" My fingers reached toward the thin yellow paper, wanting to touch it. The tight print marching across the message slip was Luka's. He'd spoken to Charlee Gibbs, a reporter from *The Observer,* while I was sleeping off last week's concussion, and had dutifully written down her phone numbers.

I hadn't bothered to call her back at the time, but I doubted the delay would matter.

Most of the hours I'd accumulated among the press corps had been grudgingly given, and I never imagined that I'd be the one initiating a story. *First time for everything,* I thought, and dialed the number.

While the phone rang I stared at the paper in my hand, a perfect square, an insubstantial remnant. *Damn details.* I forced myself not to think about the man who had taken the message.

"This better be a fucking emergency," a woman's sleepy voice rasped into the phone.

I liked Charlee Gibbs already. "How about an exclusive on the latest Undead assassination?"

"Good Christ, you're Olivia Peters, aren't you? Hey, sorry about that, I'm not at my best in the middle of the night."

"Me neither," I lied. "Forget about it. Just get here as soon as you can. And bring a photographer."

"We've got file shots of you, Ms. Peters. Don't worry about that."

"Good, because no one's taking my picture tonight. You might get a shot of the body, though, if you can get here before the rot finishes it off."

"You shot another one, huh? Hot damn!"

***

I hated having the press crew tromp through my living room almost as much as I hated having the cops here, dusting for prints and bagging everything in sight. But it had to be done. Antonio and I needed the media on our side.

Mike, on the other hand, did not, and his irritation was about to boil over. It streamed toward me, like warm breath on a cold night, his tone clipped and guarded in response to the reporter's leading questions. I did my best to ignore him.

It was getting easier.

I hardly noticed the Coroner's team bag what was left of Feine, didn't mind answering the same questions over and over. The monotony kept me from thinking too much.

I was so numb I didn't even feel Antonio approach, and when he touched my shoulder, I jumped forward, startled and suddenly uncertain.

"You've done more than I could have asked for, Olivia," he said, long fingers splayed between us, frozen on their way to my arm. "More than anybody has the right to ask for."

The half-finished gesture made him seem more human, almost vulnerable, and I wasn't exactly sure what he meant.

"I did what I had to do, Antonio."

"Yes, I know," he said, warm brown eyes smiling. "Come, Olivia, lean on me. You're exhausted."

"I would, but I think that might create more of a news story than we're looking for," I said, watching Charlee Gibbs cross the room, recorder in hand.

Antonio's power reached out to her, slick tendrils heavy with suggestion. Her aura sparkled in response. She wasn't aware of the magic, and her fingers slid through her hair, a quick touch to keep the curls in place.

"You might want to take it down a notch," I whispered. "Considering."

"Never," Antonio answered, extending his hand to the reporter. "Charlee Gibbs, I presume? I don't believe I've had the pleasure. Terrible circumstances, yes . . ."

I eased away from them, the reporter not sparing a

moment to notice my disappearance. I might take a pretty picture, and thank all the gods that wouldn't be tested tonight, but Antonio gave great press. I had every confidence he would emerge from this a hero, and that my own stock would raise more than a few points, too.

Mike didn't look nearly so pleased.

"You called her, didn't you?" His voice was a growl in my ear, reminding me of both Luka and his absence. "You compromised this investigation, Peters. What the hell were you thinking?"

"You know what, Mike? I've been through the wringer tonight, I need a shower more than I've ever needed one in my entire life, and my last nerve snapped about an hour ago. I did what I had to do, and if I'm not being charged with anything I'd like you all to clear the hell out of here. Now. Please."

"Liv, I didn't mean . . ."

"Forget it," I said, anger coiling beneath exhaustion, a copperhead creeping up my spine. "I'm sorry about that."

"No, I'm sorry. This shouldn't have happened. I should have been here earlier."

What could I say? Part of me agreed with him, the part that wanted to pull a heavy blanket over my eyes and pretend it had all been a bad dream. I settled on diplomacy.

"I wish it didn't go down the way it did, but it probably would've played out the same even if you'd been here." We both knew it wasn't exactly true. Feine would likely be just as dead, but maybe I wouldn't have been the one to shoot him. Maybe, maybe not. Still, we were both glad I'd said it.

I listened to Mike nudge the crime scene team into wrapping up, though I nearly lost my composure when it occurred to me that under other circumstances, I would have been part of that team. I was dangerously close to collapse.

Antonio read my distress from across the room. His energy stretched toward me, comforting, while he steered Charlee Gibbs and her crew out the door.

My stomach clenched as Antonio vanished around the corner, gripped by the sudden fear that he might not come back. I forced the thought from my mind, made myself focus on the here and now.

A cool breeze lifted the hair from my face, drawing my attention to the broken window, the shattered glass, the bits and pieces of wood and bone and other things I didn't care to identify. I heard a sharp inhale, like a muffled curse, and my head swiveled to the door so fast I nearly fell over.

My neighbor stood there, one paint-splattered hand covering his mouth, eyes gaping.

"Hey, uhhh, Max?" I stammered. "It's nothing, really, and, uhmm, you see . . ." My voice trailed off, an easy explanation for the sights and smells escaping me.

"Cool beans, Liv. Very, very cool."

I shook my head, the corners of my eyes crinkling at Max's reaction.

"I can't believe I missed this. Check out the floor over there," he said, walking across the room to get a closer look. There was nothing I wanted to see less, and I made an extra effort to keep my eyes focused where they were. "Can I paint it, Liv? Or snap some quick Polaroids at least? Would you mind?"

There are very few people in this world who can look destruction in the eye and still see beauty. They might not work nine to five jobs, or have an extra cup of sugar when you're baking a cake, but they'll always have a fresh perspective at three in the morning, when your nerves are shot and a breakdown seems imminent. These folks are the best kind of neighbors. Artists? Yeah, you bet. And I wouldn't have it any other way.

Twenty-seven

"Do you have someplace to stay?" Mike's voice was pitched low, but we both knew Antonio could hear him if he cared to listen.

"Yes," I lied, not bothering to lower my voice. "My neighbor offered his couch." That part was true, Max did offer. I didn't accept, but I figured that was my business.

"Your neighbor. Right. I've got paperwork waiting for me at the station." His tone told me he knew I wouldn't be spending the night at Max's. "Listen, Peters, I'll drop you at my place if you like. I have a spare room that's yours for as long as you need it."

"I don't think so," I said, my tone as gentle as I could manage. I leaned beside the doorframe, careful to avoid touching the black plastic sheeting where my door used to be. It looked slick and oily, and the dull bounce of light off its taut surface made me thankful I'd forced myself to take a quick shower and change my clothes. "Besides, it wouldn't look right for you to harbor a suspect."

"C'mon, Liv, you're not a suspect. We already know you did it." He laughed at his own joke. "Sorry, it's—"

"Cop humor," I finished. "I know."

"Seriously. Don't leave town without letting me know. You either," he said, nodding his head toward Antonio. "Not until this is settled. I doubt charges will be pursued, thanks to your little press conference, but stay local until we're sure."

Mike secured a final strip of yellow crime scene tape across the makeshift door and stepped away from his handiwork. The blood-soaked reek of rotting vampire drenched the air, making the hallway seem tight and small, and I made a beeline for the front stairs, slipping a note under Max's door and leaving Mike and Antonio behind. Whatever they had to say to each other, I really didn't want to hear it.

***

"Isn't there somewhere you need to be, Antonio?" The sun wouldn't rise for a couple of hours yet, but the first shades of morning color were already pulling at the horizon.

I resisted the urge to fall into his eyes, to let him soften the edges of my memory. My hands rested on the steering wheel, keys in my lap, not ready to leave but not wanting to stay, either. Antonio leaned against my car. He looked out of place in the parking lot, though the very ordinariness of it made his ruined clothes seem elegant despite the gore.

"Come with me," he offered. "You shouldn't be alone, Olivia. You need to sleep."

"I don't think I'll be doing any sleeping for a while, but thanks. Really." I took a deep breath, shakier now than I'd been all night. "I mean it, Antonio. Thank you. You saved my life."

Damn, but I was tired of thanking people for keeping me alive. I shook my head, trying to clear the debris. There were so many unanswered questions between us already, and now there was another, playing over and over, like an old record with a skip. And this one? This one I couldn't ignore.

"Feine said you would anger your Council if you killed him. Why would you risk that to save me?"

"Ahhh. I understand your question, Olivia, but you shouldn't concern yourself with events that didn't occur."

"It didn't, but it could have."

"Could it, then?"

I held my ground. "I think so. You came alone."

"This matter is far too complicated to explain so close to sunrise." He sounded weary, like an old man with wrinkles and loose teeth. I blinked a few times, hard and fast, surprised to see his skin smooth and fresh in the weak predawn light.

"Try."

"It's been a long night for both of us, and I must find my way home very soon." He paused, but I wasn't about to let him off the hook. "Simply put, this is my territory, and I protect my own."

"So it was obligation, then?"

"No."

I wasn't sure, but I thought I heard him sigh. I know I felt his irritation prickle in the air.

"What you did tonight saved this city, Olivia. You do realize that, don't you?"

I pulled back in my seat, fingers flicking and denial shaking my head from side to side.

"No?" he asked. "Well, maybe you can explain to me why you did what you did then?"

I thought about it for a minute, biting my lip and searching for a more complicated answer than the one that leapt into my mouth. There wasn't one.

"I couldn't have done anything else," I said, meeting his eyes, looking closer than I had in hours.

"Nor could I, Olivia." Antonio's eyes were dark pools of murky brown. The sound of swirling water filled my ears and for a few seconds I was transported to another place. Liquid sunshine sparkling over water, his reflection clear in the brilliant light, laughter spilling everywhere, a single wooden oar vibrating with the sound. "Nor could I."

Antonio wrenched his eyes from mine, and I breathed a sigh of relief, the cool breeze clearing our emotions from the air.

***

I drove away, tires not quite squealing around the corner, not believing for a second that I wasn't being followed. Whether by Antonio, or Mike, or some other force out there . . . Well, I didn't know and I couldn't quite bring myself to care.

When I pulled into Forever Crossed's lot and dragged myself up the stairs, the office was empty. As expected. The night receptionist would have left at four in the morning, and Ellen wouldn't open the office again until eight. Unless a new client had Danny chasing the clock, he wouldn't be around until much later, either. Linc's hours were less predictable, but I wasn't worried about Linc.

I started the coffee maker, drumming my fingers against a cool ceramic mug, hoping the rich scent of brewing coffee would clear less pleasant fragrances from my sensory memory. No dice. The unholy combination of human terror and rotting vampire was in my pores. It would have to be waited out, sweated out maybe, if I could muster the energy for a run.

As it was, the coffee gave me just enough momentum for the short walk to my own little closet of an office. I slouched behind the desk, stuck between thought and mindlessness. I shuffled files from place to place, organizing and reorganizing. I counted paper clips, thirty-seven, and then counted them again just to be sure.

As a last ditch effort to clear my head, I lit the battered incense cone I'd discovered in the bottom drawer of my desk. I dragged myself back to the coffee machine, waiting for my office to fill with the thin blue wisps of burning incense. Through the far window in the reception area, a pale sun colored the sky, peaking over the horizon and washing my world in new light.

A vague floral scent drew me back to my desk, the fragrance growing stronger as I approached. I'd been hoping for something moody and meditative, I realized, wrinkling my nose at the geranium-like smoke. Still, it was better than nothing.

I raked my fingers against my scalp, letting my hair free from its twist and lifting it by the handful into the scented air. I pulled it forward, segment by segment, until the whole mass was hanging over my face, the weight of it pulling my chin into my chest and creating a sweet-smelling veil so thick the light barely filtered through.

That's how Ellen found me, who knows how many hours later. Coffee corpse-cold on the desk in front of me, hands pressed into my temples and tears streaming down my face, drying in salty trails.

Without words she bundled me into her arms and led me to Danny's office. She settled me on his sofa, covering me with a worn blanket that smelled faintly of both dog and Danny's after-shave.

"I can't sleep," I told her when the tears finally stopped. A deep yawn popped my jaw, made a liar of me almost as soon as the words were out of my mouth.

Ellen's smile reminded me of pink lipstick and pearls, no matter what she was wearing, and it made me feel like crying all over again.

"Talk?" she offered.

My hand fluttered beside my mouth. I would have, but I didn't know where to begin.

"Tell me this isn't to do with the gorgeous Mr. Niere? The last time I saw you, I didn't think he'd ever let you out of his sight."

I mumbled syllables made inarticulate by sour humor

and exhaustion, but understandable to Ellen nonetheless.

"I don't believe it," she said, shaking her head.

"It's not *just* Luka," I corrected. "There's Feine, or what's left of him. Antonio. The case. Reporters. And Mike . . ." I would have gone on, but another yawn threatened to unhinge my jaw.

"Don't you worry about a thing," she said, repositioning the blanket over my shoulders. "Just sleep."

"Can't—" I yawned again. "Can't sleep."

Twenty-eight

"Good morning, Angel." Luka's voice was warm and comforting. It was a minute or two before I remembered that he didn't belong here, in this room, with me.

"Is it morning already?"

Luka didn't answer, but I could tell it wasn't. The tilt of his jaw and the warm half-smile separating his lips took the chill out of the tiny office, reminded me just how much I'd missed him.

I reached toward the desk. "Is that coffee?"

He nodded toward the steaming mug. "Even I'm not dense enough to come here empty handed. Not tonight, anyway."

It was the good stuff, too. From the coffee shop around the corner, the same beans as I used at home.

"How long have you been watching me?"

I hadn't wanted him here, would never have called him myself. But here he was, and I wasn't altogether unhappy to see him, either. I ran shaky fingers through my sleep-tangled hair and smoothed my skirt, hoping all the while he couldn't hear my stomach rumble, and knowing that he could.

"Hungry?" He made the word sound obscene.

"Yes, I am. And you didn't answer my question."

"Ellen didn't want you to be alone when she left for the day."

My left eyebrow arched so high it nearly popped my eyeball out. I needed to have a long talk with Ellen. Soon. I couldn't be sure, but I thought I remembered telling her Luka was part of the problem.

And he still hadn't answered my question.

"I didn't want you to be alone, either. I called every hour on the hour, but Ellen stonewalled all morning, said she hadn't heard from you since yesterday. I finally just drove over." He crossed his arms over his chest, and the sound of his skin sliding across the fine cotton of his shirt rubbed against my inner ear. "I knew you were here."

"I could have been at Mike's."

"Antonio didn't think so," he said, but the growl in his voice told me that he'd thought about it.

"Once I got here, I could feel your heartbeat. I caught your scent through the walls. I knew you were in this office. I knew you were asleep."

He sat beside me, his thigh pressing into mine, his words glancing across my ear. "Did you dream about me?"

I swallowed hard. My pulse raced in time with his. "I didn't dream at all."

"Good," he whispered, warm lips claiming mine. "I don't want your dreams, Angel."

"What do you want?" I asked, standing up to put a little distance between us. I needed to pace, but within two steps Danny's desk brought me up short.

I turned to cross back, only to find Luka had followed me. I leaned away, the edge of the desk cutting into the back of my thighs, an even exchange for the extra few inches of distance.

Luka planted his hands on either side of my hips, his mouth within licking distance of my own. "I think you know."

I thought I knew, too, but I needed him to say it.

"I want you wide awake, Angel," he breathed, sounding playful and dangerous and very, very sure of himself. "I won't take you sleeping until we've known each other longer. A lot longer."

It wasn't exactly what I'd been hoping to hear, but it was close enough.

***

"Where are we going?" I asked, feeling my lips soft and full, sweet against my tongue, the memory of Luka's mouth still fresh.

"Dinner?" Luka had a way of making questions sound like answers.

"Sure," I said. "I'm not really dressed, though."

He pulled his eyes from the road and looked me over, quick. "Don't tease."

Had the sunroof not been open, the atmosphere inside the Jag would have crackled and sparked. Exposed to the night, fresh air swept around us, the waning moon dimmed by the city lights. I smoothed shaky hands over myriad creases in the wrinkle-free fabric of my khaki skirt, not caring for once that the manufacturers were blatant liars.

"I'm making you dinner," Luka said.

I swallowed hard. "Do you think that's a good idea?"

"Yes." His hand flashed off the gear stick, capturing mine and holding them still against my thigh. "I can control myself, Angel."

"It's not you I'm worried about."

Luka's laughter filled me with confidence. "Not to worry. We'll have chaperones."

I wasn't surprised when Luka pulled into the narrow alley behind Feeling Blue, though I didn't think we needed quite so much supervision. Still, I was comfortable in the bar even after Luka disappeared into the back, promising me I wouldn't be disappointed with his cooking. I would have been happy with a semi-bruised apple and a bit of cheese, but I hadn't thought to raid the fridge at Forever Crossed before we left.

More than a few people in the bar seemed to be staring at me, whispering to each other and throwing nods in my direction. *Was there something stuck in my hair? Did I have bathroom tissue clinging to my shoe?* Certain that I looked worse than I thought, I made a dash to the Ladies to check out the damage.

I'd slept in these clothes, sure, but it wasn't all *that* bad. I've looked worse on plenty of occasions and not drawn any attention at all.

Luka was waiting for me at the bar when I returned. "What happened?" he asked, reading the worry in my eyes.

"Nothing," I said, thinking the hunger wasn't helping my paranoia any. "Are we eating soon?"

"Upstairs." His slow smile eased my nerves. "Our feast awaits."

As Luka steered me through the crowd I could feel him tense, knew he saw the looks and heard the whispers, too. Just before we reached the stairs, two young women stepped out from the crowd, giggling and blocking our way. Luka bristled behind me, his power wrapping around me and drawing me closer.

"Hey! You're her, aren't you?" One of them blurted out, eyes wide, hot pink fingernails framing the front page of today's newspaper.

The headline, "Lady Law Bites Back!" burned into my field of vision, pictures of my ruined apartment splashed across the page. Luka growled, mouth closed, the sound vibrating through his chest.

The second girl elbowed the first, rolling her eyes in exasperation. "You've got the wrong side showing!"

"Oh!" She flipped the paper quickly, finding what she was looking for and thrusting it forward for me to see. "Olivia Peters, right?"

The hot blush spreading upward from my chest spoke for itself. That was me, no way around it. Still, I was thoroughly jealous of the cool-looking me in the file photo.

"Wild! I can't believe it! Would you sign this?" she asked, breaking into a new fit of giggles.

What do you do when strangers want your autograph and you're not a hockey star, not some famous actress, or a ballplayer or anything?

"Sign it and start walking," Luka whispered in my ear, heat flashing through me and darkening my face once again.

"Sure," I said, taking the pen she offered and trying on a this-happens-to-me-all-the-time sort of smile. Scrawling my name across the bottom of the photograph, I thanked them and pressed forward, Luka close behind me.

"Enjoy the band, Ladies," Luka suggested. He paused on the stairs, his power flowing toward them until the giggling resumed.

***

"I don't get the fascination," I said, not smiling. "I really don't."

"You might not have noticed, Angel, but most people don't spend their free time slaying rogue vampires or getting shot on their balconies, or communicating with the dead, for that matter."

"Yeah? Well, that's my job. I have better things to do with my free time, too."

The spinach and cheese omelet Luka made for dinner was gone, the last of the grits scooped from the plate with the wedge of buttery toast I was still nibbling on.

Even as I relaxed into the soft contentment of a full belly, my mind unwinding in the safety of Luka's warm office and the certain knowledge that nothing could hurt me here, Luka began to tense.

Maybe there was something wrong with my table

manners that I was too exhausted to notice?

No such luck.

"The other morning, at the cabin," Luka started, his lips pressed together in a thin line, nervous.

So that was it, huh? Call me wimpy, but I didn't want to go there just yet. "Hmm?" I asked, letting him interpret the question however he chose.

He paused, letting out a long breath. "I'm sorry, Angel. And I'm getting tired of apologizing to you all the time."

What was I supposed to say to that? *If you don't want to say you're sorry, stop being such a jerk?* Somehow I didn't think that would help. Besides, my ignorance of the Ja'Nan and their ways was as much to blame as his jerkiness, even if I didn't like admitting it.

"I didn't know," I offered. "I was out of place. And I shouldn't have raced off like I did. I'm sorry, too."

"No, you weren't out of place. I was. I was crazy from having put you in danger. We were almost too late."

"You were right on time." I stood behind him, sliding my fingers along his jaw, down his neck.

"It shouldn't have happened that way." He took my hand from his face, turned to face me.

I swallowed hard, searching for the right words. "Maybe it had to."

"I didn't want you to see us like that, the thrill of the hunt in our teeth, like beasts in the night." His voice was soft, cradled in regret, his eyes smoky in the low light. "I didn't want your first time to be violent."

I'd been on the wrong side of a wereleopard attack long before I'd met Luka and the others, and that creature was no more like them than I was like Adrienne. We'd all been human, once, but that's as far as it went.

"My first time was almost a decade ago, but it's sweet of you to care," I said, sealing the words with a lingering kiss, remembering the taste of him, feeling the scars across my chest begin to warm. "Knowing you has altered the memory of that night forever. Really."

Strong hands gripped my hips, holding me close, giving me the chance to recall more than his taste.

The knock on the door, three sharp raps, didn't surprise me. I'd been expecting an interruption.

"Our chaperone?" I asked.

"Actually, no," Luka said. "Or not intentionally, anyway."

He swiped a hand through his hair, squared his shoulders before opening the door. Antonio filled the frame like a gift to Cardea, perfectly still but pressing forward, his power rolling into the office, claiming it. This was his territory.

"It's been years since you required a knock to announce my presence." Antonio's voice was cold, his hand on Luka's cheek possessive.

"A welcome surprise," Luka said. He slid Antonio's hand from his face and pressed it to his lips.

It was almost too much. The intimacy of the gesture. The layers of meaning in their exchange. The feel of Antonio's power washing over me, including me in his reach.

"Indeed," Antonio conceded, taking his hand from Luka's lips.

I hadn't seen him move, but there he was, sitting opposite me. "I'm pleased that you're here, Olivia."

"Back at ya, Antonio." I smiled, realizing it was true.

Beyond all reason, it meant something to me that Antonio included me, that he thought of me as one of his own. I wasn't sure what it meant, exactly, but I wasn't worried about it, either. I didn't belong to him in any sort of uncomfortable way. I didn't serve him, or owe him, or answer to him.

But he knew me, had his eye on me, maybe expected something as of yet unnamed from me. And for all my previous distaste for vampires, I liked the idea that the Undead Ruler of the Carolinas was on my side.

Twenty-nine

"I'm just glad it's over," I said, stifling a yawn and trying not to think about Adrienne.

Luka's eyes were soft, warm green in the low light.

"It is over, isn't it?" I asked, not really wanting to hear the answer.

"That depends on your definition of over," Luka said, crossing the few steps between us, resting a warm hand on my shoulder.

"Over?" I stared at my hands for a moment, uncertain. "How about no more bloodless bodies downtown? No more lunatics lurking by my back door and taking mad romps through my head when I'm not looking? You know. Over."

"Well, yes, in that sense it is over, Olivia," Antonio said, his power snaking toward me, cool and soothing. "You're in no immediate danger."

Luka rubbed his fingers along my jaw, down the back of my neck, the sweetness of his skin on mine an unwelcome distraction.

"Is it Adrienne?" I asked, using every ounce of will I had to keep my voice steady.

"You have nothing to fear from Adrienne, my dear. Nothing at all."

I could feel his determination, his power circling like a prickly wire, a vain attempt to keep me at a distance.

"You made a promise, Antonio." Our eyes locked in silent appeal. Whatever he had done with her, he didn't want me to know about it. "I expect you to keep it."

"If you insist, Olivia." He blinked slowly, gathering himself. "I will show you."

His eyes were endless dark pools, echoes of images reflecting in my own, drawing me in. Adrienne cowered in the darkness, her breath a rasp in Antonio's ear. Her skin was ashen, torn to the bone and dehydrated, unable to mend itself. I couldn't hear her pleading, but I saw Antonio shake his head, felt him steel himself.

Her eyes, flat gray slates, begged him for release, for one last death.

Blinding light, sunrise over the ocean. A quick step from the shadows at dusk, the sun dipping below white capped mountains. A warm breeze by an open window, the air thick with dancing pollen, sunlight spreading over the sill.

Antonio shook his head once more, sorrow filling the air between them.

And then he blinked, pulling his power in, breaking the connection between us. I'd seen enough to know there was no pleasure for him in this, no joy for him in Adrienne's fall from grace. Even now, grief was written across his face.

In this life, on this plane of existence, eternal damnation isn't our right. Adrienne's mind was shattered, her body wasted. Her only link to reality wrapped around excruciating pain.

"How long?" I wanted to touch him, to let him know that he would survive this despite her, that he wasn't the wretched beast he thought he was. But I held back.

Luka did what I couldn't. He settled on the edge of Antonio's chair, his arm draped around the other man's shoulder. My mind strayed, absorbing the images of past and present, Luka's fingers on Antonio's skin, his instinct to comfort familiar and absolute.

"I don't know how long," Antonio answered, drawing me back to the present. "Understand I am doing what must be done. If she doesn't suffer, if the price isn't high enough, there will be others. There will be more death, more violence, more loss. I can't have that, Olivia."

"I know," I said, meeting his eyes.

I couldn't have it, either. Antonio would defend his position against attack after attack if he had to, the Ja'Nan by his side, the whole city in danger.

I opened my mind to him, his brown eyes filling with warmth, reflecting the lighter flecks of my own. I pictured the Shamans' tree at sunrise, golden light filtering through the branches, long grass wet beneath bare feet and bird song filling the morning with life. I imagined it over and over, letting the image grow in my mind until Antonio pulled away, breaking the spell.

"Timeless beauty, such as I will never see again." His voice was wistful, and for a moment he seemed ancient once more, the weight of his years unbearable. "It's easy to forget the sun is life for so many. It has been death for me, for us, forever."

"Not forever," Luka said, smoothing Antonio's hair. "Just

for now."

"For Adrienne, it can be life again." I glanced at Luka as I spoke, not realizing until I did it that I wanted his approval. "You can give her the sun, Antonio, release her into it and set her free."

The moment passed behind Antonio's eyes, clear in the dim light, and I knew he understood.

***

"I have something for you, Olivia." Antonio reached into his jacket pocket and retrieved an antique key.

The ornate metalwork was cold against my skin, the key large and heavy in my hand.

"I took the liberty of replacing your locks."

"Thank you, Antonio, but the last time I checked I didn't have a door, either," I said, pushing the inevitable pictures of my ruined apartment from my mind.

"Yes. Well, you will have a new door before morning, and this key will open the lock." He smiled at me, gracious and warm, the master of his domain once again. "I hope you don't mind?"

I shook my head.

"Detective Rutledge agreed to contact me when his police line could be crossed," Antonio said, both of us ignoring the hiss of Luka's power at the mention of Mike's name. "After he called, I took the liberty of sending in my cleaning crew. They'll work until it's spotless, but they don't expect to be finished until close to noon."

I wiped at the tears marking twin streams down my cheeks, my instincts not sharp enough to whisk them away before they'd fallen. The idea of facing the bloodstained wreckage that used to be my home had been gnawing at me since last night. I'd imagined facing it alone, enveloped in a cloud of dread and bleach, terrified.

"Why am I not surprised you have your own cleaning crew?" I joked, my throat tight against a looming flood of emotion, and the remembered scent of old blood and rotting vampire, once conjured, wouldn't be dispelled.

"Occupational hazard," Antonio replied, and I smiled, reaching out to touch the back of his hand.

"Thank you, Antonio."

"No need, Olivia. It's the least I could do."

He had a point.

Thirty

It was hours before I realized Antonio never answered my question. I'd been the one who mentioned Adrienne. I'd jumped to the conclusion that she was the reason this nightmare still continued. Antonio had merely followed where I led.

And Luka hadn't said much at all. Even after we left Feeling Blue, he'd been quiet. Driving to his place, his power thrummed around me, a protective circle in the eerie light of the newly waning moon. The Jag slid into park, too smooth to jar me into motion, and I barely noticed Luka steering me through an empty warehouse and into a rickety lift. I just wanted to get wherever we were going.

When the creaking stopped, I stared into the dark cavernous space, unwilling to step into this shadowy void. Luka's hand on my back propelled me forward, guided me through two steel doors before he reached for the chord that sparked the lights. That's when I realized he lived in this space.

He led me past the kitchen, paused by the bathroom making sure I knew where to find towels and anything else I might need, but I only had eyes for the bed. He kissed me good-bye, and I let him go, the heat of his mouth still pulsing against mine as the door closed behind him. I made myself stay awake until I heard the first of the deadbolts slide into place, but that was all I could manage.

I'd been too tired to worry—about him, or the ever elusive *us*, or anything else for that matter. I'd seen and done too much in too short a time, and my body was rebelling. Magic, lust, death. They each exacted their own toll, and the strain of the last few days was inscribed in the folds and fibers of my body.

But now, wrapped in the warm safety of Luka's bed, with a few hours of sleep behind me and streaky sunshine pouring through the high windows, my mind wandered. Pieces of past conversations, fragments of memory surfacing here and there, like the pattern in an unfinished quilt.

Andrew's words came back to me, hard and achy, memories of my time at the cabin filling the jagged space around his voice. *He's Mr. Politically Active . . . Too ambitious for his own good . . . Doesn't need human help to find some damn rogue . . .*

No one had argued that last point. In fact, Antonio had admitted right from the drop that he could kill Feine himself, but that he simply didn't want to. He wanted Feine exposed, wanted his execution handled publicly.

But why?

Images of my apartment flashed before me. Mike Rutledge, his aura bright and squeaky clean, filth pooling on the floor, dripping down the walls. I narrowed the focus in my mind until it was just Mike and me. No cops, no Antonio, no rotting corpse. No L.V.T.

Damn! How could I have missed it? I'd said it myself and not even realized it, called that L.V.T. a corrupt bastard and not given the statement another thought.

L.V.T.s were federal agents, licensed by the government and leased out to law enforcement agencies all over the country. Mike had said he was under orders to keep this particular guy happy, said his team was walking a tightrope. Exactly how much did the good Detective know?

I sat up and tossed the blankets aside.

I was close, but there was no point in traveling down a dead-end road, especially this one. Mike wasn't a dirty cop. No way, no how.

He was on to something, though. Of that, I was sure. He'd reacted when I called the L.V.T. corrupt, but I'd been too scattered to call him on it at the time. Someone out there had invested a lot of money in this. Someone high on the food chain. Higher than Mike could reach.

But who? Who could pull the right strings and make an L.V.T. dance? I didn't know, but I was guessing Antonio had a pretty good idea. I forced myself off the bed, my bare feet protesting the cold of the concrete floor.

What to do first?

I stretched my arms over my head, tight muscles pulling against my shoulder blades. The sound of my joints popping into place echoed in the emptiness. I needed a plan.

Worse, I needed a shower.

***

Luka's apartment was barely-converted warehouse

space. Grid-like windows set high in the towering walls let in plenty of light without giving up much of view, so anyone looking in from one of the surrounding buildings would see only the opposite wall. Unless the voyeur managed some kind of an extreme angle, the interior would remain hidden. A definite plus, I thought, following the exposed plumbing to the bathroom, where a half-wall of murky glass blocks afforded at least the illusion of privacy.

Even here, in the confines of his old claw foot tub, the close plastic curtain narrowing the space and clinging to me if I stepped out from under the spray, Luka's absence surrounded me. Hot water poured over my muscles, washing away the grime of recent events, the doubts and suspicions, too. A funnel of spice-scented steam gathered toward the ceiling, and watching it rise I felt light and airy, smaller than my usual self.

The edges of my vision clouded, a burned-red stain blocking out the light. I groped for the hot water knob, palming the shower to a cool spray as I lowered myself to the edge of the tub. My head drooped between my knees, my hair trailing towards the drain in the water around my feet, like skinny snakes in a rainstorm.

I turned off the water, staring at my hair as it coiled around my toes, flat and tangled without the water to keep it moving. *Snakes in a rainstorm . . .*

Andrew had said something about snakes, too. Something about Antonio and politicians and snakes.

Damn!

I should have seen it sooner. I slid the shower curtain around its metal loop, the soft swoosh like a quiet laugh, mocking me. Did Mike know who it was? Did Antonio? I grabbed a thick black towel from the woven basket by the sink. A politician. Yes, it was obvious now.

But which one?

As I stalked through the wide open space of the half-finished warehouse, ticking through the names of every politician I could think of. None of them seemed to fit. I needed help.

I rummaged around the bedroom for something to wear, my fingers trailing across the shoulders of Luka's shirts, hung from light to dark on a wheeled metal rack. Three of these rolling barriers formed makeshift walls, moving partitions that made the bed seem like a drifting island, surrounded by open sky. I imagined the Ja'Nan here, their energy coursing through the open waters, Anya in the center, an anchor for them all.

Pain, wire-thin and jagged, gripped low in my belly, and I sank to the bed, clutching the damp towel close to my body. Pressing my palm into the tender flesh, I willed the soreness away, praying it wasn't what I thought it was.

No such luck.

A dark smear on the inside of my thigh confirmed it. I hadn't had a period in seven and a half months, and my body had to pick today? *Damn, damn, damn.* I knew the bleeding wouldn't last long, but I also knew it wouldn't be easy. It would be vicious. It always was.

I dug through the briefcase I'd hauled up from the car last night, shoved aside bottled water and bullets until I found the zippered pouch I was looking for. An old lipstick jockeyed for position with scratched barrettes and gum wrappers, three battered tampons underneath it all.

Of course, the timing couldn't be worse. The last thing I wanted was for Luka to find me curled up in bed, vulnerable, cursing the cramps I knew were coming. But on the bright side, at least I wouldn't have to improvise protection.

***

The clock on the coffee maker claimed it was seven-thirty-six in the evening. I had no idea what time it actually was, but I was certain, at least, that it was morning. Not even my body-clock was that far off rhythm.

My eyes darted over all the flat surfaces, looking for the phone. Another clock would do, but I doubted I'd find one. In the time I'd spent with Luka, I'd never seen him so much as glance at his watch. It was an accessory, a touch of black leather and platinum around his wrist.

A narrow table defined the entry way, a stack of mail on one side and a painted wooden mask on the other. I spotted the phone wedged between the two.

The moment my eyes landed on the receiver I realized I'd been scanning for other things, as well. Pictures, maybe. A pair of earrings abandoned by the sofa, or a hairbrush wound with fine strands of red or gold. Some hint of another woman's presence. There wasn't one.

The smile blooming on my lips was vanquished by a dark rush of embarrassment and a sharp stab across my belly, and I thanked all the gods for allowing me this moment free of witnesses.

I hurried to the phone and dialed Mike's number, the urge to make myself busy, to do something useful, suddenly overwhelming. I counted seven rings before I heard Mike's voice in my ear.

"Detective Rutledge." He sounded like a cop with too much on his desk and no doughnuts in sight.

"Mike, it's Olivia. Do you have a minute?"

"Yes, ma'am?"

So, he wasn't alone. I sure wouldn't have rated a ma'am if he was. And his accent was thicker than it had to be, too, which meant he was either more irritated than usual or in a particularly good mood. I doubted it was the latter.

That being the case, skipping the pleasantries seemed like the best course of action.

"The L.V.T. had orders, didn't he?"

"Yes, ma'am."

"But I got in the way, huh? He was expecting the two vamps, but he didn't know about me, did he?"

"Near as I can tell."

"How high does this go, Mike?" I could hear my voice quickening, rising higher than I wanted it to.

"Ma'am?"

"A Congressman maybe?"

"Ma'am?"

"A Senator?"

"I surely don't know about all that." Mike's voice slowed in counterpoint to my own, smoothing out like honey in hot tea.

"I'm gonna figure out who it is, Mike. And then the bastard's going down."

"Ma'am? I advise you to let the authorities handle this situation. Y'all know it's not safe for a lady to take the law into her own hands."

"Are you calling me a lady, Detective?" I was smiling now, certain that Mike was on my side, that he would be there for me when I needed him.

***

I was setting the phone back where I'd found it when I heard the lock turn, felt Luka's power pressing through the door. We stood face to face for a few seconds, drinking each other in. I was trying to memorize the sight of him, coming through the door with yesterday's mail in his hands, just about to drop it on the table.

He closed his eyes and inhaled, his head tilted slightly to the left, chin pointing toward me. He sniffed twice, quickly, and then a third time. In my mind's eye the shadow of his tail flicked through tall grass, flared whiskers tasting the wind.

He stepped closer to me, and questions swam behind his eyes, wrapped themselves around me as surely as his arms.

"What is it?" I kissed him lightly on the neck, breathing in the rich scent of him. "What's wrong?"

"I don't know," he admitted. His hands pulled through my hair, still damp from the shower. His breath was like a slow rhythm, separating the scents of shampoo and soap from my own. When his lips pressed into mine, I could feel the desire building in him, but it was more than a kiss. He was tasting me.

"Well?" I asked.

"You aren't injured, Angel, but you are bleeding."

My muscles clenched, my hand drifting over my middle in response. I swallowed hard against the swell of desire spreading through my body, a reaction I wasn't expecting. "That's right."

Luka's smile came quick, lingering like the flash from an old camera. I closed my eyes, letting him pull me close, seeing his smile bloom again and again behind my eyelids. In that moment he looked exactly like the sharp-clawed hunter I knew he could become, and my body called out to the leopard within him, heat flaming through my skin, my nerves on fire with it.

"Stay away from Antonio," he growled, his mouth along my neck, hot and demanding. "Promise me, Angel."

It wasn't a request, and I pulled away from him, shaken by the implication. I'd never found my period particularly sexy, but I never considered it a danger, either. Granted, it wasn't a regular monthly occurrence for me like it was for most women, but even so.

"Don't worry. It'll be over before I see him again. Anyway, I think you might be overreacting." I spoke softly, meeting his eyes, not wanting my meaning to get lost in the undertow. "Women don't seal themselves away when they have their periods, right? Antonio must encounter menstruating women all the time."

"You're different." Luka followed me across the room. "He'll sense the leopard in you, taste your scent in the air. He'll want more."

"Are you saying the Ja'Nan avoid him once a month?"

"No need." Something smooth and round shaped his words, not regret, but close. His arms encircled me, protective. "The leopard in you is so strong, Angel. I didn't think you would bleed, either."

"I usually don't," I admitted, jealous of the wereleopards once again. Honestly, I didn't know how women put up with this every month, I really didn't. It was hell. Like my body battling itself, an internal war for dominance. I could handle bullet wounds and broken bones, but my period? Forget about it! "Thank all the gods, it only lasts a day or so, and it only happens once or twice a year."

"So this is a treat?" Luka said, the edge back in his voice, his power thrumming against mine. "Special, just for me?"

Well, that was one way of looking at it, I thought, and suddenly, it seemed like the only way. Despite my earlier worries, right at this moment, there was no place else I'd rather be.

Thirty-one

Almost a week had passed, and Luka and I leaned on the hood of my car, eyes fixed on the building in front of us. His hand covered my own, the moist heat of contact seeping into my thigh. Shiny new window glass bounced late morning light in every direction, and I hesitated, frozen by fears I hadn't known I harbored.

"It's clean, right? I mean, they're done with, uhm, everything?" I'd asked Luka this question, or some version of it, at least a dozen times.

"Antonio's crew is the best." Luka had responded to my questions with some variation of this answer each time I'd wavered. "Did I already tell you that we found them in California? Working cleanup for the LAPD? Cost him a fortune to lure them out here, too, but it was worth every penny."

"Luka?"

"Yes?"

"You know I'm not letting this go, right?"

"I know."

"The victim's families deserve at least that much. We all do. And when I figure out who was behind this, that person will pay. You know that too, right?"

A smile played with the corner of his eyes. "Been counting on it, Angel."

Luka's power danced over my skin, and just then I did feel like an angel, all fluttery, like whispers and light.

"Let's go in."

"Race ya!" I called over my shoulder, already bounding up the stairs, Luka a half-step from my heels and the fire escape squealing beneath our feet.

We spilled into the hallway, laughing too hard to breathe. My new door looked ancient, thick and strong, the dainty glass knob belying that first impression. I fit the ornate key into the lock, feeling the catch and release, suddenly nervous again.

"It's time, Angel."

I closed my eyes and turned the key.

***

Wild flowers raced over the glass-green top of my new

coffee table, antique vases bouncing sunlight across scrubbed hardwoods and freshly painted walls, warm petals and fallen pollen scented the air. I swallowed hard, words unspoken caught in my throat, insufficient.

The first threads of my power spiraled out, tentative, searching for traces of death, looking for lingering magics beneath the oil-soap sheen on the floors and the fresh coat of paint on the walls. The rush of relief nearly knocked me off my feet—the only magic here was my own. Even Luka held his own power close, his aura a riot of thrumming green shoots, giving me time to reclaim this space.

I stretched my arms wide, spinning slowly, my power looping around us in widening arcs, finding center, marking my own.

"Welcome home." Luka's voice pulsed through me, and I wrapped my arms around him, drawing him into my circle, adding his energy to the dizzying twirl.

His fingers reached into my hair, loosed the twisted braid and set it all free. Desire sparked in the crackle of current between us, and I pressed closer, wanting more. We wouldn't be interrupted this morning, not by the Ja'Nan, or ancient prophesies, or even unvoiced fears. Not mine, and not his, either. Not this time.

The scars across my chest beat red-hot, throbbing in time with my heart, demanding. I pulled off my shirt, cool air prickling over my skin as the soft cotton whooshed to the floor, an echo of my breath.

Luka's tongue painted a hot trail along my throat, over my breasts, down my belly. My nipples burned, taut and dark, aching for his mouth to return. His hands on my thighs, my hips, slipping off my skirt, fingers finding the damp edge of my undies, impatient. He whisked them away, tossing aside the tangled twist of garments as he nuzzled lower, on his knees, pressing me back a step until the slick cool of the wall shivered up my spine.

"You shouldn't be this beautiful, Angel," he whispered, lips on fire. "Shaman aren't meant to be beautiful. It isn't fair."

Light poured through the windows, Luka's hair shining amber gold as he knelt before me. Soft lips brushing my skin, his breath hot, tongue teasing until desire leapt through my body, a wild arc, breathless.

Luka gazed up at me, a wicked smile lighting his eyes, and then his mouth was on me again, sucking, teeth bared, his tongue a roughened swirl. I buried my fingers in his hair as his hands roamed across my belly, over my hips, holding me to his mouth. A sunburst of colors behind my eyes, a flood of pleasure as need filled my throat, a soft moan escaping my lips.

His tongue traced the length of my body, all the way up until his mouth covered mine, swallowing soft sounds as he swallowed my pleasure, long fingers slipping inside me, slowly, ever so slowly. His lips tasted of me, and I wanted to taste him back, wanted more than the waves building inside me as I rocked against his palm.

"Don't stop," I whispered against his lips, my hands reaching under his shirt, hungry for the feel of his skin on mine.

He smiled that wicked grin again, and slid his hand up my belly, a slick trail winding around my breasts. He licked his fingers, eyes locked on mine, my scent hot in the air between us. "I can taste the leopard in you, Angel."

Desire coiled low in my belly, and maybe it was the leopard in me, maybe not, but right now I didn't care. I pulled Luka's shirt from his body, tried to steady my fingers as I unbuttoned his jeans. He was hard, burning with a need I finally understood.

The pulse in his neck danced as my hand closed around him, light strokes teasing. Skin to skin, power lit along the length of our bodies. His heartbeat crashed through my chest, throbbed through my fingers, an ache that matched my own. I shifted, slipping him between my thighs, sliding over him, the rhythm of our bodies hot and slow. His eyes flashed, and then his mouth crushed mine, possessive, unleashing a fierce wave deep in my belly.

He lifted me, my back sliding along the sweat-slick wall, my legs tight around his hips, fingers buried in his shoulders, his chest, his back. "Angel," he hesitated, the tip of his erection already inside me. His teeth grazed my throat, tongue on fire. "Are you sure?"

Sure? Oh, yeah. If he stopped now I'd kill him with my bare hands. I slid lower, sinking around him, gasping for breath, inhaling his spicy-sweetness. He groaned, half purr, half growl, thrusting, iridescent eyes finding mine.

"More," I demanded, and he thrust again, deeper, melting into me, his body boneless, reshaping my desire. "I want to hear you, Ra'Jahn."

Soaked in power, Luka's roar crashed over me like liquid fire, the thrill of the hunt etched in my soul, timeless and wild, like the sound of forever.

Epilogue

In the dream I am an old woman. Wide-eyed children surround me like a long and noisy skirt, laughing and tugging, calling my name.

In the dream my name is Nana, and the idea fills me with hope and yearning, and a pleasure so deep I think I might never resurface. Even so, I know these beauties cannot really be my grandchildren. I know this because the doctors told me years ago that they could never be.

In the dream, my hair is pure white and braided through with tiny purple flowers. I'm telling a story filled with adventure and courage and extraordinary creatures, and the children's faces open and close with the rhythm of the tale.

The littlest girl crawls onto my lap, whispers something in my ear. Her eyes are a familiar shape, and so green it nearly breaks my heart, but her words are too important to let go. She is telling me a secret about the Goddess of Time, something she is too young to know, something that causes us both to burst into a contagious fit of giggles, until we are all adrift on a sea of laughter and hiccups in the tall grasses by my favorite tree.

I wake up smiling into the darkness, Luka's body a warm blanket beside me and the joy of my dream spilling into reality, a prayer to Kali on my lips.

Printed in the United States
47438LVS00003B/321

9 781893 896246